What's his Passion?

LOVE MATTERS

SEAN MICHAEL

Love Matters
ISBN # 978-1-78430-440-9
©Copyright Sean Michael 2015
Cover Art by Posh Gosh ©Copyright January 2015
Interior text design by Claire Siemaszkiewicz
Totally Bound Publishing

LOVE MATTERS

Totally Bound Publishing books by Sean Michael:

Bruised
The Biker's Pup

Chess Volume One
Opening Moves
Middle Game

Chess Volume Two
En Prise
Helpmate

Chess Volume Three
End Game
The Piercer's Game

Beer and Clay
Malting

Anthologies
Stand to Attention: Almost

What's his Passion?
Size Matters
Love Matters

Chapter One

Trey finished the edits on his latest novel and leaned back, head pounding. Lord, that one had been a bear. Nearly six months he'd been fighting this novel and he was finally going to send it off. Hallelujah.

"Brian, are you out there?" He waited for the sound of his assistant's steps on the tile.

"Right here, boss. What do you need?"

"The edits are done. They'll go to Andrea. I need to make sure that the new headset I ordered will be here Monday. I need my phone and a cup of coffee with cream and then you can have the rest of the week off."

"Oh. Oh, wow. Trey. Thanks. Five day weekend!" Brian was clearly pleased at the prospect.

Trey nodded, smiled. "Oh, can you please make sure that Dodger's food is on the counter where I can get it, too?" It wouldn't do to let his guide dog and best friend on four legs go hungry because he couldn't find the kibble.

"Sure, boss. Do you need me to get you some supper?"

"No, I'm going to call a friend." He'd finished another book. He and Lucien had a standing appointment and this time, he not only wanted what the man offered, he needed it. He'd wait for Brian to leave, though. This was not a conversation to be had where he could be overheard.

Relaxing, he asked his computer to turn on his music. Bach poured over him, rich and heavy, and he nodded along, humming. He couldn't wait to make that call, to hear Lucien's gruff voice. To feel... His cock filled, swelled and he wiggled on his chair. *Keep it together, man.*

The sound of Brian's footsteps on the tile coming closer helped him get his erection under control. The last thing he wanted to do was embarrass his assistant — or himself, for that matter.

"I have your coffee and your phone."

He heard Brian set them on his desk.

"The coffee is at two o'clock, half a foot from the edge of the desk. The phone is at nine o'clock. And your headset will be here Monday before noon. Are you sure there isn't anything else you want me to do?"

"No. No, I'm good. I'm planning on staying in this weekend. I have enough dog food, yeah?" Not that Lucien wouldn't go get him some if he didn't, but he'd rather spend his time with Lucien doing other things. Any shopping they did would not be for dog food or anything else as mundane as that.

"You do, yes. And he's out in the yard, playing. Do you want me to call him in?"

"No. No, he'll use the doggie door. We've got this down. I'll see you Monday at ten, hmm?" It was all he could do not to shoo Brian out of the door.

"I'll be here, boss. Have a great weekend!"

"You too, man." Trey sat back, waiting for the sound of the front door locking, followed by the odd high-pitched whine of Brian's moped motor.

As soon as the buzz from the moped disappeared, he grabbed his phone. "Call Lucien."

The phone rang only once before it was answered. "Trey."

"I need you. It's in — Darkness. I have until Monday morning." Five days. No working, no words fighting him, just him and Lucien. For five days. It bore repetition.

"I'll be there in twenty. And boy, you'd better have a plug in when I get there."

The phone went dead, and Trey groaned, rubbing the placket of his slacks. Oh, fuck. Fuck yes. Twenty minutes.

The only question was, did he put in the plug or not, and if he did, which one? Whatever he decided would set the tone for the next five days. If he didn't, it would be punishments and torture. If he used the large one then he would get pampered. If he used a small plug...

That was it. A sweet, little plug. Obedience, but not enough. Lucien would spend the entire weekend pushing him, putting in dildo after dildo, plug after plug, each one larger than the last. Perfect.

Trey headed out of his office, down the hall and into the kitchen. He knew his home by heart and could walk around without worrying about trying to orient himself or figure out where he was — or bumping into anything. Brian knew full well to keep everything exactly where it was.

In the kitchen, he poured himself a glass of water and fed Dodger, the sound of those click-clack claws on the tile as Dodger came in, responding to the sound of the kibble hitting the bowl, making him laugh. "Hey, boy. Your favorite person is coming over."

Dodger barked twice for Trey, as if he understood. He had no doubt that Dodger did.

"I know! We haven't seen him in months." They had an arrangement. Trey needed peace to write, needed complete order and control of his life, and Lucien... Well, Lucien stole that from him. So every time a novel was done, Trey indulged. It wasn't perfect, but it worked for them.

And if he didn't want a long weekend of punishments, he'd better get that plug in. The thought gave him a jolt of excitement. Lucien was magical, making him feel so much, getting him out of his head and fulfilling all his needs. He wasn't sure anymore how he'd managed before Lucien had come into his life.

Trey checked the time, pressing the button on his watch and listening to the readout. He still had ten minutes before Lucien would be here—and he knew Lucien well enough to know that the door would open at precisely twenty minutes from the end of their call. That gave him enough time to brush his teeth, maybe even get himself off.

He headed to the bathroom, stopping to turn the music to low. He washed his face, ran the electric shaver over his cheeks, brushed his teeth, then he searched in the bottom drawer of the vanity. There were three plugs there—one that was the size of a cock, one the size of a finger and the third... That was the one Lucien called the punishment plug. That was for emergencies—like when Lucien couldn't come over because he was out of town on business. Then there was the phone and that thick plug and tears and his own hand. Though to be fair, that had only happened once. Still, it had been one time too many.

Tonight Lucien would bring his own treats.

Trey took out the thin plug and headed toward the bedroom. Lucien had his own key and would be expecting Trey to be in the bedroom, naked, plugged and waiting. It made him feel naughty in the best possible way.

He undressed, before folding his clothes neatly and setting them on the dresser, then he slid under the covers, tracing the smooth plastic of the plug, testing the give. He slipped it into himself with the barest minimum of lube — hell, he barely felt it, but the act of sliding it in his needy hole gave him goosebumps. It was a promise of things to come.

Trey had barely seated the plug when Dodger barked, his claws noisy on the tile as he raced to the front door.

Trey curled up under the covers, focusing on the sound of Lucien's heavy steps on the floor. He heard Lucien giving Dodger his due first, loving on his mutt. *Oh, go, Lucien* — he had found the kick spot and it sounded as if Dodger was trying to dig a hole to China.

Lucien laughed. "Okay, boy. I need to find your Master. See what kind of weekend we're going to have."

God, Trey loved that sound. Lucien's laugh was full-bodied, rich, happy — like the deep voice that made his cock jerk, filling.

There was a last bark from Dodger, then Lucien's footsteps heading to the bathroom. The tap ran for a few moments, and he knew that Lucien would be washing his hands. Then, finally, the footsteps headed straight for him.

Trey smiled, inhaling the delicious scent of wood smoke and spice and wind.

"Someone is hiding under the covers. Would you like the room warmed?" Lucien's rich voice poured over him like honey.

"Good evening, Sir. I felt odd, spread out and naked."

"That's how I like you, though. A feast, just waiting for me."

Trey could hear the subtle sound of buttons sliding through their holes, and he sat up, desperate to see, to touch.

"When I'm naked, Trey."

Lucien always had had the ability to seem to be able to read his mind — or read him, at least. Was it easier if you could see? He thought it probably was.

Trey explored the blanket's edge, the puckering where the stitches were — anything to keep himself busy, to keep his hands from running over his own body, wrapping around his cock. God, the waiting was torture.

He could hear each step as Lucien undressed — Lucien's shirt shushing as it slithered from Lucien's shoulders, the zipper of Lucien's pants slowly being drawn down.

The scent of his lover grew stronger, too, like the best kind of perfume on the air. He swore he could tell when Lucien's boxers were pushed down, too, the thick cock springing out.

"You're naked now." And he wanted to touch.

"I am." Lucien tugged on his covers, and Trey let them go, felt the air brush across his body as Lucien pulled the sheets away. "And now, so are you."

His nipples tightened, the flesh sliding on the metal piercing them and he reached out, searching for contact.

Lucien's hand met his, warm and solid, bringing it to Lucien's shoulder as he straddled Trey. "Look."

Oh, he'd missed this. Broad and muscled, skin smooth as glass, with a broad nose and a square jaw — Lucien was beautiful. The heat of Lucien's body was tremendous, sexy. When Trey's fingers arrived a second time at Lucien's mouth, Lucien kissed them.

"Keep going," Lucien ordered. "Then it's my turn."

"It's good to see you, Sir." The man's eyes were wrinkled at the edges, Lucien smiling. The soft tightly curled hair was kept short, not shaggy like his.

"It's been too long."

The words weren't censure, more fact, though he knew Lucien missed him as much as he missed Lucien.

"It has. This one was challenging. I didn't feel the flow." He'd fought the novel hard, getting more and more frustrated as the days and weeks had passed and it *still* hadn't been finished.

"You should have called me. I could have helped you find your…flow."

"I should have." He tried to save rule breaking for extreme emergencies. He wasn't sure that missing Lucien and being frustrated with his novel counted as one.

Lucien's fingers landed on his face, tracing his features. Trey's body shifted, squeezing the plug. After thoroughly exploring his face and head, Lucien moved to touch his neck, his collarbones and shoulders. He pushed into the touches the way he imagined a large cat might.

All the way down his body, Lucien's touch traveled, awakening his senses. Awakening his very skin. His cock was hard as nails, pushing up toward Lucien's heated fingers. He knew that was a fool's errand. Lucien rarely, if ever, worked his penis, insisting on arousing his hole, his gland. His mind.

He was shocked when a soft kiss landed on the tip of his erection.

"Oh." He moaned, sucking in air.

"Don't get used to it," murmured Lucien, touch sliding over to his hips.

"Tease," Trey accused fondly.

"Yes."

God, Lucien made him happy.

Warm fingers brushed his balls and Trey wiggled, wanting more.

"Spread your legs for me, Trey." Lucien pushed away from his body until he complied, then settled between his legs. One hand pushed in the center of his chest, easing him back to the pillows. The other rolled his balls before heading right for his hole. "Let's see what we've got here, shall we?"

"A plug like you asked, Sir." He hadn't disobeyed. He hadn't pushed himself either. He wanted Lucien to push him.

"Good, good, but which one?" Lucien was moving so slowly, he was never going to get there.

"I started small. We have four whole days." Five, if you counted today, though it was already late afternoon.

"Don't ruin the surprise." Lucien slid the long fingers to his hole, tapping the base of the tiny plug.

"Yes, Sir." He clenched his hole, playing.

Chuckling, Lucien pushed hard on the end of the plug. Trey shivered, the tiny thing rocking deep inside him.

"You started very, very small," Lucien noted.

What was he supposed to say to that, exactly?

Lucien, it seemed, had something to say about it. "We'll have to take it to very, very large. Of course we'll do it very, very slowly."

All Trey could do was moan, his entire body tightening.

"Yeah, you like the thought of that, don't you? My little size slut."

Lucien knew what he needed, all the way to the bone.

After grabbing the base of the plug, Lucien pulled it partway out before shoving it back in again. Lucien repeated the motion again and again, fucking him with the tiny plug, making it feel so much bigger than it was. Trey hummed, his body eager, cock already aching.

Lucien began to push his fingers in with the plug, stretching the base of his hole as the little tip bumped into his sweet spot. He groaned and drew his legs up, knees bending, and every time the little plug touched his gland, it made him jerk.

Electricity buzzed through him, and he couldn't believe how Lucien could make his body feel so good. It didn't matter how many times they did this or whether they used toys big or small, Lucien's fingers, Lucien's cock, it all had him moaning and begging and needing.

"Look at you — dancing for me."

"Buzzing inside." He was — as if Lucien was filling him with electricity.

"Oh, a vibrating plug. I might have brought one of those." Lucien sounded pleased as punch.

Trey was too focused on his body to wonder where that expression came from. Instead, he groaned. "Please."

"Big and fat and buzzing inside you." Lucien said the best things, had the most wonderful ideas.

Oh, yes — Trey nodded for his lover. He was addicted to the burn, to the ache, but more than that? He wanted to be made to stretch, to take everything that Lucien thought to give him and more.

"You ready for me yet, baby?" Lucien tugged that little plug right out of him.

"God, yes. Yes, Sir. Yes."

That's all it took to have Lucien's thick heat pushing into him. Trey groaned, the fat tip popping in, opening his hole and Lucien rolled his hips, stretching him even farther. He loved that ache and burn so much. Grabbing his knees, Trey then tugged and spread himself wide. Offering all of himself to Lucien.

"Slut," murmured Lucien, so much care in the word.

"Yes, Sir. Yours." He knew his need showed on his face, Lucien had told him, many times, that he hid nothing. Which was good because he didn't want to hide — not from Lucien.

"That's right. Mine." Lucien slid deeper and deeper, pushing his thick cock all the way into Trey.

When Lucien's hips pressed against his ass, Trey moaned and squeezed as hard as he could. Lucien's groan was a huge reward. The desperate press of Lucien's lips against his own was a bigger one.

Oh, God. His love. He opened, tongue sliding against Lucien's, his entire body lit up. The kiss went on and on, Lucien absolutely stealing his breath. All Trey could do was hold on tight, ride it out and trust.

Just when he thought he would pass out, Lucien broke the kiss, resting their foreheads together as Lucien pushed into him again and again.

Without the kisses, his focus shifted to his hole and the way each thrust made his balls ache. He could feel each breath Lucien took, hot air against his face, a low panting, and the slap of their bodies as they came together. There were sounds, too, each one backing up the sensations.

Hands moving restlessly, Trey explored and tugged, pulled and touched every bit of Lucien's skin that he could reach.

"Hold my hips and focus on your ass, baby," Lucien demanded.

"God, I love the sound of that." He wrapped his fingers around Lucien's hips, the warm skin slick with sweat. He held on tightly.

"The sound of this?" Lucien slammed into him.

Trey nodded, even though that hadn't been what he meant. He loved when Lucien called him baby. The word made him feel loved and cherished, cared for. Plus it was sexy as hell in Lucien's deep, round tones.

Lucien's thick cock kept pushing into him, filling him over and over, and the urge to grab his own erection was huge, but he knew better and he wanted this easy pleasure first, before the games started — before he was punished for disobeying. That was fun, too, but right now he just wanted to come. He *needed* to come.

Eventually, Lucien shifted, the next thrust hitting his gland. A cry tore from him, the jolt sharp, heady. Perfect.

Lucien made a happy noise. "That's the spot."

It certainly was and Lucien pounded it mercilessly.

"Please!" Trey was on fire. Burning.

"You need to come? To spray for me? To cover your belly in spunk?"

"Need. Oh, fuck. I haven't jacked off in a week, knowing you'd come." The end had been near, he'd felt it, even as hard as the novel had been fighting him.

"You'll still have to wait a few more thrusts before I let you."

"Want to touch my cock, come over and over." Trey wouldn't, though.

"No, you'll come just from this." Lucien pegged his gland particularly hard on the last word.

"Lucien." Trey imagined that felt how light looked.

"You heard me." He could feel Lucien's breath on his ear now. "I won't make you wait."

"Touch me?" Trey knew better, but he had to ask. He knew Lucien wanted him to ask, to share this vulnerability. His need. He did so happily, giving himself to Lucien with abandon.

"Not this time." The low growl that came from Lucien sounded pleased.

Lucien punched in again, then again, and the third time, Trey's body gave up, spunk spurting from him.

"Oh yes." Lucien's low moans were the soundtrack for Trey's orgasm.

Wet fingers smeared spunk on his lips, then Lucien leaned in, breath hot on his face, and lapped the cum from his face.

"Love your taste, baby."

"Love. My Sir." His heartbeat. His lover. His very own Lucien.

Lucien jerked his hips, cock pushing inside Trey again. Trey nodded, the world so close, warm, cozy. Hips rolling, Lucien moved inside him, finding a new rhythm.

"You're in me." Wet and slick, fat and perfect. Trey loved it when he'd come but Lucien hadn't yet—he could concentrate on Lucien's pleasure, on the way Lucien felt inside him and around him, body pressed close.

"I am. You gonna make me come with that magic ass of yours?"

The words made him laugh—or maybe that was the lack of tension, the sweet aftershocks of the orgasm. Still, Lucien's smile felt good against him.

He licked at Lucien's lips, focusing on clenching his hole, teasing that heavy cock. If Lucien's moans were anything to go by, he was doing it right. It encouraged him to squeeze again, then again, searching for more of those noises. He loved making Lucien need as much as he loved what Lucien did for him.

"Fucking love that, baby."

"Good." He wanted Lucien to need this as badly as he did. No, he was pretty sure he *needed* it to be like that.

"Make me come so we can play."

Based on the gruff note in Lucien's voice, that wasn't going to take much.

"Yes, Sir. Anything." Trey gritted his teeth, started squeezing and relaxing, working that fine cock, over and over.

Lucien took his mouth again, tongue fucking his lips in time with his squeezes. Trey wrapped his fingers around Lucien's head, keeping his lover close as he fought to push Lucien over the edge into orgasm.

He could feel it happening, Lucien's erection getting harder inside him, Lucien's thrusts becoming less rhythmic, jerkier.

Trey wrapped his lips around Lucien's tongue—sucking—and a sound filled his mouth, Lucien slamming into him and coming, filling him with heat. He could feel it, could feel Lucien marking him inside.

Panting hard, Lucien dropped his weight down onto Trey, pressing him into the mattress. He wrapped around Lucien, with both arms and legs, holding on tight.

"So fucking glad you called, baby," Lucien said between breaths.

"Needed you. It's been so long." Too long. His stupid fucking pride not allowing him to call Lucien until he'd actually finished his novel, no matter how long that took.

"I'm not going to argue with you about that."

Trey nodded, cheeks heating. He knew. One day they would join their lives, one day when Trey knew he wouldn't become totally dependent on Lucien's strength. He just didn't know when that day was. Hell, it had been close to ten years since they'd first met and he was still worried that if he let Lucien in all the way, he'd never be able to stand on his own again.

"I have a plug to go in when I come out..." Lucien began shifting, moving around, but staying inside him.

Trey nodded, squeezing Lucien's thick heat again. He loved that idea. He knew he'd probably be filled with either Lucien or a plug for the bulk of the weekend, and he loved that thought even more.

"Ah, got it," murmured Lucien, sounding pleased.

Trey reached out, searching for the plug, wanting to feel it so he could anticipate it going in, guess how it would feel as it stretched him open, as it was settled inside him.

"Not this time. You'll feel it soon enough."

There was no way to hide his pout at Lucien's words.

Chuckling, Lucien tugged on his lower lip. That made him laugh, then try to catch Lucien's fingers in a kiss.

"Cheeky boy," Lucien accused gently.

"Yours." Trey had to smile, because he was and it was such a good thing.

"Fuck, yes." Satisfaction practically oozed from Lucien's words.

Then Lucien pressed the plug against his ass, near his hole, near the place where Lucien and he were joined. The plug felt larger than Trey had expected and his lips parted, as if he was trying to make room.

Lucien traced Trey's lips with his hot tongue, then began to pull out of Trey. His entire body clenched, instinctively trying to keep Lucien in.

"Easy, Trey." Lucien's words were soft and easy, soothing, and yet there was a note of steel threaded through him, making it an order. "You'll be happy with my replacement, trust me."

"I do." He did, and more importantly, his body did, relaxing at the firm words.

"Good boy." Lucien slipped his cock the rest of the way out before pushing the plug right in, not giving Trey any chance to even feel empty. The plug was thick and long, bigger than Lucien.

"Oh." He curled up, his hips fucking the air for a few thrusts. He'd expected them to work up to one this size. Not that he was complaining—this felt amazing.

"I knew you'd like that one." Lucien sounded smug. "My size queen. My slut."

How could Trey argue? He lived for this, for the touch and sensation and loss of control. Besides, Lucien had long ago convinced him that those words were compliments, that Lucien liked that he was a size queen, that for Lucien he was a terrible slut.

Playing with the plug, Lucien pulled it partway out, twisted it, and pushed it back in again. Then he pulled it out to the widest part and held it there. God, Trey loved how Lucien played with him, pushed him, made him take things he thought he couldn't.

"Bear down on it, boy," Lucien ordered.

Trey pushed, his toes curling, the stretch going to his soul.

"I love the look on your face right now," murmured Lucien.

"I don't know what that means."

"It means that you look blissfully happy and I know I put that look there. It's hot."

Oh. "I like that." His brother had always told him the looks on his face were wildly inappropriate, but he couldn't really understand that, either. Lucien would always try to explain things he didn't get to him, though.

"Yeah, I do too." Lucien turned the plug, rubbing him on the inside.

His body tried to move with it, follow the motion. He didn't want to lose the plug, not for a second.

"So hungry." Lucien's voice was deep, soft and thick.

"I can't help myself." Trey maybe could have, but his body was moving, responding to Lucien of its own accord.

"Good. I don't want you to."

Lucien's words made him smile and reach for him, needing the connection, needing to know they were together. Lucien's hand wrapped around one of his and brought it to Lucien's broad chest. Beneath his hand, Lucien's heart thumped—the rhythm solid, steady.

"Better?" Lucien asked, as he seated the plug properly inside Trey's body.

"Yes. Yes. You heartbeat is like a song."

"Are you getting sappy on me, baby?" Lucien teased.

"Of course not." He was just feeling. He couldn't help it if he was a writer and sometimes got poetic.

"Damn." Lucien chuckled. "And here I thought I'd melted your brains."

"Well, I couldn't tell someone what you looked like," he teased back. His knowledge of Lucien was all about feeling and hearing and smelling, tasting.

Lucien's soft chuckles turned into laughter and Trey loved that. He added his own laughter to Lucien's, warm and happy.

Settling next to him, Lucien then drew him close, hands warm as Lucien dragged his fingers over Trey's body.

"Lucien…" Trey hummed softly, cuddling in. He felt so warm and safe wrapped in Lucien's arms.

"Don't get too comfortable," warned Lucien. "I have plans."

"Plans?" He nuzzled the curve of Lucien's throat, not concerned. Whatever Lucien had in mind, it was what he needed.

"Oh, yes. I'm going to drive you wild."

He liked the sound of that. He liked the sound of the low, wicked tone of Lucien's voice even more.

"It's just too bad we have to fit it all into a couple of days…" murmured Lucien.

"Shh." Trey shook his head. It would be far too easy to give in and let Lucien take over. "You know where I stand on that. I could learn to need you, so quickly.

Lucien's chuckle was wry. "And would that be such a bad thing?"

"What if you begin to resent me? What if you hate me? You've never lived with a blind control freak nutbag."

This time Lucien's laugh was more natural. "Blind control freak nutbag?"

"That would be me," Trey pointed out, just in case Lucien didn't know.

"Oh, good. I was worried there was another blind control freak nutbag here." Lucien nipped at his nose. "Be nice to yourself."

"I am." Sometimes. Maybe.

Lucien snorted. "If you were really nice to yourself, you'd let me see you more often."

God, he'd love that. Love that. So very much. Too much. Far, far too much. "You know I can't. You're an addiction."

"One that's not illegal and doesn't kill brain cells. There's no bad here," insisted Lucien.

Trey reached out, tracing the warm, familiar features. Fuck, he loved this fine son of a bitch.

Lucien let him look — Lucien always did, like he totally understood Trey's need to see the best way he knew how — then Lucien's warm lips began chasing his fingers, taking soft nips out of them.

Trey's ass clenched around the plug, working the invader hard as Lucien's mouth made him shiver lightly.

"Looking at you." He traced the length and breadth of Lucien's broad nose.

Lucien's soft laughter at his words warmed him all the way through.

"Besides that," said Lucien.

Trey went for innocent, but he really didn't understand expressions and he had no clue what his face was doing as he said, "Huh?"

"You're playing with that plug."

"Would I do that?" He didn't call Lucien sir, just to see where they were in this game. Sometimes Lucien pushed harder than others.

"You so would do that. And if you're angling to get moving on to the punishment side of things, *forgetting* to call me 'Sir' is a great way to go about it."

"I wasn't angling." He was more...curious.

"No? Are you sure?" asked Lucien.

"Pretty sure." He nodded. He honestly hadn't been fishing for punishment. "I just wasn't sure where we were."

"In your bedroom."

Lucien's wry words made him chuckle. "Turd."

"That's me. Sir Turd. Don't forget the sir—it's important."

"God, I love you." The words blurted out of him, uncontainable. Sometimes it just needed to be said.

Trey felt Lucien still, then his mouth covered his, Lucien's kiss fierce. Trey spread, lips opening, tongue sliding against his lover's and Lucien grabbed hold of his tongue

The entire time they kissed, Trey's ass worked the toy inside him, squeezing and relaxing. It was so big and felt so good. It felt even better when one of Lucien's hands slid around his body, grabbed his butt. Those fingers dug in, feeling his glutes, testing him.

"Go ahead and do it again, boy," Lucien told him. "I want to feel your muscles working."

That was no hardship, and Trey squeezed the plug, let it move inside him.

Lucien groaned for him. "Oh, that's sexy.

"Feels so good, Sir. Always better with your plugs." He had a collection of his own—hell, Lucien had bought them for him—but it was never the same.

"That's because I sprinkle them with magic."

"Sprinkle them with magic?" That was *so* going in a book.

"Yep. Lucien's special magic plug dust."

Trey started laughing, just cackling madly. God, he really did love this man, so very much.

"God, that's an amazing sound," Lucien said softly.

"You make me so happy, Sir." He thought Lucien knew that already, but he needed to be sure, because it was important.

"That's my mission." Lucien's slid his hands over Trey's body, making his skin alive.

He felt on fire, burning top to bottom, lit up inside and out.

"You ready for more, baby? It's been so long and I have so many plans for your hot little bod."

"More. More, please. Sir. Love." Now. Now would be good. Trey wanted everything Lucien would give him.

"I think maybe we need to put a ring on this needy cock of yours."

"Please." Trey loved that—not being able to shoot, to feel the pressure in his balls.

Lucien nuzzled his neck, then murmured into his ear. "Slut."

The word sent a jolt of lightning through Trey, making him spread and moan. He loved the things Lucien said to him, loved how they made him feel.

Lucien moved away for a moment, one hand on his arm so he knew his lover was still close. Shifting back against him, Lucien let him feel the cock ring first, dragging it over his belly, then across his nipples. It was leather, cool at first touch, but warming quickly from his skin. It felt heavy, thick, and he licked his lips. The scent of leather was heady and it gave the cock ring even more weight.

"You like the smell of that?" asked Lucien. "The feel of it?"

Trey nodded. Of course he did. It was delicious.

Lucien rubbed his nose along Trey's cheek again. "I love how sensuous you are."

"Well, four out of five, hmm?" He had never had five senses.

Lucien slid the leather cock ring around his growing erection. "You make up for it."

That right there was one of the things Trey loved about Lucien—the man didn't pity him. Not for a moment.

"I do." Trey arched up into the touches around his cock.

Lucien continued to drag the cock ring over his skin and his cock jumped and jerked—whether to get away or get more of Lucien's attention, he wasn't sure. He did know that Lucien would do as he wanted, taking as long or short a time as it pleased him to get the cock ring around Trey's heat.

Humming, Lucien finally wrapped the ring around the base of Trey's cock, and the sound of the ends snapping closed together was loud. The cock ring bit into him, pressing into his skin just enough.

"Little pain slut," murmured Lucien.

"N...not. Not." He wasn't—he was Lucien's size slut.

Lucien laughed loudly. "You are too!"

"Uh-uh." Trey moaned, sliding his fingers down to touch his cock.

"Are you going to give that a light pat or a pinch?" Lucien asked.

"Huh?" The ring was tight, already pinching him. Not too hard, though, just right.

Lucien's hand stopped his. "What's your plan for those fingers, babe?"

"I just wanted to see the ring on." He needed to 'look' at it.

"Ah. That's allowed." Lucien let go of his hand and instead stroked his belly, the touches soft but not ticklish.

Trey reached for his cock again, exploring it and the ring at the base. "It's tight."

"It's supposed to keep you from coming."

"Do you like it?" Did it look good? He didn't want Lucien to think it utilitarian.

"Mmm-hmm." Lucien touched the cock ring, fingers sliding on his. "It looks amazing against your pale skin."

Trey wasn't sure what that meant, exactly — pale — but Lucien sounded pleased, so he didn't worry about it. Then Lucien stroked his erection and that was better than any tone. Trey rolled his hips up, his hands falling aside.

Humming again, Lucien shifted, moving away from him. Then Lucien ran his nose along Trey's cock, skin and air both teasing him.

"Sir!" Trey's entire body arched, following Lucien's touches.

"Mmm." God, he could almost feel the vibrations from Lucien's sound.

There was nothing like his lover, his Sir, like this. If he was beautiful, sensual, if he was anything it was because of Lucien.

Lucien's touches became licks, tongue hot and slick on his skin. Trey gasped with the touches of Lucien's flicking tongue. From the tip of his cock, down to his balls, Lucien licked him everywhere, but oh so very slowly, thoroughly.

The air felt cold in his cock wherever the wet licks passed. Then Lucien blew over his skin, increasing the sensation of cold.

"Sir…" Trey drew his knees up to his chest in a silent plea for more. He didn't even care what exactly he was begging for — he just needed more of Lucien.

Licking from his balls to his hole, Lucien left a long line of cooling damp behind.

"Sir." He said it again as his balls drew up, so tight, almost tugging inside him.

"Yes, boy?"

"I…" Trey shook his head. He was a fucking writer, for God's sake, and he didn't have words. Lucien did that to him. What a power to hold.

Chuckling, Lucien continued licking. The heat was so intense it almost felt like electric shocks. Then Lucien took one of Trey's balls into his mouth. Trey's breath caught in his chest, his whole body stilling, freezing in place.

Humming, making his whole body vibrate, Lucien sucked gently.

Oh. Oh, fuck. Oh, God. Trey couldn't even breathe.

Lucien's humming got louder, the vibrations moving through Trey becoming stronger. He cried out, gasping as he finally sucked in a deep breath.

Lucien eventually let go of Trey's testicle, only to take the other one into his mouth. The contrast between the cool air on his wet orb and the heated mouth on the other one was maddening — pure insanity. Lucien was taking his sweet fucking time, too, like they had all day for him to just explore Trey's cock and sac.

Trey was so hard he ached, and the plug inside him shifted as he continued to work it.

Then Lucien added words to the mix. "I love how much you need, how you ache for my every touch."

He did. "Every second of every day."

Was that vibration a little growl?

Trey moaned, caught in pleasure. The vibration came again, Lucien clearly trying to drive him out of his mind. His legs moved restlessly, like he was swimming on the sheets. After spreading his thighs wide, Lucien licked at his hole, at where his skin was stretched around the plug.

"Sir." The single word was a whisper, and Trey barely heard it in his own head.

He felt Lucien's hum against his skin, though. God, that mouth — that tongue — was magic.

Trey's ass worked the plug over and over, the pressure inside him perfect. Delicious.

Then Lucien's nose nudged his balls as Lucien continued to lick around his stretched hole. Trey called out to his lover, over and over, begging for this, for more — for it never to end.

Lucien's fingers danced over his belly, but it wasn't enough to distract him from that hot tongue on his ass. He let out a slew of vicious curse words, trying to release the pressure inside him.

"Such a dirty mouth," accused Lucien, sounding so calm while Trey was in a storm of sensation.

"Fucking need you!" He shouted the words and it felt good to let them loose.

"I'm right here."

He nodded, swallowing over the lump in his throat. Right here. He could feel each of Lucien's breaths against his skin. Here. Real. His. God.

Without warning, Lucien swallowed him whole, his cock pulled into heat. Trey jerked, hips pumping violently, taking Lucien's mouth. Lucien let him, let him fuck that amazing mouth.

Trey screamed inside his head, his body taking what it needed. Lucien's hand wrapped around his hips, encouraging him to keep moving, to do it faster, harder.

"Lucien. My Sir. Fuck. Your mouth. Fucking heaven. Couldn't write anything so big." His words were failing him.

Lucien responded by sucking harder and Trey's lips opened and closed, his hips driving until his muscles screamed with the effort.

The feel of Lucien's fingers undoing the ring around the base of his cock was huge and oh, sweet fuck, he was going to shoot. He was.

Lucien sucked harder, as if he knew, and pulled the ring right off.

"Sir." Trey bit out the word as Lucien rolled his ball sac and spunk sprayed out of him in waves.

Lucien took him in, swallowing down everything he had to give.

Finally, Trey slumped to the mattress, his chest working like a bellows. Lucien kept sucking his cock, licking and cleaning it, mouth like a firebrand on him.

Trey was spent enough, though, that he couldn't even work the plug.

Lucien eventually let go of his flesh and slowly kissed his way back up to Trey's mouth. The kiss they shared this time felt sloppy, lazy, and Lucien's body was heavy against his, solid and comforting.

"Rest, baby. I'm here."

He nodded, smiled. For four whole days. Trey could pretend like it was forever.

Chapter Two

Lucien held Trey as his lover dozed. Three orgasms in a row would do that to a man. Of course Trey still had about nine hundred and eighty-four left to go to catch up on all the ones he'd missed over the last six months. Six months — it felt like it was taking longer and longer for Trey to finish each book.

Lucien still wasn't happy with their arrangement — he wanted more of Trey, wanted them to be proper lovers, to be able to see each other every evening after work, to sleep and live together — but it was what it was. He cared for Trey too much to make any sort of ultimatum. If this arrangement was what Trey needed, then so be it.

He placed a soft kiss on Trey's forehead and traced every feature with his gaze. His lover looked exhausted, worn, worried.

Lucien had to admit he didn't understand why it was so important to Trey to be on his own. He respected his lover's wishes, but he didn't like them — at all.

They'd met ten years ago. Ten. Trey had been an instant addiction and Lucien had known immediately that he was going to love the man until the end of time. Trey's parents, though, had been evil long before Lucien had known him, accusing Trey of choosing a man because he was afraid of taking care of himself, not because he was gay or in love.

Trey had taken the accusations to heart and refused to let Lucien move in, be a part of his day-to-day life. So now they had time whenever Trey finished a book and Lucien would take it. He just wished it wasn't so long in-between books. This last time, he'd thought Trey would never call.

He was going to blow the man's mind for the next four days. Maybe, if he was lucky, this time Trey would ask him to stay. He was going to do what he could to make that happen.

"Oh, Lucien. You're here." Trey's lips spread into a satisfied grin as he woke.

"I am." Lucien took Trey's hand and brought it to his face.

"I was dreaming." Trey's fingers explored him, lazily but so very thoroughly.

The way Trey's blue eyes moved fascinated him, usually so restless and searching, but focused and still now, trusting his fingers to do the work.

Lucien waited until Trey had finished exploring and began to kiss the lovely, sensitive fingertips.

"Is it morning? Still night?"

"Still night, baby. In fact it's only about nine. You only had a catnap."

"Oh." That smile widened, Trey relaxing. "I didn't waste any of our time."

"Nope. Although maybe we should start tacking on time at the end for sleeping." Four days could become eight that way.

"My body would never survive." Trey nodded, though, agreeing.

"Excellent. Eight days it is." He wasn't letting Trey take his agreement back, either.

The last couple of times they'd shared their lives, Trey had begun letting him in deeper, agreeing to outings to the coffee shop, around the block to walk Dodger and introducing Lucien to the assistant. And now he had eight days. A whole week and a day. Who knew what inroads he could make with that?

He rubbed Trey's belly, loving the tight little tummy.

Trey arched into his touch. "Mmm. You have the best hands."

Lucien knew that wasn't true. Trey's fingers were like magic. "Yours are better."

"They have to be," Trey pointed out.

"I know." Lucien began to tease Trey's fingertips, mouthing them with his lips.

He got a blissful smile, Trey's nipples hard as little rocks, muscles exposing how Trey was working that plug once again. Lucien was glad he'd left it in. "God, you're insatiable."

"All your fault."

Laughing, he rubbed himself against Trey, letting his lover know that it wasn't a complaint.

"Are you hungry?" Trey asked. "I'm sure there's something in the fridge."

"I'm hungry for you. And when I've had my wicked way with you, we'll forage or order or something.

"Forage. You and me in the backyard, hunting mushrooms."

He snorted. He'd bet his picky lover wouldn't know a mushroom if he dropped one in Trey's hand. Besides, they always ordered, Trey a creature of habit. "I imagine the only mushrooms in your backyard are the psychedelic variety," Lucien noted.

"I guess? I've only been out there a couple of times."

He hadn't known that, hadn't known that Trey had this big backyard he never used. "Then we need to spend time out there over the next week." This was one of the reasons he wanted Trey to let him in. Everything was so structured. Every day was the same when he wasn't around.

He moved his hands over Trey's body, offering his lover as much sensation as he could. He loved to watch Trey move, so completely unselfconscious, so honest. God, he was so in love.

"Missed this," Trey moaned. "You."

"I'm yours." Lock stock and barrel, he belonged to Trey.

"So glad." Trey twisted, body pushing into each of his touches.

Lucien watched, utterly fascinated by Trey. There was such an unconscious grace in the slender boy, in each of Trey's movements.

He circled Trey's belly, watching the muscles jerk and flex beneath his fingertips.

A pink flush climbed up Trey's cheeks. "Good."

"I..." Trey couldn't argue with that. Trey would be lying after all, if he did.

"Going to have to take the plug out, clean you up, find another one." He took good care of his boy, made sure Trey didn't get sore.

Trey groaned and shook his head, but that ass kept working the plug, telling an entirely different story.

"Oh yes. I want to watch you walking with that thing in your ass." Lucien was always fascinated by how having a plug in totally changed how Trey walked.

"Perv." Trey swallowed, over and over, as if there was a lump in his throat.

"Yes, absolutely." Lucien wouldn't deny it.

He teased Trey's erection, swatting it lightly, moving it back and forth.

"We'll shower together in-between plugs." He knew his sensual lover enjoyed the way the water falling around them changed the sensations.

Trey spent a lot of time jacking off in the shower. Lucien had no doubt. It would be the easiest way for him to keep things cleaned up.

Pressing a kiss to Trey's cock and grabbing his lover's hands, Lucien then tugged Trey up into a sitting position. It said a lot, that Trey let him do it without tensing at all. His lover trusted him implicitly. Lucien picked Trey up, loving how Trey's legs wrapped automatically around his waist.

Trey's house was big, simple — the only things on the wall in Brian's little office. Lucien ignored it all and headed for the bathroom, kicking one of Dodger's balls down the hall for the pup.

"I hear someone's ball!" Trey was good at that. He could decipher so many different sounds and what they meant.

"I sent it into the living room — keep him from under foot so I don't trip over him as we go to the bathroom."

"Does the house look good? Everything's holding up?" Trey asked.

"You know it looks fantastic. Your assistant is keeping things up." And there was a housekeeper to make sure it all stayed clean.

"I hope it does. I want it to. He's a good kid, honestly. I'll be sorry when he's finished his studies and wants a real job."

"I believe you. And I'm doing something wrong if you're worried about the house instead of trying to rub off against my belly," he noted.

Trey stopped then laughed for him. "You are absolutely right. I just... I can trust you, implicitly, with everything."

"Oh, that was a good answer. You should be a writer," he teased, turning on the light as he carried his burden into the bathroom. All but one of the light bulbs were out, so he made a mental note to change them—Brian used the bathroom at the front of the house and, as far as Lucien knew, never used this one.

"Maybe I'll think about going into that...writing."

Chuckling, he carefully set Trey down on the toilet seat. Trey's fingers searched the vanity, the wall on the other side, his lover always looking.

Lucien got the shower going, turning the spray of water nice and hot like he knew Trey liked it. "Did I tell you about the shower toys I saw?"

"No. No, tell me. Where did you see them?" Curious boy.

Lucien loved how Trey wanted to know about everything.

"Online. You can get a shower head that detaches and there's all these different heads that go on in its place." It was sexy as hell and he could imagine using them on Trey, feeding the different heads into his lover's ass.

Lucien took Trey's hands again and brought him into the shower.

"Really? Like cocks?" Trey's eyes were wide, then they closed as Lucien tugged him into the spray.

"Yes. Like cocks and all sorts of plugs, things to fill you with water. Ones with one hole, with two, with a whole bunch. They were pretty neat."

The water fell around them. "Warm enough?" Lucien asked.

"It's perfect." Trey held onto him with one hand. "Did you... Did you get some?" That meant Trey was intrigued.

"I didn't. I needed to check your set up here to make sure I bought the right stuff." But he had days now, and he could take the time to do that and to get them here before he was banished again as Trey started his next book. "They had overnight shipping."

"Do they? That's expensive."

"You're worth it, baby." He did love how that made Trey's cheeks go pink. "Just imagine, by the day after tomorrow we could be pushing plugs that spray water up your ass." Okay, that had sounded sexier in his head.

"Lucien!" Trey's eyes went wide, moving around madly.

"I've got you." He wrapped his arms around Trey.

"Sorry. Sorry. I—" Trey chuckled, cheeks heated. "You say things."

"I'll tell you a secret. I say them because I like the way you react." He loved that Trey was so open with his feelings.

"Like a shocked idiot?

Lucien laughed and held Trey tight against him. "You could never look like an idiot."

"No? You promise?"

"I promise. You are beautiful, Trey. Always. You take my breath." Lucien meant every word, too.

"I worry. I worry about it. About things."

Lucien knew. Trey worried all the time. Not so much when he was there, though. "You need a handsome man in your home, telling you how wonderful you are." Trey needed someone who helped him leave the house, travel. Trey needed him, damn it.

"You make me feel almost normal," Trey admitted.

"That would be because you are."

"Almost." Trey leaned into him.

"Almost." He kissed the top of Trey's head before picking up the soap.

Trey's fingers were moving constantly, looking, searching. Lucien loved the little touches and wanted them to be a daily thing.

He started soaping Trey up, doing some looking of his own. It made him wild, how his fingertips confused Trey's hands, distracted that curious focus. He teased his fingers across Trey's cheeks. Trey followed him, head pushing into his hand, lips open, seeking.

"They're soapy, baby, you don't want them in your mouth."

"No. No, that's nasty." Trey wrinkled his nose, the expression adorable.

Chuckling, he kissed the tip of that adorable nose, then put soap bubbles on it. Trey blew them off, the foam floating off in the air. It made him chuckle and he put more on Trey's nose.

"Stop it." Another blow, and this bunch of bubbles went up toward Trey's forehead.

"No, you look cute with the bubbles."

"Cute? Cute? I thought I was a stud!" Trey flexed, gritting his teeth playfully.

God, it was all Lucien could do not to crack up. His lover was fine and sensual, hot and sexual, but a muscle man? No. Of course that wasn't what he was going to say to Trey. He went for, "You are a stud. But even Mr. Universe would look cute with bubbles on his nose."

"Mr. Universe is like you, huh?" Trey put bubbles on Lucien's nose.

Laughing, he rubbed their noses together. "Mr. Universe is way more muscular than I am."

"Really? More than you?"

"I know it's hard to imagine…" He mock flexed his arm muscles.

Trey nodded, though, face so serious. "I've never seen anyone with more muscles than you."

"And you never will." He wasn't letting Trey touch anyone but him. So no 'seeing' anyone else—Mr. Universe or not.

"No. No, I don't want this with anyone but you."

"Good." Lucien knew that, but it was still good to hear.

He took a hard, fierce kiss. Trey arched into him, whimpered softly, tongue sliding alongside his, and their bodies rubbed together, Trey slick with soap.

"Love how the soap feels on your skin," Trey told him, starting to sound somewhat breathless.

"Yeah? It makes everything nice and slippery." Lucien certainly enjoyed the way their bodies moved together with the soap to ease the way.

"Slick and…" Trey paused, tilting his head slightly until he figured out exactly what he wanted to say. "It's like I can feel everything."

"More than you can without the soap?" Lucien asked. The way Trey saw fascinated him.

"There's nothing stopping the feelings, making them everywhere."

He considered that, sliding his own hands on Trey's slick skin. "I think I know what you mean."

"It's amazing." Trey dragged his fingers down Lucien's sides, digging in.

He groaned, pushing into the touches. Trey began to sing, the words barely audible, focus clearly on his skin. Moaning, he pressed closer, the combination of the hot water and Trey's fingers magical.

His lover held his cock, squeezed it, weighed it, then Trey wrapped those long fingers around his ball sac. This time his moan was louder, a sweet shudder going all through his body.

"I won't hurt you. I just like to explore."

"That wasn't from hurt, baby." He loved the way Trey touched him, whether it was just to look or to arouse him.

"Good." Trey carefully slid down, then his lover was kneeling before him, plugged ass on Trey's heels.

"Oh, fuck. Trey…" Was there any sight better than that? Lucien didn't think so. In fact he knew there wasn't.

"Sir." Trey leaned forward, cheek sliding on his shaft. His baby was still clean shaven, cheek smooth and soft.

It looked as if the water and Trey's touches had washed away any soap on his cock, so he nodded. "Yes, please, baby. Taste me."

Trey's lips started at the base of his cock, teeth carefully tugging the black curls around it. It made him groan. He did love the way Trey explored. The first time they'd made love, he'd been stunned at how amazing it felt to be trapped in Trey's focus. It had spoiled him for anyone else. Hell, everything about

Trey had, and Lucien wasn't the least bit unhappy about it.

"You smell good," Trey told him. "I forget sometimes how much I love the scent of you needing."

"I could send you texts to remind you." He could move in, sleep next to his lover, take Trey out and about.

Trey chuckled, lips sliding over his balls. Lucien bit his lower lip, spread his feet wider apart.

Trey buried his face in Lucien's body, breathing deep — the motion purely erotic, so incredibly sensual. Humming, the pleasure too big to be completely contained, Lucien stroked his hand over Trey's head. The wet, heavy strands of hair tangled around his fingers, tugged at them.

He stroked Trey's cheek with his other hand. "Don't stop, baby."

"Not going to." Trey licked and nuzzled the base of his, chin nudging his balls.

He had almost forgotten how Trey could torture him with his slow explorations. His lover touched him like there was nothing on earth he'd rather do. Was it any surprise he wanted this full-time?

Slowly, Trey worked his way up to the tip of Lucien's cock. The entire way, Trey rocked, working the plug inside him. Fuck. This was... stupendous. Stunning. Everything Lucien wanted.

Trey held his cock in both hands, thumbs on the tip, tongue exploring the slit. A shudder rocked Lucien, a low moan coming out of him. Oh, fuck. So sweet, so good. It was going to make him stupid.

He started babbling, "Trey. Love you, baby."

"Love." The single word was whispered against his cockhead, then Trey took him in, swallowing around him. This strangled sound came out of him.

Trey sucked hard, moving like the world's most perverted angel in front of him. He reached out, bracing a hand on the wall as he began to slowly rock into the suction.

"Don't think I've forgotten why we're in here, boy." He forced the words out, knowing they'd drive Trey insane. "Gonna clean you, put a bigger plug in, make you need." Then they could find the site with the shower toys and order them for immediate delivery.

He closed his eyes and rocked again, pushing deep, taking Trey's mouth. Trey groaned, fingers digging into his hips, pulling him even closer. He wrapped his free hand around Trey's head and moved faster, and suddenly he was rutting, fucking Trey's mouth, needing nothing more than completion.

"Fuck! Trey!" It was the only warning he managed before he came, pouring spunk down Trey's throat.

His lover drank him down, swallowing convulsively, over and over. He watched Trey's face, the bliss and pleasure there. Lucien needed this man more than breathing.

When his orgasm let go of him, he leaned against the tile, panting. Trey rested against him, quiet and heavy.

"Well... My pipes have been cleaned," he teased, voice still thick from his orgasm.

"Oh, that was bad." Trey popped the tip of his cock, gently, making it bob and sway next to Trey's face.

Chuckling, Lucien grabbed Trey's hand to keep him from doing it again. "It was."

Trey wound their fingers together and stood, swaying a little, cock hard like a lance, jutting out from between Trey's slender hips. Lucien helped his lover up, letting his body support Trey.

"Time to take care of you now." He'd made promises he intended to keep.

Trey kissed him, the buss a bit desperate.

Stroking Trey, Lucien offered the comfort of touch. "Easy, baby. I'm going to take care of you."

"'Kay." Trey's word was carried out on a moan.

"I need to take out the plug and clean you inside." It was time.

"Do you have to?"

"Yes. Why don't you want me to?" he asked, surprised.

"It... It's so big, so hard to control."

"But I'm taking it out, so wouldn't that be a good thing?" Although he was putting another one in again.

"I mean the cleaning, Sir. The process."

Lucien was good with that. "Ah, excellent."

Trey's eyebrow rose. "Is it excellent?"

"It is. I like making things huge for you." Lucien maybe needed to.

Trey nodded, unseeing eyes moving furiously again.

Lucien kissed Trey's forehead and slid his hand down to Trey's ass. Pushing close, Trey hid against him. It wasn't going to work, though and Lucien played with the base of the plug. He could feel Trey ripple against him as he manipulated the plug.

"I love cleaning you out. It's going to be even more fun when I get the shower attachments."

Trey's moan was pure, unadulterated need.

Tugging at the base of the plug, Lucien pulled it right out—it was time. Trey offered him a low cry, a shudder, cock throbbing against his belly.

"My sweet, needy boy."

Trey's answer was a series of soft, wanton pants.

Lucien used two fingers, pushing them into Trey's sweet body. Trey's hole trembled against his fingers, shaking, drawing him in farther. Groaning, he pressed them deeper yet, pushing against Trey's gland.

"Fuck." Oh, filthy words.

He loved them from Trey's mouth because they were fairly rare. Watching Trey lose control was one of his favorite things — ever.

He spread his fingers inside Trey, then pushed against the little gland again. Trey jerked, nearly climbing him.

"Mmm. Yeah, you need this. So badly." He kept working Trey's little hole, encouraging Trey's body to squeeze and jerk, to push out his come he'd trapped inside with the plug.

"I... Sir." Trey moaned low, eyes rolling.

"Should I clean you out with the tubing, baby? Then I'll clean you out with my tongue."

"Lucien!" Trey shook his head, gasping for breath. Such a wonderful reaction. Trey couldn't hide anything from him, it was always written there on the lovely features.

"Yes, baby. That's exactly what I'm going to do." Lucien knew there was equipment for it in the cupboard under the sink, pushed to the back, hidden and out of the way. He'd brought it himself last time he'd been here. He'd driven Trey utterly insane at the time.

"No. No. I." Trey was sawing that needy cock against him, looking dangerously close to climax.

Grabbing Trey's balls, Lucien tugged on them, giving the movement a little twist at the end. "Not without my permission."

"Sir!" Oh, that was a lovely desperation in Trey's voice.

Lucien tugged a little harder. "I mean it."

"I-I..." Trey's little struggle was delicious.

"Yes, baby? Go on."

"I need you, Sir."

And that made things so much more fun.

"Good." Lucien kissed Trey softly then returned his fingers to Trey's ass, pressing two in again.

Trey moved on his touch like a dream, focused on him and him alone. He found that sweet gland once more, making Trey's whole body jerk for him.

"Sir. Oh, right there."

"Here?" He pushed his fingers against that spot again.

"Uh. Uh-huh." Trey's eyes were heavy lidded now.

Lucien loved being able to make Trey incoherent. Grinning, he continued to work Trey's sweet spot. There was no question where Trey's focus was now. Zero.

Lucien stretched his fingers wide, then hit that sweet gland again. Trey went up on tiptoes, almost falling. Lucien had his boy, though — he wouldn't let Trey fall. Never. He was put on earth for this.

He tugged at Trey's upper lip, letting his teeth scrape along it as he continued to finger-fuck the sweet little ass.

"I-I need to... It's big." Trey was ramped up, and Lucien loved it.

"You're not allowed to come." He brushed his lips against Trey's ear. "You can't come until after I clean you, until after I plug you up again." He let his fingers fall away as he spoke.

Trey moved almost frantically against him. "Need you. I need you, Master."

"Just stay here, baby. I'm going to get the stuff to clean you out." He couldn't possibly reach from the shower.

Trey moaned, but that pretty cock didn't flag, not for a second.

Taking Trey's hands, Lucien placed them against the tile. "Don't move."

Then he slipped out of the shower. The equipment waited right where he'd left it, and he wrapped his fingers around it, tugging the tubing out of the cupboard. He grabbed soft towels, too, leaving those on the edge of the tub as he climbed back into the shower.

Trey was waiting right where Lucien had left him and he reached out, touched that beautiful ass. Trey didn't say a word, but Trey did push back, offering that pert ass to him. It was stunning, the trust Trey gave him. Had given him since the beginning.

"I have what I need. I'm going to put the tubing into you."

"I trust you," Trey told him.

Lucien knew. "That's what makes everything we do so special." Trey's trust left him a little breathless, to be honest.

He slid his fingers back into Trey's ass, wriggled them around. Trey reacted to each touch with soft sounds, with desperate little wiggles. Needy little slut.

Pulling his fingers out, Lucien grabbed the tubing. "I'm going to feed the tube into you now."

He felt Trey tensing, but it didn't matter, the tube was going in. Trey needed to be cleaned if they were going to keep playing with the plugs. After pushing two fingers back into Trey's ass, Lucien spread them and put the tubing in between them. Soft panting filled the air, Trey's forehead pressed against the tiles.

"You're doing great, Trey." Lucien kept feeding the tubing in. This was the easy part, after all. It was what came next that made Trey work to keep it together. "Okay I'm going to start filling you."

Trey didn't argue, but there was a hint of a moan on the air. Lucien loved that about Trey. While sometimes Trey liked to play, to complain or be coy, he owned the fact that he was a bottom, a size queen and a bit of a pain slut. The lack of shame was sexy as hell to Lucien.

He only opened the valve partway, wanting this to take time. "When I get the shower attachments, we'll have one that plugs you. You won't be able to push the water out until I say you're allowed to." He whispered the words against his boy's ear.

He loved the sound of Trey's needy moan.

"I'm going to fill you all the way up with water." His lovely size queen should be able to take a lot.

"No..." Despite the negative, Trey sounded like he was flying.

"Yes, and when you think you can't take anymore, I'm going to keep filling you." He knew how to keep Trey on edge.

Trey rocked, moaning, moving against him. He put his hand on Trey's belly, rubbing it in circles as the soapy water continued to fill his lover. A dark flushed climbed up Trey's body, coloring the pale skin a deep rose.

"You're doing so well and you look so sexy." He kept talking, knowing it helped Trey to hear his voice.

"I do? You mean it?"

"I don't lie to you, Trey. You make me need." He rubbed his hard-on against Trey's hip as proof. Trey's submission itself was aphrodisiac enough for a hundred men.

He went back to rubbing Trey's belly, feeling it there as Trey began to be filled. Moaning softly, Lucien continued to rub against Trey's thigh. "There so many things I want to do to you."

"Tell me? Please?" Trey begged.

"Well, I can't wait to rim you and fill you with the vibrating plug I brought." He hummed happily. "I'm going to drive you crazy." Maybe they'd go down to the coffee shop with it in. Wasn't that a lovely thought? He could buzz it inside Trey at random times. It made him laugh happily.

"What? What's funny?" Trey was on edge.

"Not laughing because of funny. Laughing because I can't contain my happiness." And it was all because of Trey.

"Oh. I get that. I do."

"Good. That's how you make me feel." He kissed Trey's shoulder. "And when we're done this evening, we'll go shower toy shopping."

"Uh-huh. Please. I'm full."

He pressed his hand a little harder against Trey's belly. "You can take a little bit more." He took Trey's flaccid penis in hand, beginning to stroke gently. "You were hard moments ago, baby."

"Uh-huh."

And it wasn't taking much to bring Trey back, either, that pretty cock eager for attention. Lucien rubbed the tip, letting just a little more water into Trey's ass. Trey's lips parted, his hips rolling in tiny motions.

"Yeah, you're getting it now, baby." Lucien stopped the water, making Trey hold it and fight the urge to thrust into his touch. "Just a little longer, Trey. Hold on until I say you can let go." He kept his fingers moving, even as he eased Trey out of the tub, toward the toilet. "You're doing great, baby. Just great."

He got Trey sitting on the pot. "Now hold it until I say."

Trey panted, hands gripping him fiercely. It was sexy as hell, watching Trey fight to obey, knowing his lovely boy put Lucien's demands ahead of those of his own body.

Lucien pressed a kiss to Trey's lips. "Okay, baby. You've done amazingly. You can let go."

Trey's eyes moved furiously, panicked, wild, like they were trying to light on something.

"Easy, baby. You have this." Lucien made soft, soothing noises, his hand petting Trey's arm.

Trey sucked in shallow, hysterical breaths, but they were easing, the panic beginning to fade.

"Just let go now. It's just fine." *Trust me, boy. In all things.* "I love you, baby."

"Love." Trey let go, hiding his face in his hands.

Lucien tilted Trey's head up and took a kiss. "There is no shame in this." He watched the emotions flash across his lover's face—worry, shame, arousal, panic. "No shame. You did great."

Tears trembled on Trey's lashes, but Lucien cleaned up, flushed, then he got his boy back in the shower.

"You'll get used to it," he promised. He was putting the cleaning into regular rotation. There was no reason they couldn't do this every time, especially if he got to stay a week or more from now on.

Trey pushed into his arms, holding on tightly.

"I've got you and I'm not letting go." Lucien spoke the words fiercely. Trey was *his*. They might be unconventional lovers, but there was no denying that they belonged to each other.

He pressed kisses over Trey's face, and Trey chased them, following Lucien's lips. Finally, they were kissing, Lucien working to bring Trey back to life, to arousal. Trey's sweet cock filled, his lover's hands sliding over his arms. That was it. He needed Trey focused on the here and now.

Lucien needed his lover to burn with need.

"Want to taste you, boy."

Trey nodded, moaning and reaching for him and Lucien took the kiss he wanted first, tasting Trey's mouth. Trey slammed into his embrace, tongue sliding against his. Pushy. Sweet, beautiful, needy pushy boy.

Grabbing Trey's ass, Lucien then spread it, teased a finger from each hand into it. He needed to get them to bed, but the hot water was holding out, the steam bubbling and it felt good, right here.

"Hold onto the tile again." Lucien turned Trey back around, helped his baby spread his legs. Then he knelt down, nose dragging along Trey's spine.

"Oh." The tiny word made him smile.

Smiling, Lucien kissed the base of Trey's spine. "I'm going to make you moan for me." He kissed each ass cheek.

Trey gave a breathless little laugh. "That won't be a challenge for you."

"Good." He dragged his tongue along Trey's crack.

Trey spread for him, ass offered freely and Lucien grabbed an ass cheek in each hand and pushed them apart, flicking his tongue out to lick at the little hole. It didn't take any time at all for Trey to press back against him, begging for his tongue.

Lucien continued stroking until Trey's sawing motions became a little desperate, then he pointed his tongue and pressed it into Trey's body.

"Sir! Lucien!" Trey's tiny hole gripped him tight, grabbing at his tongue.

Lucien moaned his reply, knowing the vibrations would shake Trey. He heard Trey's hands slap on the tile, heard his boy's need and that urged him on. He fucked the little hole with his tongue, pushing it as deep as he could while Trey humped his face desperately, slamming back against him. Grabbing Trey's hips and holding him in place, Lucien pushed in deep, and wriggled his tongue around.

"Please." The word was desperate, wanton.

Lucien wriggled his tongue a bit more, then backed off. "Need to put the plug into you."

"Lucien, I need."

"I know. Plug first. Then I'll make you come." In fact, he'd use the plug to make Trey come. He knew the stimulation to Trey's ass and gland would do the job.

"Here or on the bed?" Trey asked.

"Bed." He could take his time that way, and Trey would be more relaxed.

"'Kay." Trey didn't move, though.

Chuckling softly, he blew across Trey's hole. That earned him a delicious, full body shudder. So he did it again.

The water was starting to feel less hot, though, so he turned it off and helped Trey out of the shower. Grabbing a towel, he spent his time drying Trey off. "You're doing great, baby. Just wait for this plug I brought. You're going to love it."

"You spoil me."

"I try." He thought Trey deserved a little spoiling — or possibly a lot. Definitely a lot.

His lover grinned. "You do. I'm always stunned when you're still waiting for me. Most guys would give up."

"Most guys are idiots." He might not be a hundred percent happy with their arrangement, but he loved Trey and that was what mattered.

"Most guys are," Trey agreed. "I care about what you think."

"And I love you, baby." Bringing their lips together, Lucien kissed Trey.

Trey smiled for him, beamed.

"Come on. There's a vibrating plug with your name on it in the bedroom." He took Trey's hand, leading his lover down the hall.

"Is it big?"

Slut. Beautiful, wonderful size queen.

"Of course it is — I know my baby."

Trey grinned. "No punishments for me, today."

That had him laughing. "No, if you'd wanted punishments, you wouldn't have been ready and plugged for me when I got here."

"Maybe tomorrow I'll earn some." Trey leaned into him, and they both chuckled.

"If we're lucky." He kissed the top of Trey's head, stopped, putting his boy's hand on the mattress. "Hands and knees for me."

"Yes, Sir." Trey settled on the bed, hips already rocking a bit.

"Eager slut." He ran his hand along Trey's back and over his ass.

"Uh-huh. I need it."

"I know."

Trey always needed it. Of course it was months in between their bouts of lovemaking so maybe that wasn't at all unusual. And Lucien knew Trey. Trey craved pressure, pain, submission.

Right now, he started slowly, lubing the plug, then rubbing it against Trey's ass. He didn't turn the vibrations on, planning on making Trey wait for it. Turning the plug, he pushed the tip against that little hole, getting the very tip in, then tugging it out again.

"Tease," Trey accused.

"Yes." He was going to make this last and last. He wanted to watch his lover stretch.

He rubbed the tip into Trey's ass again, pushing it a touch deeper this time. This plug was thick, but short, and had strong vibrations in it once it was turned on. Twisting it, Lucien pulled it almost out, then pushed it a little deeper.

"Thick." Trey moaned, thighs parting.

"Oh yeah. I know how you like it."

Trey would be complaining if he didn't. Not that that wouldn't be fun tomorrow, but he was sure Trey would earn a punishment or two over the next week.

He pushed more of the plug into Trey's body, not quite sending it in completely. Trey's thighs tensed, muscles rippling. Lucien twisted the plug around and around until Trey relaxed a little, then he pushed it all the way in. Trey rocked forward, moaning low.

"Yeah, baby. Do that again." Lucien let Trey's own movements pull the plug from his ass, push back in again.

"More, love. Please." Trey begged so well.

"I know." He pulled the plug out and started fucking Trey with it. He twisted it, holding it at the widest part. Then he slammed it in hard.

Trey cried out, voice raw, needy.

"Yeah, baby, that's it." Lucien did it again.

"Please. Oh, God. Sir."

He continued fucking Trey with the plug, pushing the thick toy in again and again. "No coming until I say so." Not until he had filled his beautiful size queen a few more times with this nice, thick plug.

"I have to."

"When." He thrust the plug in hard. "I." He tugged it out again. "Say." He slammed it back in. "So." Out and in hard once more.

"Now!" Oh, someone was ready to push.

"No." He slammed the plug in again. "I said not yet." He grabbed Trey's balls, tugged hard. "You'll come when I say so." He waited for Trey's whimper, then slowly let the sweet balls go.

Trey pulled away, just a bit, letting Lucien know he wasn't pleased. He knew. He knew Trey wanted to come, badly. But he also knew Trey loved this, the push and pull, the need and desperation.

He kissed Trey's ass. Trey shifted, just barely responding.

"When I say you can or you get punished."

"Okay!"

Chuckling softly, he tapped the end of the plug.

Trey was frustrated now, and he had to decide whether to push his lover or back off a bit, let him breathe. Lucien gave the sweet ass a kiss, then moved, sitting with his back against the headboard and pulling Trey down into his arms. "Come here, baby."

Trey pushed in and he knew he'd chosen wisely when Trey started to shake.

After tugging the covers over them, he started running his hands over Trey's body. "I've got you, baby."

"I... It was hard, this one."

"It's pretty damn thick." He'd save the vibrations for later. For when Trey was feeling less shaky and had forgotten about that aspect.

"No. No, the book. The book."

"Oh! Sorry, baby." He kissed the top of Trey's head. "It took longer than usual. Five months from start to finish. I missed you so bad."

Trey nodded, those poor empty eyes moving restlessly.

"Why was this one so hard?"

"It just was. It felt like pulling teeth and I was... I don't know." The frustration in Trey's voice was clear.

"I'm sorry. Maybe it's time to switch things up."

"Maybe." Trey sounded exhausted, worn out.

"I want to float the idea of me coming to live with you, not just in between books."

Trey shook his head immediately, body tensing. "You know that I can't. I'll depend on you for everything. It would be so easy." It was always the same worries.

"I don't believe you would." He honestly didn't. Trey was the most independent, capable man he knew.

"I do. I would want to be your sub all the time." Trey said it like it would be a bad thing.

"You already are my sub, all the time. That doesn't make you weak, you know?" Lucien didn't think Trey did know and the tension in Trey's body said that he was onto something.

Trey didn't answer — he just stayed close.

"There's another alternative" Lucien suggested, more than willing to compromise, to make the next step one Trey could be comfortable with. "We can get together more often than just when the books finish." Once a week... Hell, once a month would be better than the current setup. And he wanted to prove to Trey that they could work, being together more often. That it wouldn't turn Trey into a needy, dependent man who couldn't write anymore.

Trey took a shaky breath, fingers tracing restlessly over the top of the comforter, a worried little frown marring his forehead. "Right now I just need you to hold me. This isn't a place to make decisions."

"I just wanted to put the ideas in your head, that's all." He kissed the top of Trey's head.

"So. These shower attachments. Should we take a look?" Trey asked, clearly ready to change the subject.

"I'd like that." Lucien was fine with moving on — he really did just want to have Trey consider things. He knew change was hard, and it was even harder for a blind man.

Learning over the side of the bed, Lucien grabbed Trey's laptop. "Okay, let's take a look."

Chapter Three

Trey woke up plugged and sore, so he stumbled to the bathroom to soak in the tub. His head hurt, his heart felt tender, and the emptiness after this book was huge—bigger than usual, which was probably why he'd agreed to extra days this time.

Extra days. Eight instead of the usual four. Was he doing the right thing? What if that made it even harder to write? What if the next book took even longer to wrangle into control?

He could hear his mother's voice in his head from when he'd come out, telling him he just wanted a man to take care of him, that he wasn't ready to live on his own and be independent—that he probably never would be.

Well, he'd more than proven her wrong. He worried, though, that that was why living with Lucien was such a huge draw. Which was crazy, because he knew he loved Lucien, right?

A soft knock sounded at the door. "Baby?"

"Hey, love." He wiped his eyes. He'd been crying.

"Hey now." Lucien's fingers slid over his cheeks. "What's wrong?"

"Nothing. Nothing, I'm okay." Just empty, emotional.

"I'm coming in with you."

Lucien shifted him forward and settled behind him, pulling him back against his solid chest as Lucien's strong arms wrapped around him. Trey let himself lean back, breathe in Lucien's strength.

After a while, Lucien pushed him forward so that Lucien could top up the water with more hot. Then he settled back again. "Talk to me, Trey."

Trey thought about asking what about, but that would be disingenuous, so he didn't bother. "I feel empty, scoured out. I'm lonely and I miss you all the time. This time I wrote about stuff that scared me. Really scared me and... Am I making any sense?"

"Yeah, it makes sense. You could have called me. Any time. I wish you had."

"I know. I wish I had, too. My soul feels like part of it is missing."

Lucien's arms tightened around him. "That sounds awful."

"Yes. Yes, it does and it's stupid. I know it is. I write books — just books. But that's how I feel."

"It's not stupid, baby." Lucien nuzzled his neck. "It's real and I hate to think of you here all by yourself needing me. I can't let you keep doing that."

Trey sucked in a breath, licking his lips.

"I don't have to move in, but you not seeing me, not talking to me at all while writing, isn't working anymore." Lucien spoke softly, and it didn't feel pushy.

"I've always imagined living with you, how it would work," Trey admitted.

"Oh yeah? Tell me about what you've imagined." Lucien nuzzled his neck, all soft touches and kisses.

"I've imagined everything. I mean, from little things like having breakfast together to the big things — going places with you, traveling. Being your sub twenty-four-seven. That's like a fantasy. Waking up, knowing you're here with me."

"Oh God, Trey. That's my fantasy, too." Lucien's groan tickled his skin a little.

"I've never been to your gym."

"We never have the time, but this time you're giving me eight days, right? I'll take you. At the end of the week."

"I'd love to. I want to... Lucien, I want to see things." He'd been born blind — he knew better — but his life was so predictable.

"I want to take you places. I want to show you the city. I want to show you the world."

God, Trey wanted that, too. He wanted to get the fuck out of this house — and not just for a walk around the block or over to the coffee shop. Sure he'd been on a book signing tour, but he hadn't had time to do anything but sit and sign books and it had been so stressful, not being able to see. Now he just stayed home and did virtual book tours. Thank God for the electronic age.

"Will you take a chance when the next book starts and not wait until it's finished to call me?" Lucien asked. "Maybe we can take a vacation a couple months in? Hell, bring your laptop and split the time sightseeing and working."

"I think I'd try. I want to try."

"Really?" Lucien sounded surprised, but also really pleased. "Oh, baby, I'd love that. We can spend some time deciding where we want to go, what we want to do. Half the fun of a vacation is planning it. And I'm taking you to the gym on Friday next week. Plus, I was thinking tomorrow we should go to the lake. It's supposed to be a beautiful day and the sunshine will feel so good on your face."

They usually spent their time together indoors. In bed for a lot of it, really. Of course, it was usually only for four days—five at the most—and he seemed to remember he promised Lucien they'd make it eight last night. Lucien was certainly under the impression they would still be together at the end of next week. Trey didn't have the will, or desire, to pull back from that.

"I haven't been to a lake since I was a teenager," Trey admitted.

"Then let's go. If there isn't anybody selling food on a cart or out of a truck, we'll find somewhere to eat at on the way home."

"Okay. I bet the dog would love that." Dodger never went anywhere either, thanks to him.

"Yeah? Awesome!" Lucien sounded so pleased and he shifted, the water lapping at their skin. "It'll be a lot of fun, I promise."

Trey nodded. How could he not be excited?

Lucien kissed the back of his neck. "How's that plug feeling? You need some vibrations?"

He'd forgotten about it, honestly. Completely. Lucien stretched and a moment later the huge plug in his ass began to vibrate, ever so slightly. He sucked in a breath, his body working the plug.

"Good?" Lucien asked. "You need more?"

"Please."

"I've got you, baby." Lucien made the vibrations deeper, the buzz moving through Trey's whole body.

"Oh… Oh, yes." He rocked, chin dipping down.

Humming, Lucien wrapped a hand around his cock. It didn't take thirty seconds for him to start filling.

"Mmm. There's my needy boy."

"Sorry. Sorry that I'm in my own head so much." The words pushed out of him.

"I love you for who you are, you know?"

"I do." Trey did. He knew.

"Then don't apologize for being you, huh?"

"I know, but I…"

The vibrations amped up and he groaned. Lucien's hand kept moving slowly on his cock, even as the vibrations ramped everything up higher. His head fell back, his mouth open as he focused.

Lucien's lips, warm and soft, were a counterpoint to the vibrations in his ass and the stroking of his cock. He barely noticed the kiss, though—his focus was almost entirely on the buzzing in his ass. He couldn't believe it could buzz any harder but suddenly it did, without warning, just boom, bigger.

"Sir!" Trey jerked, the water splashing.

"Yeah, I've got you, baby. Know how to make you fly." Lucien's legs pushed up between his, spreading him wide. "You're allowed to come." The words came with even faster buzzing.

"I-I-I." He wanted to stroke himself off.

"Tell me, baby. I want to know everything."

"Touch me?" he begged. He was going to scream if Lucien said no this time.

"Mmm. I do love touching you." Lucien's hand wrapped around his cock, loose and warm.

"Yes. Yes, Sir." He panted, caught in the vibrations.

When Lucien's hand finally tightened around his cock, it was perfect. His hips moved in short, fast thrusts.

"That's it, baby." Lucien's mouth closed over his shoulder, sucking hard.

He nodded, teeth clenched together. *God, yes. Yes.*

Lucien bit at the mark on his neck then went back to sucking, thumb working the tip of his cock. All Trey could do was pant and moan and try to shoot. Lucien pushed against the base of the plug, jostling the vibrating thing.

"Sir. Sir. Sir." Trey kept moaning the word, over and over.

Humming around his neck, Lucien continued jacking him and playing with the plug. The vibrations eased, then began to grow again. Between that and the thumb at his tip, the mouth at his throat, it was a circle of pleasure. Trey rode it, letting the pleasure cycle, spin inside him.

"Beautiful size queen. Sweet slut."

Yes. Yes. He was. Lucien's size queen. Lucien's slut. He wasn't like this for anyone else. He never could be.

Trey burned, his legs beginning to tremble.

"Let go, Trey. Give me your pleasure."

"Yes. God…" *Please.*

Lucien pinched the tip of his cock, hard and that was all she wrote, spunk spraying from him.

"Yes. Yes, baby. Just like that. So damn sexy."

Trey came and came, his entire body seeming to burn.

The buzzing finally slowed, then stopped, Lucien's mouth simply resting on his throat.

"I love you," Trey said, the words not big enough for how much he felt for Lucien.

"Oh, baby. I love you too. So much."

"That's never been our problem. Loving each other." He'd loved Lucien almost right from the start.

"Nope. Never." Lucien spread soft kisses over his shoulders and neck.

He leaned back and sighed, so fucking happy.

Lucien licked along his right shoulder. "You need to get some sleep — we're going on an adventure."

"I do. I couldn't before. I could sleep now, though." The emptiness from the novel being finished and out of his hands was fading rapidly.

Excellent." Lucien dropped a last kiss on his shoulder and pulled the plug on the tub.

Before he knew it, Lucien had him all dried off and was moving him, helping him toward the bed. His lover climbed in with him, and there was that spot for his head on Lucien's chest that fit him just perfectly, Lucien's arm around him.

"Love you." His head was so heavy and it felt so good to let Lucien hold it up.

"Me, too. Go to sleep, baby. Tomorrow we have an adventure."

"An adventure." And with that, he was asleep.

Chapter Four

Lucien was excited as hell. They were not only leaving the house, but he was taking Trey to the lake. It was going to be fantastic. He just needed to get Trey out of the door.

"You look great, baby. Let's go."

"We got water and stuff for my boy, right?" Trey touched Dodger's collar.

"Yes, baby, we do." Lucien had to smile. They had a huge amount of things in the car for a simple afternoon out.

"I'm sorry. I'm just... You know."

Lucien did know—Trey had become trapped in his house.

"I know. I'm here, though, and I'll be right by your side. If we need anything while we're out that we didn't bring with us, I'll take care of it." There couldn't possibly be a single thing they would need that they hadn't packed.

"I know. I know. I'm excited." Trey offered him a genuine grin.

"Then let's go."

Lucien led Trey to the car, putting Dodger into the back, then Trey into the front.

They were really doing this. He hadn't ever been allowed to drive Trey somewhere. Never. This was a triumph of magnificent proportions.

He got into the driver's side and started the engine. "Here we go."

"Yay!" Trey was trying, so hard.

"Yeah. It's about a forty-five minute trip. You want some music?"

"I do. Can you drive with music on?"

"I can. As long as it isn't too raucous." He turned on the radio, the eighties classic rock channel he'd been listening to on his way to Trey's coming on.

Trey sang along, then those long fingers began to explore the interior of the car. It was fascinating, watching Trey discover new surroundings. The glove compartment popped open beneath Trey's questing fingers and Trey jumped, then started laughing.

Lucien chuckled himself. "That's the glove compartment. It's got the manual for the car in it. My registration and insurance papers. And some wet wipes."

"Neat. What's a registration?"

"Proof that I own the car. I need to show it if we get pulled over by the cops." There were so many things that he took for granted that Trey had no idea about. He wanted to be able to teach Trey about everything.

"Ah. Yes. That makes sense."

"We're just hitting the highway now and will be out of the city momentarily. If you have any questions, please ask, okay? No question is out of bounds." He wanted Trey to be totally comfortable.

"What do you see?"

"At the moment it's just cars and highway. There are walls built next to the highway to keep the sound of cars down for people who live close by."

"Oh. It that why it echoes?" Trey asked.

"I hadn't actually noticed any echo, but that would be my guess."

"No? I hear one, I think." Trey tilted his head slightly. "And the road. I hear that."

"That's pretty cool, actually."

Trey nodded. "I used to go with my folks, in the car, but it's been a long time."

Lucien should have suggested something like this earlier, but this was the first time they'd have more than just a few days together and he'd been greedy enough to want to spend them all making love and cuddling and just being naked and close with Trey.

"I'm glad we're going today," he admitted.

"Me too. I was nervous earlier, but you seem like a good driver."

"I am. Besides, I have precious cargo, so I'm being extra careful." He would make sure Trey was safe.

"Thank you. Is Dodger okay?"

"Yep." Lucien glanced at the dog in the rear view mirror. "He's sitting on the back seat with his nose pressed against the window."

Trey chuckled, expression truly tickled.

God, they were going to do this as often as possible. No more denying that there was a life out here in the name of independence. He wasn't going to let Trey hide anymore. His lover needed more than just writing and sex. And they needed to experience things, together.

He needed to remember to keep Trey apprised of what he saw, their surroundings. "We're out of the city now, lots of grass on either side of the road."

Trey nodded. "You can tell—not about the grass, but the noise is less."

"I love how you use your other senses to make up for sight."

"Do I? I mean, I'm sure I do, but I've never had to see."

Had to see, not been able to see. There was no self-pity there.

"Yeah… I can't imagine what that's like." It kind of blew his mind when he thought about it. No matter how much Trey 'saw' things, he'd never actually see them the way the rest of the world did.

"Just like I can't really imagine what it's like for you," Trey pointed out.

"No, I guess you can't." Lucien chuckled, glanced at the oncoming road sign. "About ten more minutes, I'd say, before we get there."

"Cool. I can't wait."

"Have you ever been to the lake? Do you swim?"

"When I was little, I think? I don't know. I haven't been in the water in…fifteen years? Longer?"

"Oh man, that's a shame." Lucien actually laughed, his excitement building at being able to do this with Trey. "This is going to be so much fun."

"I wonder if Dodger knows how to swim."

"I think it's instinctive." Lucien had never seen a dog in the water who flailed instead of doggy paddling.

"Yeah? You can swim?"

"Yeah, I love it. I go a few times a week." He liked alternating his work out routines. It was better than doing the same exercises repeatedly. "I'd be happy to take you once in a while."

"I don't want to be trouble."

"Are you kidding me? I love spending time with you. Swimming with you would be awesome." In fact, Lucien thought it was a fabulous idea—a great way to get Trey out of the house and exercising more than just his brain.

"Maybe. Maybe I'd suck."

"Could be. But it's not like you're going to be going for the Olympics or anything. You just need to be able to propel yourself in the water."

"More like you just need to not drown."

God, Trey could make him laugh. Lucien loved that about Trey. "Exactly."

Trey reached out, found his side then dragged his fingertips down from just below his armpit to his waist.

He wriggled, laughing more. "Tickles!"

Trey headed for his leg. "Better?"

"Careful, baby. I'm driving." He didn't want to have an accident because he was distracted. And Trey's touches were distracting, no doubt about that.

"Sorry. Sorry." Trey pulled back, curling in on himself.

"Oh, don't feel bad, please. It would just be so easy to forget I'm driving and get too into your touches."

"Uh-huh. I understand that."

"Cool. You can touch me all you want when we get there." He'd encourage it in fact.

"That's fair. Are we close? I can smell water." Trey's tilted his head slightly, sniffing.

"Yeah, it shouldn't be much longer." In fact there was a sign for their turn just ahead. "Are you excited?"

"I am. I thought I'd be more scared, but you're here." Trey's face proved his words were truth.

"That's right, baby. You're safe with me."

Look at that smile. He'd done that. He took the next right and even he could smell the water now. Okay, that was fucking cool. Trey taught him so much.

He found the public parking lot and pulled up into it, fairly close to the beach so they could spend their time on it, not getting to it. The place was deserted, just two other cars in the lot, though there was no one on the beach as far as he could see. They must have walked farther up.

Turning off the engine, Lucien then turned toward Trey, all smiles. "Are you ready, baby?"

"Yeah. Yeah, we'll let Dodger off the harness so he can play too."

"Yeah? That's great."

Trey was going to trust Lucien to lead. That meant so much to him.

"Yeah." Trey got out of the car, hooked the leash to Dodger's collar and waited for Lucien to come around.

Grabbing the bag with the snacks, Lucien then tossed it over his shoulder, made sure the car was locked and came around to put Trey's hand on his arm. Trey held Dodger's leash, the pup wagging furiously. It looked as if someone was more tickled than either one of the humans.

They moved onto the beach.

"It's warm enough to take our shoes off if you want." And the beach was clean as far as Lucien could see.

"It's safe?"

"Yeah, there's lots of sand and I can't see any garbage." He bent, letting his hand trail along Trey's body so his lover knew where he was, then he undid the Velcro on Trey's runners. Trey stepped out of them and his socks, expression surprised as his feet hit the sand.

Lucien spent a moment just looking, then he put Trey's hand on his shoulder and got the shoes and socks into his bag. His own shoes and socks were next, then he stood again, putting Trey's hand back on his arm.

Trey was wiggling and curling his toes, sliding them in the sand.

"What's it feel like?" Sure, he could feel the sand against his own feet, but he wanted to know what it was like for Trey.

"Alive. It moves like it's alive."

"Pretty neat, isn't it?" He started them walking, slowly. They could take as long as they wanted.

"It's fascinating." Trey stopped and bent down, touching the sand, let it trail through his fingers.

"When you're ready to stop, we can sit and build a sandcastle."

"I can't do that, can I?" Trey laughed, and they moved on. "Don't you need a bucket and a shovel?"

"I just might have a bucket and shovel in my bag. And of course you can build a sandcastle. I'll help."

"Cool. Okay, yeah."

Lucien walked them over just a few steps, letting the hint of water brush Trey's feet. He loved Trey's gasp. "That's the waves. It's not as strong as it is at the ocean, but there's little ones. Feel how wet the sand is here? Feels really different underfoot, doesn't it?"

"I—" Trey's eyes were huge, wide open.

He moved them slowly, letting Trey feel it again. Then he went a little closer to the water, so it lapped at Trey's feet a little more. Trey's toes curled, both Trey and Dodger dancing in the water. Laughing, Lucien just watched, thrilled with what he was seeing.

"Oh my God… That's so cool." Trey's face showed wonder.

"So you like the beach." It wasn't a question.

"Can we feel more?"

"Yeah. A lot more. Let's go in a little into the water so it comes up over your ankles." Lucien bent and folded up the bottom of Trey's pants.

"There aren't fish to bite me, right?" Trey could always find something to worry about.

"Not this shallow." Lucien couldn't stop his smile.

"Cool. I don't want fish to bite me."

"No fish are going to bite you. I promise." He angled their path to go a little deeper into the water.

It lapped at Trey's ankles, and his lover made amazing noises. Lucien waded them in just a touch deeper. Based on this, he had a hunch going to the pool with Trey was going to be wonderful.

Dodger licked the water, splashed, tail wagging madly.

"Your pup is enjoying this almost as much as you are."

"Oh, God. He's definitely wiggling."

Lucien laughed. "You want me to take him?"

"No. No, he's good right now."

"Let me know when you want to stop and we'll build that castle."

"Okay. Not yet. I want to feel the water still."

"Feels good, doesn't it?" Lucien loved the way it felt, as if some of the sand was being stolen from beneath his feet by the water.

"It's incredible." Forget wonder, Trey's face was a study in joy.

He'd done that. He'd given this to Trey. And he could keep giving this kind of thing to his lover. It made him more determined than ever to change things. "It is incredible." And because it was the middle of the day, they had the place to themselves. Trey grabbed him as a tiny wave hit his calf. "Lucien!"

He slipped his arm around Trey's waist. "It's okay, baby. I've got you."

"It is!" Trey kissed his jaw. "It's glorious."

"*You're* glorious, baby." He kissed Trey's nose, then laughed as another wave moved against Trey's calf. "Oh, there's a lovely rock here." Bending, he picked up the oval, totally flat stone and put it into Trey's hand.

Trey handed him Dodger's leash, focusing on the rock.

"The flat ones like that can be skipped. You throw them against the water in just the right way and it'll skip along the surface."

"I don't understand, Lucien."

"Yeah, it's a hard one to explain to someone who can't see. Rocks are heavy, they usually sink down in the water."

Those clever fingers traced the stone, petting it.

"But if you throw it right, you can make it jump across the water for a couple of skips. People who are really good at it can make it jump a lot more times than that."

"Can I have it?"

"Keep it, you mean? Of course. It's a nice souvenir."

"Cool. Thank you." Trey grinned at him, slipped it into one pocket.

Putting Trey's hand back on his arm, Lucien led them back along the beach.

They headed to a sunny, drier spot, one they could sit at. Lucien pulled a blanket out and spread it on the ground. "I've just put out a blanket for us to sit on."

"Do I just sit down?" Trey asked.

He helped Trey sit. "Yep."

"Cool. Come on, Dodger. Lie down."

Dodger obediently lay down next to Trey and Lucien reached over to rub the dog's head.

"He's a good boy." Trey's fingers twined with his.

"Yeah, I think he's great."

Dodger woofed at them.

"Are you great? Is that your best friend, Lucien?" Trey asked.

Dodger woofed again. Lucien thought Dodger would be thrilled if Trey let them be together all the time. The pup was panting, wagging, and Lucien would swear it looked like Dodger was smiling.

"All right, baby. How about that sandcastle? You wanna give it a try?" He wanted Trey to get his hands dirty.

"You know it. I want to do it. I want to do *everything*."

Lucien laughed in delight. "Then that's what we'll do. I'm going to pull the blanket back up against your legs so you can get to the sand." He did that, then gave Trey one of the little buckets and a shovel. "Okay. Put sand into this until it's full, I'm going to fill this other one up with even wetter sand. I'll only be going a few feet away."

"I can do that."

He watched Trey for a second, watched his lover explore the shovel, the bucket. When Trey started pushing at the sand with his shovel, Lucien walked over to where the water met the sand and began filling his bucket with wet sand and water.

Then he went back to Trey. "How are you doing?"

"Good. Good. The sand is…silky almost."

"You should feel the difference with the really wet sand here." He put Trey's hand on the edge of his bucket.

"Oh. Oh…" Trey dug in, the wet sand dripping from his fingers.

"You like that?"

"So cool! Show me more!"

"Okay. Let's take your full pail and turn it over. That's going to be the base of the castle." He took Trey's hands and helped him turn over the pail. When they took the pail away, the shape held. "Okay, gently now, feel this."

Trey's lips opened, and Trey gasped. "It held!"

"Yeah, pretty damn cool, huh?"

"Uh-huh. Do it again." Trey handed him the bucket.

Laughing, Lucien filled the bucket, then he grabbed Trey's hands and helped him turn over the bucket again.

This time Trey explored more closely, making the pile crumble. "Again!"

"Again? Sure."

They did it again, then again, Trey's delight absolutely amazing. Trey was filthy—covered in sand and starting to burn, but so happy.

Lucien showed Trey how the wetter sand could be used to make additions to the castle base, and once they'd built a several buckets big castle, Trey smashed it up, the two of them laughing.

"Oh, God, that was fun, baby."

"It was. Oh, please, can we feel the water again?"

"You are going to have a hell of a sunburn by this evening." Still, Lucien helped Trey up and they went into the water, Lucien taking them in until it was up past their ankles.

"I like the water!" Trey splashed, laughing as Dodger bounced along.

"Then I'm definitely taking you swimming." They could do it every week. Trey needed a break while writing anyway, some time doing something active, physical.

He could tell that Trey was starting to drag now, though—activity and sun and water slowing him down.

"Come on, baby. Time to find some food." He headed them back toward the car. "What do you feel like eating?"

"Can we have burgers and milkshakes?"

"Oh, that sounds good. There was a pub just a few miles from here. I bet they do great burgers."

"Am I too dirty?"

"We'll pop into their bathrooms and wash the sand off. I bet they get lots of sandy people in."

"Okay." Trey nodded and that was that. No arguments.

Lucien couldn't remember a day when he'd seen Trey look happier.

Trey squeezed his arm. "Thank you. Thank you for today."

"And thank *you* for today. I've had an amazing time." It had been...magic. Pure, simple magic.

Lucien prayed with everything he was that there would be many more days like this one.

Chapter Five

Okay, sunburn hurt. Lots. Trey slipped out of the bed, uncomfortable and achy, itchy. Water. Shower. Cold shower.

"Baby? Where are you going?" Lucien asked.

"Shower. I hurt. My cheeks hurt."

"Aw, baby. Come on. I'll help you. And I've got aloe for you when we're done."

"It was worth it. It was totally worth it." The beach, the water, the sand—it had been wonderful.

"It was a fun day."

Trey could hear the smile in Lucien's voice as they made their way to the bathroom.

"Amazing. Perfectly amazing." Now he needed a shower.

Lucien turned the water on and helped him in. It was cool, almost cold, but it felt so good. He shivered, grabbed Lucien's arms.

"Okay, baby?"

"A little cold."

"Feels good, though, doesn't it?" Lucien asked.

"Uh-huh." Trey started shivering.

"Just a few minutes to help pull out the heat."

"Mmm-hmm." He was floating a little.

Before his shivers got to him again, Lucien turned off the water and began to dry him off, patting his skin gently.

"Did I say thank you for today?" Trey asked.

"You did." Lucien's fingers slid over his face, just barely touching. "I have aloe vera gel. It'll help."

"Okay. Cool." He wasn't sure what meant, exactly, but he'd go for it.

Something sticky was spread over his cheeks and nose, the effect of cooling immediate. Goosebumps rose up all over him.

"Better?" Lucien asked.

"Oh, God. That's like sex. Like a scene."

"Oh, that *is* good." Lucien picked him up.

Trey arched, the sudden change of direction fascinating, perfect.

"Sexy boy," murmured Lucien, walking down the hall.

"Am I?" He felt pretty damn sensual, actually. Maybe it had been the cold shower, maybe it had been their lovely day.

"You are. The sexiest boy I know." Lucien kissed his cheek.

"Good. Good. I worry sometimes that you'll get bored."

"Of you? Never! Is that why you only let me see you in between books?"

"There are a lot of reasons." A lot. Trey had a million and one reasons.

"I'm not going to get bored of you, baby."

"I hope not. I…" *Need you.* "You're important." More than he was probably willing to admit, even to himself.

"You're important, too, baby. You mean the world to me."

Trey felt his cheeks heat. *Okay, wow.*

Lucien spread him out on the bed, Lucien's warmth pouring down on him as his lover straddled him. He reached out, hands sliding over the furry thighs.

"Mmm. Gonna make me need," Lucien told him.

He could feel Lucien's cock firming against him. "Again?" he teased.

"God, yes. I want you more than anything."

"I'm right here." He cupped Lucien's jaw, exploring. "Here and empty."

Lucien nuzzled against his palm, the touch so familiar it made him ache. "Don't worry, baby. I'm going to fill you with me."

He didn't even bother to pretend not to be eager. "Please."

Lucien's smile pressed against his lips, the kiss quickly going deep and eager. He opened up, letting Lucien's tongue in. Lucien tongue-fucked him and it made his hole ache. He wanted to stretch now, stretch and feel.

Lucien fumbled with something on the bedside table and a moment later one of Lucien's long fingers pushed into him.

"Sir…" *Yes. God, yes.*

"Mmm. Right here. Right here." Lucien pressed a second finger in with the first.

He moaned, the sound happy, hungry.

"I want you to take my whole hand, boy. I want to fill you that big."

Trey cried out, shoulders leaving the mattress. "Sir!"

"I'm right here, ready to give you what you need."

He nodded, hands opening and closing. "Sir. My sir."

Lucien leaned away again, then settled between his legs and pushed three fingers into him this time. His hands landed on Lucien's chest, fingers stroking and petting and searching. He tugged the tiny nipples in time with the thrusts inside him.

"God, you know exactly how to drive me wild," Lucien told him.

After so long, Trey hoped so.

"Ready for more, boy? Ready for another finger?"

"More. Master." His hips rolled, his body eager.

"More it is." Lucien worked his little finger in, the stretch becoming huge.

He parted his lips, a deep groan escaping him.

"I love stretching you because I know how much you need it."

Trey nodded. He did. He craved it, ached for it.

Twisting his fingers, Lucien pushed them deep into him. Trey jerked and drew his knees up, fighting to make room. His movements sent Lucien's fingers deeper and they hit his gland.

"Master. Master!"

"Yeah, still right there." Lucien pushed against his pleasure point again and he sucked in a breath, trying to relax. "Easy, baby. We have all night long."

All night... Christ, he'd explode.

Twisting and pushing, stretching, Lucien slowly opened him up. His body relaxed, the pressure easing, growing, then easing again.

"You'll take my whole hand soon," Lucien promised.

Trey would say he couldn't imagine, but that would be a lie. He could. He did.

A soft kiss landed on his lips, then on the tip of his erection.

"Oh." The heat was sudden, surprising. Perfect.

He felt Lucien's smile against his cockhead, then another kiss graced his belly. "How's that stretch, baby?"

"Good. No, better than good. Amazing. Stunning. Right."

"God, I love you." Lucien pushed his fingers in as deep as he could, spreading them apart inside Trey's body.

Trey soared, the pressure singing in every cell of his body.

"You're ready for my whole hand now."

"Will it hurt?" He wasn't one hundred percent sure he cared.

"No, I'm not looking to give you pain, baby. I want to give you the ultimate experience. Give my beautiful size queen my hand."

"Please." He craved it, so hungry for it.

"Okay."

Lucien's fingers slid out of him, his hole closing over the emptiness with an audible sound. He reached out, needing the sensation back.

"I'm adding more lube, baby. I need to make sure everything is nice and slick." Lucien's familiar, sexy voice was like a touch, like velvet across his nerves.

His entire body responded to that voice. He could wrap himself in it, rub it all over his skin.

"I'm back now. Don't tense up. You crave these sensations. Let them happen." Lucien's fingers rested against his hole.

"Yes. Yes, Sir. Please, take me."

"I'm coming in, baby." Pushing into him, Lucien slowly spread him and spread him and spread him.

Trey fought to breathe, to suck in more air.

"You're the most amazing man, I know," Lucien told him.

"Yours. Your man. So full, Sir."

"All mine." Lucien's hand felt so huge. Just enormous.

As the widest part of Lucien's hand held his hole open, Lucien stilled. Trey wanted to scream, to beg, to plead.

"Sorry, baby, but I had to stop and look. To see my hand inside you."

"Tell me. Tell me, sir. Please."

"How it looks? Unbelievable. Your hole is stretched so wide and all I can see of my hand is the base of it. My fingers and thumb aren't visible at all."

Trey whined, the sound tearing out of him. Like that was what he'd been waiting for, Lucien pushed his hand all the way in. Trey could feel his skin practically snap closed around Lucien's wrist.

"Oh, God. God. Sir. Master. Lucien. Please."

"Tell me what you're feeling," Lucien demanded.

He didn't know. His lips opened and what came out was, "You're everywhere."

"Oh. Oh, baby. Yes." Lucien kissed the tip of his cock again.

Trey's lips parted, his toes curled. He was soaring.

Then Lucien began to move his fingers, wriggling them so deep inside him. His breath caught in his chest. The sensations got even bigger when Lucien curled his fingers into a fist, moving his whole hand now. He reached down, touching his own belly.

"It's okay, baby. You can touch my wrist, feel the place where it disappears into you."

Trey's body squeezed tight, just the thought of those words making him insane.

Lucien's free hand took his, slowly moved it down toward his hole, toward that place where they were joined. His hips tried to roll, but he was caught by Lucien's hand.

"Easy, baby." Lucien guided his fingers right to his stretched skin.

"Sir. Lucien. Oh, God."

Lucien's hand felt even bigger to his fingers, that wrist like a tree trunk. His head shook, side to side, breath catching in his chest.

"I know. It's unbelievable, isn't it?"

"Uh-huh." Unbelievable. Huge.

As he touched, Lucien moved the large hand, and he could feel the tiny movements inside him and beneath his fingers.

"Breathe, baby. Come on. Slow, easy breaths."

That was easy for Lucien to say.

Then Lucien's mouth covered his, Lucien breathing into his mouth and Trey's chest opened, and he breathed deep.

"Mmm. Better." Lucien's hand kept moving, little pushes and pulls.

Soft sounds hiccupped from him, his body jumping and jerking.

Lucien licked the shell of his ear. "You're allowed to come."

"It's so big inside me. There's no room to come."

Lucien's mouth dropped over his cock, sucking hard as that huge hand continued to move. Trey threw his head back, screaming as his nerves were overwhelmed. Lucien kept sucking, kept moving his hand, and Trey could feel this enormous pleasure building in his balls. Sounds tore from him, his hands slamming on the bed.

Nudging his balls with his free hand, Lucien's suction got harder, more insistent. He fought for a breath, then he cried out, slamming up so that his cock bumped the back of Lucien's throat, lightning shooting through him. He poured himself down Lucien's throat, his body squeezing down hard on Lucien's hand.

The room went gray and he melted, simply fading away.

It was the sound of Lucien's voice that brought him slowly back to himself. Lucien's voice and the emptiness inside him.

"Stay. Please," he begged, needing Lucien's hand back.

"I'm just slicking up my cock, baby. I'll be back inside you in a second."

"Oh." It felt like that orgasm had lasted for days.

"I took my hand out while you were out of it, before you could tighten up." Lucien's cock was suddenly pressed against his hole, hot and solid and oh God, so good. "You up to this, baby?"

"Yes. Yes, Sir. Lucien. Love. Please." He wanted to keep flying.

"Good boy." Lucien pushed into him, the thick cock spreading him open again.

Every inch of his body felt loose and relaxed and he couldn't really thrust back, but he tried. Lucien's warm lips touched his own as Lucien thrust, driving into him deep. He offered Lucien a lazy kiss, moaning as it slowly deepened. The warmth between them was undeniable, Lucien making him feel like the center of the world. It was a study in contradictions — the slow easy kisses compared to the wild thrusts into his ass.

"Love how hot you are inside," Lucien told him.

"Love you." He did, completely.

"Good. Good." Lucien moved faster, fucked him harder. "So good."

So good. Trey nodded, the sound of Lucien moving against him like a song.

Lucien kept pushing into him for a long time, but eventually he groaned. "I need to come, baby."

"Fill me up. I want you."

"Gonna plug you with my seed inside you."

Trey nodded, almost hurting his neck with the ferocity of the motion. He loved that. It was so hot, so sexy — and so necessary.

"Fuck." Lucien jerked, shoving hard.

Trey could feel Lucien's cum, spraying inside him. The idea of it filling him up, made his poor, spent cock jerk.

"Love you," Lucien whispered into his ear.

"Love. I swear. Love."

Lucien licked along the shell of his ear. "You want the big plug, baby?"

"Uhn…" Uh-huh.

"That's a yes, please, Sir. You're lucky I speak orgasm addled Trey."

Lucien stretched away from him without sliding out of him and he heard the bedside drawer opening.

"Lucky." God, yes. He was the luckiest man alive.

"And I do love it when I make you incoherent."

Something heavy was placed on Trey's belly, rolling a little as Lucien kissed him again. The sensation tickled him, and he laughed, the sound husky and lazy and right.

"God, I love it when you laugh. I love knowing I made you laugh."

He reached out, searching for Lucien's face. Lucien nuzzled against his palm as soon as he found it, and his lover's wide smile felt right against his thumb. His heartbeat, sure and strong, steady. His Master.

"The plug is on your belly. Check it out while I get the lube." Lucien stretched away from him again.

Reaching down, Trey found the plug, the huge thing soft, giving, warming to his touch.

"Good choice?" Lucien asked, fingers joining his.

"Uh-huh. Big. Soft."

"It's going to fill you and keep my cum inside you."

His ass clenched around Lucien's cock and he got a soft moan for his troubles.

Lucien rubbed their cheeks together. "So hot, baby. You're make me want and want and want."

"That's good. I don't want you to get bored."

"You keep saying that—why do you think I'm going to get bored?" Lucien picked the plug up from his belly.

Trey worried. His life was so structured, so repetitive. What if Lucien couldn't handle it?

"Baby?" He could feel the plug, pressing against the place where he and Lucien were merged.

"Hmm?" He bore down.

Lucien slowly slid out, the plug pushing into him immediately, keeping him spread.

"You didn't answer my question. What makes you think I'm going to get bored?"

"Mmm." He didn't want to answer. Maybe Lucien would let it drop. Things were working just like they were, why did they have to change it?

Lucien lay down, tugged him against the amazing, solid body. "I'm not, you know."

"I don't want to talk about it, okay?" He just wanted Lucien to hold him. He didn't want to risk changing things and lose Lucien in the end.

"We can table it." Lucien kissed the top of his head. "I'm not going anywhere."

"Good. I miss you." And what if missing Lucien was part of what made the writing work?

"You know I miss you, baby. The time between your novels is…really long."

"Yeah." And it was getting longer as the book ideas grew. As the monsters seemed more real. Were they manifestations of his own fears of becoming too dependent on Lucien? Or was it just that Lucien wanted to change things and that was terrifying in and of itself.

"I want to revisit the rules, baby. I really do. I want to have date nights. I'm totally amenable to having things canceled if the writing is going like gangbusters and you don't want to stop." Lucien held him close. "I'd like to at least try."

"Date nights." Oh, that could be… He was so scared that he'd be on his knees begging Lucien to stay. But still… Maybe the time away from Lucien wouldn't seem so terribly hard that way. "Yeah. You know, every Friday night. Sometimes we go to things, sometimes we stay in and get busy. Then on Saturdays I could take you swimming. You get a break from the writing. We get to see each other…"

It was so tempting, the way Lucien had put it. "I want to, so much. I don't know what's changed with me." He used to be so sure of what he needed.

"Maybe because after ten years, you want more."

"Ten years. Can you imagine?"

"I can. They've been wonderful years. The only thing I'd change is getting to see more of you."

Trey found himself nodding, agreeing.

"I was hoping you'd think so, too. We can start after our time together is up. What do you want to do on our first date?"

"We could go get coffee?" They'd gone a time or two, to the shop just down the street.

"That was our very first date. Do you remember?"

Of course he remembered. "I do. I was so scared. I'd never ever done anything like that before."

"I'm so glad you took a chance on me. But look how good it worked out. You should take another chance on me."

"I give you all my chances. You know that, don't you?" He let Lucien in where no one else belonged.

"I know. I'm just trying to be logical and shit over something that means a whole lot to me."

"I can handle emotional. I mean, seriously. I can." It might actually feel good, to have Lucien be less than perfect.

"Then I want to see you more. I love you and I want to spend time with you. A lot more time than we do."

"Are you scared? I mean, about having a full-time sub?" Unless that wasn't what Lucien wanted.

"I have some nerves, but mostly I'm eager for it. Excited."

Trey pressed close and rested against Lucien's chest. "I'm a little scared. I could totally lose myself in you."

"You don't need to worry, baby, I'll always be able to find you." Lucien's hand stroked over his skin, warming him and easing him. "You think you can sleep, baby?"

"Uh-huh. Thank you for the beach. It was the neatest thing ever."

"Yeah, I loved showing you that."

"I'm inside my head all the time." And Lucien made him fly, took him other places.

"Well, we're going to change that, yeah? Add some times when you're not inside your head."

"Uh-huh." His cheeks felt so tight, so hot.

"Cool. That makes me happy, baby. So happy."

"Me too." He waited for a minute, then asked, "Can I have more aloe stuff?"

"Yes, of course." Lucien shifted him to the pillows and got up. "Back in a second."

"Thank you." He explored the bed, the sheets, the pillows, feeling the warmth where Lucien had been.

Lucien was soon back, spreading the cooling gel over his skin. "Better?"

"Uh-huh." His eyelids were so heavy now.

"Good." Lucien kissed him softly. "Sleep, baby."

He nodded, cuddled in, utterly worn out. Lucien's arms wrapped around him, holding him close and safe. Now he could sleep.

Chapter Six

Lucien was excited. He'd half expected a call from Trey all day, canceling on their first date. It hadn't come, though. So here he was, dressed in a suit, at his lover's door for what was, really, their first date. He knocked, grinning at the sound of Dodger's barks.

He waited patiently, and it was Trey's personal assistant who answered the door. "Hey, man. He's changing shirts again. I was just on the way out. Come on in."

"Thanks, Brian. Have a good weekend." Bending, he gave Dodger some love.

"I hope so, yeah. Boss... He's giving me Fridays off from now on. How much does that rock?"

Lucien grinned widely. "That rocks a lot." Every Friday. His baby was really committed to doing this.

"Yeah. You need anything, man?"

"I've got it from here. Thanks, Brian." He knew how to take care of his baby.

"Cool. See you Monday, boss!" Brian called out before waving to him and bouncing down the stairs.

Chuckling, Lucien closed the door and threw Dodger's ball for him, sending the dog down the hall. Then he headed for the bedroom.

Trey was 'looking' at two shirts, one soft and bright red, the other a tight, lightweight sweater in black.

"You'll look great in either, baby."

Trey jumped, proving how distracted he was, not having heard Lucien coming down the hall. "Lucien! Which one?"

"I like the red one. Is it silk?"

"Uh-huh. It's my favorite. I wear it when I miss you."

"You should call me over when you miss me." He was going to keep flogging this particular dead horse until it got up and rode. He lifted the shirt, helped Trey slide it on. "You like how it teases your skin, hmm?"

"Uh-huh."

Dropping a kiss on Trey's cheek, he helped do up the buttons, holding Trey against him. Trey's nipples went hard and Lucien smiled. So that was why Trey loved it. He wasn't going to do anything about that right now. He thought a little need would make their supper taste all that much better.

"Are you ready to go, baby?"

"I am. You have on a jacket. Am I okay? I look okay?"

"You look fantastic. We're going somewhere quiet and fancy and you're dressed perfectly."

"I like quiet. Let me get Dodger harnessed up."

Lucien had picked the fancy restaurant deliberately, knowing that it wouldn't be very busy until later in the evening, and that the quiet atmosphere would likely be easier for Trey to deal with. He'd called to make sure they wouldn't freak about Dodger, and that they could put them in a corner where the dog could lie next to Trey's chair without being in the way. They had been very accommodating.

"The food there is supposed to be excellent." Lucien had heard a lot of good things.

"What kind of food?" Trey harnessed Dodger up, the pup's demeanor immediately different, more alert.

Lucien waited until they were out and Trey had locked the door before giving Trey his arm. "It's new American fusion. The chef is one of those young up-and-comers. And it's close enough so we can walk. I thought that'd be nicer than having to worry about parking."

"Oh, yeah? Cool. I'd love to have a walk."

He knew Trey walked to the coffee shop and back quite often, but he didn't think his lover did that much more walking when they weren't together. And when they were... Well, they were usually focused on indoor activities as they only had those few days every few months.

"It's a nice day, too. More sunshine, but it looks like your burn has settled into a tan."

"Does it?" Trey took Lucien's arm, a happy, eager smile on his bright face. "I hit my word count for the week."

"That's great. Hey, maybe this new arrangement will actually make you more productive." He had no idea, but he was going to accentuate all the positives.

"Maybe. We'll just have to see, I guess."

"Well, I'll see," he teased, nudging Trey.

Trey cracked up, the sound tickled.

Dodger stopped them at the corner.

"We're crossing this street and the next, then we go right." Lucien knew it was important to orient Trey, who nodded, and he knew Trey would remember that, remember how to get home.

They continued on and it felt like they were a normal couple. Like this was life. Him. Trey. He wanted it so much, wanted this to be their life. They already had the kinky sex, the BDSM relationship, he wanted the normal everyday stuff, too.

"Can you tell me anything about the new book?" He loved Trey's novels, had even before they'd known each other.

"It's a ghost story about a man who lost his brother."

"That has the potential to make me shiver. I can't wait to read it." He devoured Trey's books so much faster than his lover could write them.

"Yeah? I hope so. It's going surprisingly well."

"That's great." They crossed the next street and turned right. "It's just down the street from here."

"What's it called?"

"The Grey Dove."

"Oh, what a pretty name. That would make a great title."

"Not for a horror novel, though, I wouldn't think."

"No? Maybe a western…"

"Yeah, that would work better." He opened the door, and the smell of garlic and bread hit him square in the nose. It smelled fantastic. This was going to be even better than he'd anticipated. "We're here."

"I can tell. Yum."

"Yeah, that smell kind of makes you drool a little, doesn't it?"

"God, yes. All of the sudden, I'm starving." Trey laughed happily.

"We have reservations," Lucien told the hostess. "Lucien Delacroix."

"Yes, I have you in our alcove. Follow me, please."

Trey didn't tense, Dodger moving easily to guide him through the tables. So far this was going even better than Lucien had been hoping.

They followed the hostess to their table, and Lucien held out Trey's chair, put his lover's hand on the back of it. "You're here. I'll be sitting right across from you."

"Can you please sit next to me? I'm more comfortable with that."

"Yeah, sure. Miss, can we move my chair here, please?"

She looked concerned for a moment before nodding. "Sure."

He dragged the chair from across from Trey to next to him, then helped Trey and Dodger get settled.

"Thank you. I know it's weird, but..."

Lucien covered Trey's hand with his own. "Whatever you need, baby."

"You're good to me." Trey twined their fingers together.

"Well, I love you."

"Good. What is there to eat?"

"So the menu is a single sheet. It's a four course meal and we have four options. Vegetarian, seafood, chicken or beef."

"Oh. What sounds the best? You know my tastes pretty well."

He didn't know really if that was true when it came to food. He and Trey tended to order out when they got together, pretty much exclusively. So he decided to go with his own favorite. "Let's get the seafood. It's a very sensuous food."

"Works for me. I'd like a glass of pinot grigio too."

"Good choice, I'll have one, too."

"Nice and light and harmless, right?" Trey grinned. "I like how it goes with most food — even pizza."

"Cool. And I've got to say, God, you look good." He couldn't stop smiling himself, having Trey out on a date like this.

"Yeah. I like this shirt. It's soft."

"Oh, it's more than just the shirt, baby."

Trey's hair was short, adorable, the sweet belly lean and trim. Lucien loved every inch of the man. Smiling, he took Trey's hand. "Are you looking forward to going swimming tomorrow?"

"Uh-huh. I'm a little nervous, but you'll be there. You won't let me drown."

"Nope. Not into necrophilia."

"Ew." That made Trey laugh, though, loud and happy.

God, he loved being the one to make Trey laugh like that. "Yeah, that's how I feel, too."

The waiter brought their waters, eyes wide at the sight of Dodger. He was wearing his harness, though. The waiter would figure it out, Lucien hoped.

"Good evening. How is everyone this evening?"

Trey smiled, dark glasses turned toward the waiter. "Just fine, thank you."

"Yeah, we're good." Lucien's gaze kept returning to Trey.

Trey didn't look nervous or worried at all. In fact, his baby was relaxed and smiling.

"Have you decided what you'll be having to drink?"

"We'd like to share a bottle of pinot grigio, please," he answered, and Trey nodded.

"Good choice, sir. Have you chosen your meals yet?"

"Yeah, we'd both like the seafood, please," Lucien answered again for both of them.

"Excellent choices. Shall I bring bread?"

"If that's what smells so good, yes!" Trey said.

Laughing, Lucien nodded his agreement.

"Very good, the bread and your drinks momentarily."

"Excellent." God, he was having a ball.

He touched Trey's foot under the table.

"Are you playing footsie with me?" Trey asked.

"I am. Are you going to play back?"

Trey chuckled and nudged Lucien's toes. "Tag."

Grinning, he slid his own foot up along Trey's calf. "Can anyone see?"

"Nope. Dodger's giving us plenty of cover."

Trey reached out, fingertips touching his knee.

"Mmm. My sweet, bold boy."

The wine arrived shortly after that, along with bread and salads.

"Thank you." Lucien put Trey's salad right in front of him, his wine to the top right of his plate, his bread to the top left. Then he told Trey where to find everything, "You want me to butter your bread for you?"

"Please." They'd shared many meals together over the last ten years, although ninety percent of them had been pizza.

He knew Trey was pretty good with his fork, though, one hand holding it, the other subtly moving over the plate to find food, guide it to the utensil. The motions were small, careful.

He buttered Trey's bread, then his own. "The butter is brown. I think that means it's caramelized." He took a bite, and sure enough, it was sweet, the bread crunchy, still warm and delicious.

"Huh. Interesting." Trey's fingers moved across the tablecloth until they found the base of his wine glass.

"I used to go out to eat with my friends from school a lot, but it's been a while."

"Why did you stop?" He thought it was because as Trey got older, he'd become more and more in need of control. But it was just a theory.

"I lost touch with a lot of them and I just... I write. A lot. The world outside changed and got bigger."

"It's not so big if you've got someone at your side. I want to show you everything."

Trey's eyebrows lowered. "You know that it isn't about not wanting to come out, right? I mean, the last few years?"

"No? What's it about?"

Trey folded his napkin, smoothed it out, folded it again. "I mean... I... Is that what you thought?"

"Well, yes."

"Oh."

He wished he could see Trey's eyes. "I was wrong, huh?"

"Yeah." And that was it, Trey went quiet, and Lucien knew his lover was back inside his own head.

He reached for Trey's hand, squeezed it. "Baby, talk to me."

"When I left home to go to school, it was tough, but cool, because everyone was like me. But after graduation, everyone expected me to go home and I didn't. I was gay, I wrote scary books—my people weren't ready, you know? It was hard to learn how to be on my own. I don't even know the difference between a hundred dollar bills and a fiver without help."

"There was no one who could help you?"

"I have assistants. I've been lucky. I have online friends, my agent. You know."

"I know. But you haven't had a chance to do things outside of your house aside from book signings and the coffee shop."

And Trey had never asked him to do things.

"I know and I want to, I've always wanted to, but I didn't want to… I mean, I need you for so much and it would be easy to be your sub, all the time."

"Okay, that's two things, I think. First of all, my taking you places, like this tonight, isn't being my sub. It's two lovers doing things together. And second, what would be wrong with being my sub all the time?"

"I don't know. I just… We've never had enough time for things not to be about sex." That was the answer to the first question, at least.

"You're absolutely right. That's why I wanted to change our arrangement. I need more of you than just a few days in between novels." Lucien wanted every part of Trey, all of him.

"Yeah. Yeah, I just hope I can continue to put out the amount of words I need. Only time will tell."

"If we were living together full time, I could help keep you focused on the writing when you need to be."

"I'm scared of learning to depend on you completely and then losing you."

"Then we need to make sure that doesn't happen." Lucien meant either possibility.

"That's what I've been trying to do, make sure it doesn't happen."

"Baby, not being completely dependent on me doesn't mean keeping me at arm's length. I want you to have both."

"I don't know how and I don't know how to figure it out. I've tried. I've Googled everything."

God, that was adorable. Possibly the dearest thing he'd ever heard.

"But you never asked me. Two heads are better than one, aren't they?"

Trey nodded, reached out toward him, and Lucien took his hand.

"I have no problem helping you become more independent—teaching you how to go to the pool on your own and swim. How to go to a restaurant and order by yourself, figure out where everything is and pay for it yourself. We can start on our next date." Of course his first reaction was to take care of Trey, but he could learn how to take care of his boy by teaching Trey how to do things for himself.

"I don't want to have a date by myself."

"No, but you can take me out. You can research where you want to take me, figure out how to get there. Order for us. Pay."

"I know how. I mean, I do. I used to go out with my friends." Trey grinned. "I've even done book signings."

"Well then. You're in charge of dinner next Friday night. Oh, that reminds me. Brian told me you gave him every Friday off starting next week."

"Yeah, I did."

"That's awesome, Trey. Thank you."

"I wanted you to know I was serious."

"Yeah, that's exactly what it did. Let me know you want this, too." It made it real. Possible.

Trey found his bread, tore a chunk off, and nibbled.

Lucien focused on his salad, the dressing totally delicious. "I might have to change my position on greenery."

"Is it good?"

"The vinaigrette is good enough I want to lick the bowl clean." Oh, his bread could do that for him. He grabbed a piece and began to sop up his bowl.

Trey carefully found the salad with his fork, leaned over to take a bite.

It was really neat to watch his lover navigate eating in public. Trey did a fantastic job of it. "You eat more neatly than a lot of people."

"Yeah? Does it look weird?"

"Nope. Not at all. Your sunglasses inside give you away more, I think."

"Yeah. I used to not wear them, but it wigs people out.

He touched the side of Trey's face. "It doesn't bother me."

"Well, I hope not. You get to see my eyes a lot!"

Chuckling, he stroked his fingers along Trey's skin. "Yeah. I think they're beautiful. I've never seen a blue quite like yours."

"I imagine blue is cold."

"It is what they call a cool color."

"Tell me what it looks like," Trey demanded.

"Wow. That's really hard." He considered it, tried to figure out how to describe it without using sight as a reference. Blue was... It was blue. Then he figured it out. "It looks like how the ocean feels on your skin."

"Like regular water, but it leaves a little roughness behind from the salt?"

"Yeah, that sounds about right."

Their waiter swooped in and took their plates. "Your appetizers will be along shortly."

"What were the appetizers?"

"I don't know exactly. We got the seafood plates — the whole meal was set and there was just the one choice. I wasn't paying total attention to the menu." He grinned. "It's an adventure."

"Hooray adventures!" Trey lifted his glass in a toast.

Lucien clinked them gently together, more in love than ever. "I'm so glad we did this, babe."

"Yeah? Me too. It's like…a mini vacation almost."

"You know it's also our first date, really."

"No, our first date was at the coffee shop. The best day of my whole life."

"Yeah? This just seems more like a date than the coffee shop—that's having coffee." Taking Trey's hand again, he squeezed it happily. "It was the best day of my life, too. Well, no. Best day up until then. Each one with you is the new best."

"The new best. I like that."

The waiter appeared at their table again. "This is scallop ceviche with a lime salsa, with crispy Israeli couscous."

"That sounds delicious." Lucien was eager to try it.

"It smells good. Tart."

"It looks amazing, too. The scallops are paper thin. I think they've deep fried the couscous. The plate is right in front of you, your appetizer fork to the left of it."

"Okay. Is it in a bowl?"

"It's a plate with a wide brim." He wasn't going to have any until Trey had started.

"Okay." Trey explored gently with his fingers, then picked up his fork.

"We'll take our first bite together." Lucien had never had raw scallops before.

"Sounds like a plan." Trey got a forkful. "Is this a scallop?"

"You've got scallop, a bit of the salsa and two of the couscous pearls. A perfect bite."

"Thanks. You ready?"

He gathered up his own bite. "I so am. On three. One. Two. Three."

The main flavor was citrus, a hint of heat and the scallop just melted on his tongue. It was rather spectacular.

"Oh my God," he managed.

"Uh-huh. It tingles."

"I haven't ever tasted anything like it." He had another bite, eating slowly – this wasn't the kind of food you gobbled up.

Trey managed to eat one bite for every two of his, his lover so careful. Still, the food was delicious and they were having a great time.

"Man, this is good."

"It's fascinating. So bright."

"It is. I'm looking forward to seeing what the other three dishes are." There was no way the rest of the food could be as good as this, but he'd like to see them try.

"Can I have another piece of bread?"

"Yeah. The butter's nice, eh?" He grabbed another piece from the basket and buttered it for Trey, handed it to his boy.

"Thank you." Trey used it to scoop up the ceviche.

Lucien finished his own plate, setting his fork across it and sitting back so he could watch Trey. He found his lover endlessly fascinating. Trey was so careful, fingers moving constantly.

When they were done, the waiter brought their next course.

"Ethically raised sea bass in a delicate fish broth with microgreens. Enjoy."

"So... It's fish soup?" said Trey.

Lucien chuckled. "I guess. With a big piece of sea bass in it."

"Are there bones? I can't cope with soup *and* bones."

Lucien checked his fish. "Nope. It's a big chunk in the middle of the bowl, but it flakes nicely. Did you want me to break yours up so you can have a bit of fish in each spoonful?"

"Do you mind?"

"Of course not." He reached over, flaking the fish apart with his fork, moving it so it would be pretty easy for Trey to get some fish on his spoon, no matter where he dug it in. "There you go, baby."

"Thank you." Trey's cheeks were pink, hot.

"Hey. Stop that. I think it's amazing that you're out at a strange place, eating food you've never eaten before. I'm proud of you."

"I just… One I can handle. Two is too much."

"You're doing great with both, I promise."

"Thank you." Trey tasted the soup, nodded. "It's nice."

"I liked the scallop dish better," Lucien admitted.

"Me too. Lots."

"Well, there's another main and a dessert still to come, so if we don't finish this, we won't starve." He didn't hate it, but frankly, he'd rather have another piece of warm bread with the caramelized butter melted on it than more of the soup. He set his spoon in his dish and moved it to the side to let their waiter know he was done.

"Do you think it's okay to not finish it?" Trey asked.

"I do. We're paying for the food. I don't see why we should eat it if we don't want to."

"Oh, good. Good. I don't want any more."

He leaned over and pushed Trey's bowl slightly to Trey's left. "Now they'll know to take it away and bring us something we like better."

"Cool. I hate wasting it, but..." Trey shrugged.

"But the first course spoiled us for the second." He wrapped their hands together again. "I'm holding hope out for the third."

"Oh, the soup wasn't bad."

No, it just wasn't *good*.

Their waiter came just then. "Were the soups not to your liking?"

"I'm afraid the scallops spoiled us." It was as diplomatic as Lucien was going to be.

"Hopefully the lobster dish will live up to them, then."

"I'm sure it will. The soup wasn't bad." Lucien had to admit, Lobster did sound good.

"Thank you, sir." Their waiter gave a little half bow and took off with their mostly uneaten soup course.

"I love lobster," Lucien admitted. "Have you ever had it before?"

"No. No, I mean, I know what it is, but that's it."

"Cool. I'm hoping it comes out of the shell." He leaned forward, lowered his voice. "I'll admit, I hate having to fight my food out of the shell."

"Shell?" Trey looked panicked.

"Don't worry, baby. If it's in the shell, I'll take care of it for you." He glanced around. "I don't see anyone else fighting their food."

"It has a shell?"

God, he forgot sometimes that Trey could only truly know what he explored personally. He would have no idea what the lobster having a shell meant.

"Yeah, an exoskeleton I think they call it. I tell you what, I'm going to buy us some lobsters for when we're home, so you can explore them in the shell, really see them."

"Exoskeleton? I... Okay. Okay, that would be cool. I could write them then."

His brave lover. Lucien was more than a touch stunned by Trey. "You amaze me, baby. Every day that we're together you amaze me."

"What did I do?"

"Everything."

Trey laughed, and Lucien closed his eyes to hear it fully. "God, you're beautiful." He could see it with his heart.

"I love you, Lucien, even if you're a dork."

"I hope you love me even if I'm not a dork, because I'm not a dork." He all but stuck his tongue out at Trey.

Trey giggled for him, the sound charming the fuck out of him.

"Your third course, gentlemen." The waiter startled Lucien, but he smiled and nodded at the man.

"Lobster Alfredo with angel hair pasta. And as the chef was sorry you didn't like the last course, there's also crab cakes on the side."

"Oh, he didn't have to do that." Lucien felt bad now.

"Nonetheless." The waiter gave a little bow and left them.

"Are there skeletons?"

"Nope. The lobster is in pieces and all through the pasta, and there are two claws and the tail sitting on the top, not a shell to be found. And then there's the little plate with a lovely little crab cake beside it." He tried to figure out if it would be easier for Trey if he cut up the angel hair.

"Claws and a tail? Lucien, I... How do I do it?"

It's just meat like any other meat, only softer so easier to cut. Did you want me to cut the meat and your noodles up? Make them easy to scoop with the fork?"

"Will you? I'm sorry, but... This is my favorite shirt. Pasta is so hard."

"If you wanted, I could move the lobster itself to the same plate as the crab cakes. Then you don't have to worry about the pasta at all."

Trey looked so upset, so embarrassed.

"Baby." He squeezed Trey's hand. "Please, there's nothing to be embarrassed about."

"I'm sorry. I... Did you know, when I was a little boy, I thought dirty dishes disappeared?"

"You mean like magic? If you ate everything on your plate they just went poof?"

"Yes. Yes, exactly."

"Oh God, that's adorable!" He loved hearing things like that, learning about his lover. He cut Trey's pasta as they chatted, making it as easy as he could. Then he passed Trey's fork to him. "Eat. It looks amazing."

"It smells good."

"Yeah, it does."

He watched, making sure Trey was able to get some food onto his spoon and into his mouth before he had his first taste from his own plate. Creamy, rich, with a lovely sweetness from the lobster—it was luscious. "Oh God. This makes up for the soup like a thousand fold."

"It's yummy. Rich, huh?" Trey carefully ate, just a little bit at a time.

"It's delicious. I'm glad I didn't fill up on the soup."

"Like that soup would have filled you up."

"Are you saying I'm a pig?" he teased.

"Nope. I'm saying you're a solid guy who works out all the time."

Lucien chuckled. "Not *all* the time."

"All the time." Trey was getting more confident, scooping up a bite that had a huge chunk of claw meat.

"I'm not working out now," he pointed out, grinning as he watched Trey eat.

"Nope." Trey chewed. "That was big."

"Nice and sweet, eh?" He slipped a whole claw into his own mouth, enjoying just the lobster meat on its own.

"Uh-huh." Trey touched the crab cake. "What's this?"

"That's the crab cake—the waiter said to make up for the soup."

"A cake—what's in it?"

"Crab, I assume. Probably breadcrumbs, an egg and spices," he guessed. "I can call the waiter back and ask."

"No. No, I'll just try it."

"I'm so proud of you," he told Trey again.

Trey grinned, pinched off a bite with his fingers. "It's crispy."

"Yeah. Fried food pretty much always rocks."

"Yeah. You know how I feel about French fries."

"Oh yeah, they're awful." He grinned. They might order pizza for a lot of their meals together, but they usually had a side of fries, too.

"Yep. Hate 'em. Pizza, French fries, Eggos. It's nice to have something not finger food."

"It is, actually." He rubbed his foot against Trey's. "It's just nice to have some time with you doing something different."

"Yeah. Yeah, it's almost like a new relationship, huh?"

"It is. Dates, going out. Learning new things about each other."

"What did you learn?" Trey asked.

"That you're even more amazing than I thought you were."

Trey's laughter rang out, pure joy.

"And that I love the sound of your laughter more than just about any other sound."

"Oh." Trey looked so pleased.

Lucien rubbed Trey's thigh beneath the table. Trey beamed, leg moving a bit, just like Trey was rubbing him back.

"I can't wait to get you home," he admitted, which sounded silly when he'd been so enthusiastic to come out. This was supposed to make them being together at home better, though, so maybe not so silly.

"One course left. Dessert?" asked Trey.

"I sure hope so. And hopefully it doesn't include any seafood." He squeezed Trey's thigh.

"Oh. Oh, man. It won't, right?"

He chuckled. "I hope not. Probably not."

"Yeah. I hope not too, because whoa."

They were still chuckling when their plates were taken away and replaced by two little dishes with crème brûlée in them.

"A traditional crème brûlée to finish off your meal." The water gave a little flourish as he presented the food.

"Thanks. Man, Trey, this looks delicious."

"Oh, this I know. It has the crunchy sugar on top, right?"

"It does. All nice and caramelized."

"That's my favorite part." Trey explored the edges of the ramekin, then dug in.

"I like the sound it makes when you break through it." He hit it with his spoon in a few places, listening to the crack.

"Does it look like ice?"

"Nope. Well, maybe a little, but it's the wrong color."

"Ice is white, right? What color is this?"

"Brown. Because the sugar is burnt—that's what makes it go hard like that."

"Brown, like dirt. Cool."

Lord, the way Trey's mind worked was fascinating. Weird, but fascinating.

"Doesn't taste like dirt," Lucien teased.

"No. No, it doesn't. I totally know that. It doesn't smell like dirt either, although they both smell good."

"You like how dirt smells? I like it in spring."

Trey nodded, licking a sliver of sugar off his lips. "I think it smells fecund. I love that word."

"You love all the words." It was one of the most fascinating things about Trey. Lucien ignored the fact that he found everything about Trey fascinating. Fas. Cin. A. Ting. Christ. He laughed at himself for being a dipshit, laughed at Trey for the way the dessert disappeared completely. They were a pair.

"God, I love you," he told Trey. This should be their life, being with each other every day, going out, staying in. All the things couples did.

"Yeah? I love you, too. Honest."

"I know." He squeezed Trey's knee under the table before finishing off his own sweet.

Their waiter was pretty attentive, coming right away to clear away their plates.

"Can I get you anything else?"

"No, I think we're good. Baby?" He looked over at Trey who was nodding for him.

"Very well. I hope you enjoyed your meal, aside from the sea bass, of course."

"It was great, thank you. And thanks for the crab cakes."

Giving them a short bow, the waiter promised to be back with their check momentarily.

"Do you want some money?" Trey shifted, moving to dig out his wallet. "I have some cash."

"You can pay next time. This was my date."

"If you're sure…"

"I'm sure, baby. We'll take turns. That'll make it fair. This weekend is mine. You plan next weekend and you can pay for it."

"That works for me, yeah." Trey reached out, touched his side. "Thank you for supper."

"You're welcome, baby. It was my pleasure."

He took Trey's hand and squeezed, only letting go when the waiter brought over the machine and he pulled out his card.

Trey got Dodger up and ready to go, the dog shaking himself hard.

"He deserves a treat when we get home." Lucien couldn't believe just how good Dodger had been.

"Always. A treat, supper, maybe we can throw the ball."

He was stupidly pleased that Trey was inviting him in for that simple, normal bit of life.

"Sounds like a great way to work off our meal."

"Yeah?" Trey beamed, and Lucien thought he wasn't the only one loving this.

"Yeah." He put Trey's hand on his arm and they walked out into the night.

This had been a great idea.

Chapter Seven

Trey stood beside the car, feeling completely wrong without Dodger. Lucien was here, sure, but still... It was weird.

"Are you ready?" Lucien asked, taking his hand.

"Sure." He shook his head, though. *God, no.*

"Your mouth is saying yes, but your body..."

"I haven't gone outside without Dodger in a long time."

"Oh, baby." Lucien held him tight for a moment. "I promise not to let anything happen to you."

"I know that. I do. I just have to do it and then it'll be neat and I won't be scared anymore."

"All right then, let's do it." Lucien walked him forward and he could smell chlorine.

"It's outside or inside? The pool."

"It's inside. I thought it would be good to have a place you could get used to and use year round."

"Okay. And you can smell it out here? Is that weird?"

"They use a lot of chlorine. And you have a pretty special sniffer. I can smell it, too, though, faintly."

"Oh." A door opened and he could smell people, chlorine, antiseptic, soap, a hint of mustiness. *Wow.*

"We're going to the counter to pay."

"Okay. I didn't bring stuff. Was I supposed to?" God, he'd fucked up again.

"I figured you didn't have a bathing suit and bought one for you. I brought you a towel too. We're good."

"I-I'm sorry."

"What for?"

"Not being prepared." That was the secret to survival, wasn't it?

"You had no idea what you needed to be prepared, but I have it covered, so we're good. I like that you weren't, actually."

He squeezed Lucien's arm. That was sweet, trying to make him feel better.

"You want to know why I like that you weren't prepared? Because it means you trusted me to make sure you were okay."

"I do. I trust you with everything." Everything.

"Thank you."

A kiss landed on his head, then Lucien talked to someone, paying their entry fee to the pool.

After that they headed into an area that echoed, their footsteps so loud.

"This is the pool. We're going to a changing room just a few feet down from here.

"Okay." God, he was unnerved. Really.

"There's no one else here—just you and me, and the lifeguard on a chair about halfway along the pool."

They turned a corner and things got quieter, less echo-y.

He took a deep breath. "What's in here?"

"A few showers, lockers, changing rooms and some benches." Lucien led him a few more steps in. "There's a bench here, right behind you."

"Okay." He felt behind him, sat. "Okay, so... Lucien, I'm really wigged."

Lucien knelt in front of him, one hand on his cheek, the other on his thigh. "I know. I've dressed and undressed you a lot of times before, though. Admittedly, undressed more than dressed."

"You promise not to leave me alone in the water, right?"

"I'm gonna stick with you this whole adventure. I'm not even going to let you pee on your own."

"Okay. Okay." He took a deep breath and just made himself experience this. "So, naked now? Do I do it here?"

"Yes. I can help." Lucien's lips covered his, the kiss sweet, quick. Then Lucien tugged his T-shirt up over his head.

"Is there a place for clothes? That's the locker part, right?"

"Yep. That's where I'm putting your stuff. I'll show you where it is once you're changed into your bathing suit." Lucien tugged open his jeans.

"Do I just go barefoot? Are..." God, he hadn't worn swim trunks since he was a teenager. "What do the suits look like?"

"Like shorts." Lucien helped him stand and tugged his jeans down, then let him sit again, working off jeans, underwear and his shoes. "We'll go barefoot."

"Sure. Is there a cock sling like the ones I had before? The mesh?"

"Yeah. I was tempted to get you a pair of Speedos actually. You'd look sexy in them."

"Those are the bad ones, right? The ones that don't cover?"

Lucien chuckled. "They cover everything that needs to be covered and they aren't bad—just sexy."

"I'll just wear the ones you brought."

"Well, I hope so, because your other option is naked and while I'd enjoy it, I have a feeling the lifeguard might be a bit shocked."

"Yeah and there are probably laws."

Chuckling, Lucien helped him into his swim trunks. "They're blue with splashes of red, like someone flicked a red paintbrush at them."

Trey nodded, as if that meant something, but it didn't, not really. Lucien couldn't understand that he didn't know what those words really meant any more than he could understand the words. Wow, that was circular.

"Okay. You want to see where the locker is?" Lucien led him over, put his hands on the metal door.

There was cold metal, and it felt flimsy. It was like the ones from school, but smaller. "You have a lock for them?"

"We're the only ones here. I don't think we need a lock, babe."

"Oh. Okay." If Lucien thought so... He didn't know this place.

Lucien put an arm around his waist. "Okay, let's go swim."

The floor was cold and damp, hard under his feet.

"It's flat all the way to the pool," Lucien assured him.

Trey nodded. Flat. He could hear the water lapping at the sides of the pool.

"There's a ramp that will take us into the water. It's about three feet deep at the shallow end where we're going in.

Trey held on tightly, refusing to show how scared he was. He knew himself – if he did this, he'd be fine.

"Water's coming – and the ramp."

"Uh-huh." It was a close thing, but he managed not to gasp as the water lapped at his feet, and then he laughed, stepped deeper.

They moved down, Lucien careful. Then suddenly they were in the water up to his thighs and the ground was flat again beneath his feet. He reached out, touching the top of the water, and it seemed to come up, meet his touch.

"You like it?"

"It's different, yeah. Yeah, so far." He laughed as he spoke. "Everything sounds so different!"

"Yeah. It always echoes in a pool. Let's go deeper." Lucien took his hand and led him deeper.

The water went past his waist, soaking into his shorts, and that was different. They kept going until it was up to his shoulders. Lucien's hand stayed holding onto his, though.

Still, his breath came faster, the water everywhere, surrounding him.

"Do you want to try putting your face in it?"

"Sure." Trey bent his knees and ducked his head, popping up immediately, blinking hard. Oh. In his eyes, his ears.

Lucien laughed, hugged him. "Good job!"

"I… Cool. Cool."

"You want to try floating?" Lucien asked, sounding excited.

Trey nodded. He wasn't sure how, but he'd try.

"Okay." Lucien's hand landed on his back, fingers spread wide. "I want you to lean back against my hand. I'll keep you up until you're in floating position, okay?"

"Don't let go."

"Don't worry, Trey. I'm not going to let you drown or panic."

He nodded, leaned back toward Lucien's touch.

Lucien's other hand came up to join the first, pushing at the base of his spine. "Let your feet come up off the ground."

That was harder than advertised, to pick his feet up, to trust that he wouldn't fall.

"The water will hold you — you're buoyant. And I won't let you drown," Lucien told him again.

"I know." His brain knew. His body thought this was bullshit.

Lucien's hands were big, though, and both on his back now and when his feet finally left the bottom of the pool, his legs floating up, Lucien had him.

"Now just spread your arms, like a starfish."

What the hell did that mean? He reached back into his memory. Starfish. Hard. Bumpy. Stiff. Okay. Stiff.

"Sorry, baby, that didn't help, did it?" Lucien kissed his nose. "Your arms and legs should be spread out like I have you tied to the bed."

"Oh! Not stiff and hard." That he understood, stretching out wide.

"Yeah, I just meant the shape of it." Lucien chuckled. "You feel how the water is keeping you afloat?"

"No." All he could feel was… It was almost too big to be wet. In fact, he really only felt wet in the places that were out of the water.

"Well it is." One of Lucien's hands disappeared.

"Don't leave me." His butt sank into the water.

"I'm not going anywhere—just relax."

Relax. Okay. Right. Slowly his ass lifted again and he breathed, focusing on the sounds, the weird echoes. He almost missed it when Lucien's other hand drifted away. Almost.

He wasn't sure what to do, so he didn't do anything.

"You're floating," Lucien murmured. "What does it feel like?"

"A little scary. No. More unnerving."

"Yeah? Not neat?"

"It's neat, too, but so different. Are you holding me?"

"Nope. My hands are underneath you in case you start sinking. But you're floating on your own."

"Weird." But cool.

"Do you like it?" Lucien asked.

"Uh-huh." He did. Especially if Lucien stayed close.

"Cool. When you're comfortable with the floating, we can try swimming."

Trey nodded and water splashed on his face. He tried to sit up, and everything went wrong, water going everywhere as he flailed.

Lucien was right there, though, pulling him against Lucien's strong body. "Okay, baby. I've got you."

"Oh. Oh. Okay. Okay, scary."

"I imagine it'll happen again. You just need to get comfortable getting back into your floating position."

He nodded, but he wasn't sure that he could do that—be comfortable in the water like this.

"Oh, I want to show you something. It's an on your stomach floating that you can do, that's easier to get into position for if you lose the floating again."

"On my stomach? Really?"

"Yeah. You go onto your stomach, and let your limbs go all loose. Your head is in the water. And when you need to take a breath, you just have to lift your head up, breathe, and then relax back into the water again. Do you want to try it?"

He nodded, shook his head, nodded again. He did, but he really didn't at the same time.

Lucien shifted him, big hand on his belly. "You'll have to get your face wet again, but it's very peaceful. Give it a try. I'm right here."

Peaceful. Right. No panic.

Lucien shifted him, moved him so his belly was in the water, still holding on, though.

"Okay, spread your arms and legs so it feels like you're tied to the bed face down this time."

He panted, his head up high to keep it out of the water.

"Now take a deep breath and hold it, put your face in the water and count to ten in your head, then bring your head up again."

He nodded, but his head wouldn't do it. It wouldn't go down.

"I promise you won't drown," Lucien whispered next to his ear.

"I'm scared, Sir."

"I know. But you've overcome so many fears. I know you can overcome this." Lucien kissed him, tongue pushing into his mouth. "I believe in you."

"Hold me." He squeezed his eyes shut, took a deep breath and put his head in the water.

Lucien's hands were on his waist, right there.

One. Two. Three. Four. His toes curled. Five. Six. Seven. Lucien's hands tightened, giving him the strength to count to ten.

He threw his head up, gasped for air. "I did it."

"You did!" Lucien's lips felt so warm against his.

He pushed close, taking comfort. "This is okay here?"

"It's just the two of us, baby. We can't get all hot and bothered, but being close, some kisses, that's just fine."

"Okay. I wasn't sure." He wasn't hot and bothered now, he simply needed some kisses. Some comfort. Contact.

Lucien moved him so his legs were around his lover's waist, the big arms holding him easily, Lucien's hands linked behind his back. "I'm so proud of you, Trey. I can't imagine doing this without being able to see." Lucien kissed him softly, then rubbed their noses together.

"I did it. I did." He was so proud of himself, too.

"You did. We'll have you swimming in no time flat." Lucien moved in the water, going deeper so the water drifted up as high as his nipples.

He held on, hands on Lucien's shoulders. This was less frightening, was exhilarating. Deeper and shallower, Lucien wandered, sometimes bouncing, sometimes spinning and the water flowed around Trey in cool waves, Lucien's body warm and solid, his center.

It was so fascinating, to relax, feel, throw his head back and laugh. Lucien's laughter joined his, low and sexy. He could feel that sound deep inside.

"This is fun!" He was having a ball.

"It is." Lucien began jumping, getting him completely out of the water and then sinking down again, warning him just before his head dunked. He was soaring. Soaring.

Sometime later, breathless, laughing, Lucien stopped. "You're having fun now."

"Uh-huh!" He was having a ball. "Say we can come again!"

"Every Saturday at eleven a.m."

"Thank you." He kissed Lucien hard, so happy.

Opening to him, Lucien accepted his kiss, tongue tangling with his. Oh, they shouldn't, but he wanted to thank his lover, his best friend.

The kiss went on and on and then Lucien pulled away, pressed their foreheads together, Lucien panting hard. "I love you, Trey."

"Love you. Thank you for this. It's... Wow."

"I'm so glad." He could hear the happiness in Lucien's voice.

"Me too. God, me too." He'd been worried, but it was wonderful.

"We have a bit longer. You want to keep going or are you ready to go?"

"I would keep going."

"Cool. Me too. I want to sink down and get our heads wet, okay? Bobbing up and down. You wanna?"

"Uh-huh. Okay." He took a deep breath, squeezed his eyes shut.

Lucien kissed him. "Don't forget to take a new breath whenever we pop back up out of the water."

"Okay. Okay." His heart sped up again. So exciting.

"Okay, here we go. Grab a breath."

They bounced up then down again, the water rushing up around his face, over his head. They weren't down very long before they popped out of the water again, then down once more beneath the water.

Exhilarating. This whole thing was exhilarating.

They bounced up and down over and over, and in the end he got brave and spread his arms wide, leaned back a little. Trusting that Lucien would keep holding him, he just let go.

Chapter Eight

They got home from the pool and Lucien thought he hadn't smiled this much in a long time. He'd been smiling so much his cheeks were hurting. The pool had been a great success and he figured eventually he'd have Trey swimming on his own.

"It's a beautiful day. Let's go sit in the backyard in the sun." He wasn't sure if he'd ever actually been in Trey's backyard except maybe a couple of times to throw the ball for Dodger.

"Okay. I-I hope there are chairs."

Lucien chuckled. "Me too. You don't sit out here at all, eh?"

He went to the back, Dodger flying out of the doggie door before he could even unlock the bolt. Chuckling, he opened the door. "Oh, you have one of those little outdoor sheds. That's new." Since last summer, anyway.

"Is it? Brian hired a lawn service and a pooper scooper. He must have had it built."

"Yeah. I'm going to see if there are any lawn chairs in there. Oh! You've got a grill. We can cook out here." It was like discovering a new place.

"A grill? With fire? Really? Is that safe?"

"I should be able to manage it, baby. Let me go see if you've got any deck chairs." He put Trey's hand on the deck rail.

"Okay. Can I come, too?"

"You want to come down to the shed? Sure." He took Trey's hand and set it on his arm. "There are two stairs down into the yard."

Trey followed, face up to the sun.

He opened the shed door. "There's a lawnmower in here and several deckchairs, including a couple of long ones that you can lie out on. Perfect." There was a standing umbrella, some older gardening tools. Decent stuff.

"Who bought them?"

"Baby, I don't know. Brian, I guess. The yard's been cared for, so I guess there's a gardener..." If he lived here, he'd have known.

"Oh. Cool. I know Brian comes out here with his girlfriend sometimes when they had a date and I needed help."

"It would be neat to have some vegetables and herbs out here. Fresh veggies rock." He'd loved to cook more often for Trey, and given there was a grill out here...

He grabbed the chairs, manhandling them under one arm so that he could still guide Trey back to the deck.

"Vegetables grow on farms."

Lucien laughed. "They'll grow anywhere there's dirt, though."

"Oh. Let's do that. I can touch." Trey was throwing himself into the whole idea of new things.

"All right. I'll find out where we can find the stuff we need and we can go tomorrow, get started right away." He was also loving this spending the weekend together thing.

"Okay. Okay, sure. Yes. Can there be tomatoes and green peas?"

"There can be anything you want. Anything." He would give Trey the world.

Trey smiled, sat in the chair Lucien offered, the sun making his lover glow. He'd have to either get the sunscreen or make sure they weren't out for very long.

"What else would you want to grow? You have a huge backyard, so we could do a lot of stuff."

"I... I grew a bean from a bean in school once."

"I remember that one. Looks like it's a universal lesson. So tomatoes and green peas and beans."

"And cucumbers. Those are neat."

"You just like the shape," he teased.

"Yep. Nice and thick. Firm."

"Perv." He couldn't keep the laughter out of his voice.

"God, yes!" Trey hooted, the sound ringing out as Dodger ran around in circles.

"He's happy you're out here," Lucien noted. "Excited." He found Dodger's ball and put it in Trey's hand. "Lob it straight out in front of you."

Trey grinned and threw, surprising him with the strength in Trey's arm. Dodger went nuts, bounding out to get the ball. After grabbing it in his mouth, Dodger loped back and left the ball beside Trey's chair.

"Good one! Both of you."

"I played baseball at school." Trey threw again.

That brought Lucien up short. "I thought you were blind all your life?"

"I was born blind. My optic nerves never developed—you know that."

"Then how did you play baseball?"

"Dude, beep baseball! You've never heard of it?"

"Beep baseball? Really? That's pretty cool." He learned the most interesting stuff from his boy.

"Yeah. The balls beep and the bases make this buzzing noise. The pitcher and catcher can see, but it's a lot of fun."

"Very cool. I'm impressed."

"I haven't played since college, but it was good."

"I could try to find a recreational league in the city, if you're interested in going back to it."

"Oh, I don't have time for that sort of thing…"

"We are introducing a lot of new things. Maybe we can revisit it later."

"Maybe. Maybe. I'll have to see. I can't do too many things."

"I know. We've got weekends, Friday night dates, swimming. Great sex."

"Scenes." The word was offered to him, softly.

Warmth filled him. "I'd love to do scenes with you outside our usual end of book get-togethers."

"Me too." Trey shifted in his seat, chuckled softly.

"Is my boy hard, just talking about it?"

"Always, Sir. Always."

"Then we'd better head inside." He moved toward Trey, letting his shoes hit the deck so Trey knew he was being stalked.

"Already…" Trey stood, cock obvious hard in the thin shorts.

"We're in no fit shape to be outdoors, baby." He slid a finger along Trey's cock when he got close.

"Yes…" Oh, his boy was needing him. Now.

"Bed, boy." Before he changed his mind and they gave the neighbors a show.

"Master." Trey's body rippled and he headed in, headed for the bedroom.

He followed, eyes on Trey's ass. His sweet size queen. He had to wonder how much courage it had taken for Trey to ask for this, when so much had changed. If he hadn't already loved Trey before, he would now.

Catching up to Trey just before they reached the bedroom, he slid his hand over that amazing ass.

"I wasn't sure how to ask."

"You know you can ask me anything, don't you?"

"I do. I don't want to miss this part of our lives."

Once they were in the bedroom, he turned Trey around and brought their mouths together, opening Trey's lips. Like he'd ever let them miss out on their connection.

He slid his hands down to Trey's waistband, started tugging Trey's T-shirt out of his jeans. He loved exposing that sweet, lean little body. Humming, he touched Trey's nipples, flicked his fingers across them. Mmm. He should clamp them, make Trey wild.

"Don't move," he ordered, before kissing the top of Trey's head and moving around to the bedside table on the other side of the bed. That was where he kept the things he brought to play with.

Trey's head tilted, the man listening closely.

"I know what you're doing," Lucien teased.

"Hmm? Who? Innocent little ol' me?"

Lucien chuckled. "You left innocence in the dust about ten years ago."

God, he loved Trey's laughter.

"Besides, I can see you trying to track what I'm doing, listening to every step. You want to know what I'm up to."

"I do. I get curious."

"You're just going to wait until I come back to know what I'm getting for you." He was going to have to be careful. Trey would recognize any noise. He cleared his throat as he picked the clamps up.

"Oh, that was clever!" Trey looked absolutely tickled.

Chuckling, he moved back to Trey. "I have to be sneaky."

"Hey, I can't even see!"

"I know! And somehow that makes it even harder to surprise you!"

Trey chuckled, reached out toward him. He wrapped Trey's ass in one hand and brought their mouths together, tongue sliding into Trey's mouth. It started easily, gently, and then the kiss deepened, Trey hungry for him.

He slid the clamps into his pocket and brought his free hand up to pinch Trey's little nipples. Trey nodded, lips clinging to his, tiny nips going hard as rocks. Sliding his hand back into his pocket, he grabbed one of the clamps, readying it to go around Trey's nipple.

He waited until the expression on Trey's face was open, unfocused, before fastening it on.

Trey arched, eyes wide, huge. "Sir."

"That's right." He flicked the clamp.

Trey's eyelids fluttered, cock hard as stone.

"Ready for the other one?" He pinched it, let it know what was coming.

"Yes, Sir." Trey swallowed, over and over.

He grabbed the second clamp and dragged it up along Trey's skin. Trey went up on tiptoe, rocking back and forth.

"Needy boy." He loved how eager Trey was.

"Yes. Yes, Sir. Aches so good."

"You always did have sensitive nipples." He let the second clamp close.

"Uh. Uh-huh."

"Have your words abandoned you, baby?"

"Sorry." Trey's fingers squeezed tight.

"No, don't apologize. I love being able to make you incoherent."

"Love you." He loved those words in Trey's voice.

"Oh, baby. I love you, too." He stroked Trey's cheeks, loving on his boy.

Trey pushed into the touches, keeping his chest well away from contact. It made him chuckle and slide his fingers up along Trey's torso, not letting his boy know yet which nipple he was going to pull on.

Trey's breath caught, sped, his boy wiggling. Chuckling, he skirted the right nipple, keeping Trey guessing, on edge.

"Sir..." Trey panted, lips open, body arched and waiting.

"You need something, baby?" He danced his fingers in random patterns, still keeping away from where Trey most wanted his touches.

"You. I need you. Your will. Your everything."

"Oh, good answer. You always have good answers." Taking Trey's mouth again, he flicked the right nipple clamp, hard.

Trey's cry tasted good in his lips — wild, desperate.

He flicked the other nipple clamp, then did it again. "I want you to bend over the bed, boy, legs spread wide." He wanted that hole, wanted to make his boy need. He flicked Trey's nipples again, making the clamps wiggle again.

Trey jumped, turned to bend over, lean against the mattress.

"Oh, look at you. So sexy, Trey." He slid his hands along Trey's back, all the way down so he could cup the sexy ass.

His boy pushed closer, rocked into him. As he leaned over, he reached for a tube of lube on the bedside table, keeping one hand on his boy.

"You've been empty too long, boy. Poor needy hole." He slicked up his fingers, pushing two in, just like that.

"Sir!" Trey was ready for him.

He spent a few minutes, working on Trey's hole, stretching it for his cock. He loved the way the sweet body clung to him, to his touch.

"I can't wait," he told Trey as he tugged his fingers away.

"Don't. Don't wait. Yours." He didn't wait, pushing his cock into Trey's hot, tight hole.

Trey took him, the soft cry filling the air as their bodies slammed together.

"Oh, God, yes." He slid almost all the way out, before pushing in more slowly this time.

He made sure to vary his touches, his rhythm, keeping Trey on his toes, literally. Every now and then he'd pull right out and rub the tip of his erection over Trey's hole. That made Trey growl. Chuckling, he pushed back in, loving the way Trey's body opened up to him.

"Teasing me. Always teasing."

"You love it." Lucien breathed the words.

"Love you. Please."

He pushed in a little harder, then again, punching in this time.

"Yes. Yes." Trey met his thrusts, again and again, begging for him.

"Needy, beautiful size queen." He loved Trey for it.

"Yours. You made me. You made me need."

"Oh, no, baby. You needed all by yourself." He kissed Trey's spine. "I'm the one who gives you what you need."

"God, yes." Trey nodded. "Thank God."

Nodding, he increased his thrusts, moving harder, faster, taking that sweet ass with all he was. He wanted to fill Trey up then plug him. Groaning, he held tightly to Trey's hips, leaving marks as he shifted, as he found Trey's gland and nailed it. The low groan let him know he'd found it and he stayed there, slamming in, over and over.

"You're gonna come for me without a touch to your cock."

Trey shook his head, nodded, shook his head again.

"You are, baby. I'm the one calling the shots and I say come just from this." On "this" he slammed in as hard as he could, banging right up against Trey's gland.

"Please! Again. Again. Again."

He gave his boy what Trey craved, pounding in with everything he had. He wanted his boy's pleasure and he wanted it now. Trey cried out, entire body jerking, spunk spilling, spraying against the bed.

"Yes!" Lucien shouted the word.

Trey's orgasm pulled out his own and he pumped, filling Trey with his cum. Trey held him, milking his cock and squeezing him.

"Fuck, baby." He rested his cheek against Trey's spine. "Making love to you is better than breathing."

"Less necessary, though."

Laughing, he nearly came out of Trey before he was ready. He swatted one perfect ass cheek. "Practical boy."

"Infinitely."

He grabbed the plug he'd brought over. "I have one you haven't tried yet."

He loved exploring the Internet and sex stores, looking for new and interesting plugs and dildos for his sexy size queen.

"Let me see?"

"I'm trying to decide if I want your fingers or your ass to feel it first…"

Trey rolled his hips, gripped his cock tight.

"Is your ass voting?" he asked.

"A-another nation heard from?"

God, he loved laughing with Trey, loved that quick mind.

"Here." He put the dildo into Trey's hands. He did love it when Trey explored new things.

This one was shaped like a bullet—tapered at the end, then thick all the way to the base where it went small quickly.

"It's going to keep your entire ass stretched wide."

"Oh, God. Sir. It's… It's big." Trey's body worked his flagging cock, his lover's excitement ratcheting up again.

He rubbed Trey's hip. "Yeah. I think it's the biggest plug we've ever had." He'd bought Trey a dildo that was somewhat bigger, but never a plug like this one. "I think you can take it, though. I think you'll beg for it."

In fact, he knew Trey would. His baby was a size queen, through and through, and the bigger the better would be a good motto for him.

"I can't wait to watch you walking around with it, sitting with it…" He leaned in. "Maybe next week I'll get you to swim with it in." Maybe that would help with the floating and the dead man's float, if Trey had something to distract him a little from the fact of trusting the water to hold him up.

"Sir!" Trey's voice sounded scandalized.

Chuckling, he took the plug from Trey. He was getting softer and he didn't want to lose any of his seed from inside Trey. He slicked it up, getting ready to watch it slide into that tiny hole.

Setting the tip beneath where his cock disappeared into Trey's body, he then pushed just the very tip in, then began to pull his cock out. Trey panted, hips moving in unconscious little jerks.

"Needy lover." That need was one of the things he loved about Trey. One of many. God, he loved this man through and through.

"Yes. Yes. Need you. What you give me."

He worked the plug slowly in, twisting it, turning it, taking his time. He added more lube, keeping his boy slick so he would spread. The plug seemed huge as it opened Trey. Still, he kept pushing, playing, knowing Trey could not only take it, but was loving it.

Trey's head was hanging down between his arms, chest working like a bellows. He slid his free hand along Trey's spine, up all the way to his neck, then slowly down again as he continued to work that plug in.

Trey moaned. "So much."

Lucien stilled, letting Trey's motions pull the plug in. His fingers stroked the skin just above Trey's ass, then slid them along that knobby spine again.

"It's big. So big."

"It is. Bigger than me." He stroked the stretched hole, where the plug pierced it. "And the base is tiny. Your hole's going to snap around it."

And Trey would be aware of it, there's no way he'd be able to forget for a second that it was in.

"How will it come out?" Trey asked.

"There's a little base that I'll be able to grab onto."

Trey was still moving, taking the plug in.

"Fuck. You are stunning, Trey. Unbelievable."

"Full. Full for you." Trey moaned softly, legs beginning to tremble.

It was time to get it all the way in and seated so they could lie together while Trey got used to the sensation. "Press back for me, baby. Take it."

"I'm trying..."

Resting his hand back on Trey's spine, he encouraged his lover to rock back. He didn't have to push. He had patience enough to make this good. Slowly but surely, he got Trey rocking, moving back and taking more and more of the plug in.

Deep, hungry sounds were leaving Trey, escaping his boy. Then all of a sudden, Trey's body swallowed rest of the plug up and the tight muscles snapped closed around the thin end, leaving only the base outside of Trey's body. It made Lucien moan, had him stroking the fine little ass.

Trey humped the air, hips moving furiously.

"You need to come again, baby?" Leaning in, he whispered, "You're allowed," before blowing on Trey's filled hole.

"Master!"

Oh, listen to that cry.

He nudged the base of the plug, eager to have Trey come again without a single touch to his cock.

"Full. Full, God. Touch me. Please."

"Come for me," Lucien demanded, rubbing his lightly stubbled cheek against Trey's right ass cheek.

"Master..."

After pulling the plug partway out, he slammed it back in. "I said come."

Trey's head slammed back and he screamed, spunk spraying from him. Yes. Yes. Bending, he covered Trey's body, pressing kisses on his lover. He loved the sound of Trey's sobs, the wild moans.

"So good, baby. You make me so hot."

"Master... Sir."

"Yeah, that's me." He was allowed to feel smug — he'd made Trey come, twice, without a single touch to that lovely, long cock.

"Love."

"You know it." He helped Trey get onto the bed, petting and stroking.

"So full, love. Heavy."

"I know." Kissing Trey's head, he pulled his lover close. He had Trey, rocked him nice and slow. "How are your pretty little nips doing?" Drawing a hand between them, he then flicked one of the clamps.

"F-fine until you touched!"

That had him chuckling and flicking the other one. "It makes you vibrate."

"It aches."

"That's a good thing, baby." He flicked them both again.

Trey curled down, as if he was trying to protect them.

"You can't hide from me." He tugged on one as proof.

"Oh..." Trey rocked back, rubbing against him.

"Love watching you move."

"Need to." Trey reached back, hand sliding on his cock.

"Now you're trying to distract me." Lucien knew this maneuver well and sometimes he let it work, sometimes he didn't.

"Me? Would I do that?"

Lucien laughed. Oh God, he did love this man. "You so would."

"Not me... I'm innocent. All blind dudes are innocent."

Lucien kept laughing, tickled. "Not you. I corrupted you." Honestly, Trey had been just asking to be corrupted.

"Maybe I corrupted you."

"Oh, that's it. I was pure as the driven snow before I met you." Hell, he'd been — not a bad man, but a bit of a user before he found himself in love with Trey, fascinated with the way Trey needed.

Tilting Trey's head, he took a kiss, eager to taste the pleasure there.

Trey turned, pushing right into him before jerking back. "Oh. Take them off, Sir? Please?"

"Yeah. Your nipples should be nice and tender for the rest of the day." He teased the right nipple, then grabbed the clamp and opened it up.

"Oh. Oh. Oh, please! Master!"

He bent and he wrapped his lips around the free nipple, sucking hard to help pull the blood back into Trey's flesh.

"Yes!" Trey grabbed his hair, hips jerking restlessly.

Taking hold of Trey's hips, he held them away from him so Trey couldn't rub. Trey sobbed, head shaking, so wild for him. Then he took the other clamp off. His lover went wild beneath him, screaming and twisting, totally free and unashamed. It was fucking stunning. Trey was stunning.

God, he loved his boy. So damn much.

He waited a moment, then wrapped his lips around the nipple he'd just freed up. Trey wrapped around him, clinging to him, groaning little nonsense words. Humming, he kept sucking, digging his fingers into Trey's ass now. He could feel Trey working the massive plug.

His own cock was half hard, growing from how sexy Trey was. It stunned him, the sheer depth of Trey's need.

He palmed Trey's balls, pushing them against Trey's body.

"Sir…" Trey moaned, spread wide.

"Wanton boy." He loved that about Trey. And he thought maybe having two days doing things together had made Trey even hotter and more eager than usual.

"Please…" Trey begged.

He needed to bind that needy cock, the heavy balls. After all, Trey had already come twice. That would be enough until morning. His boy loved being controlled.

Rolling over, Lucien then opened the bedside table drawer, looking through the cock rings.

Trey plastered against his back, his ass. He undulated, feeling Trey roll along him from shoulders to knees. His sweet boy was hard as stone, leaving wet kisses on him. He loved the heat and the velvet of Trey's erection and he undulated again, getting a bit of friction going for Trey.

"Oh, damn… My Lucien."

"All yours, baby. Like every bit of me."

"Mine. Love." Trey kissed his nape.

"That's right. Even my innards."

Trey grabbed his belly, tickling him. Laughing, he pressed back against Trey, making sure not to roll on top of his lover.

"Mmm." Trey's fingers found his nipple, tugged.

"Oh..." His laughter faded and he took a deep breath.

He got another tug, then another. He thought he'd let Trey distract him this time. He shifted, turning to face Trey again.

"Hey." Trey pressed close, kissing him.

"Hey, baby." His sexy lover.

"Love you. Love this. *Us*."

"Good. Me, too. You're the best thing in my life."

"Good." That was a satisfied sound.

"Let's hope you still think that when I've finished torturing you."

"I will." There was no doubt in Trey's voice.

"Yeah." Lucien smiled, rubbing Trey's hip with his thumb, trying to remember what he'd been doing. Oh, right. Letting Trey worship his body.

Smiling, he ran his own hand along Trey's spine, giving even as he was getting. Trey leaned forward, lips searching for his nipple. He didn't help, enjoying the glide of those lips on his skin. His sweet lover licked and lapped, nuzzled and kissed.

When Trey found his nipple, Lucien moaned, moving toward his lover.

"Mmm." That was a happy, happy noise.

"Feels good. Don't stop."

"I won't. I have you." Trey leaned in, let his teeth drag a bit.

Jerking, Lucien pushed closer. Trey's chuckle vibrated against his skin, driving the sensations higher. It was delicious, intoxicating, having Trey focused on his pleasure. He arched up, and Trey pushed him down, held him.

"Oh, pushy." His voice was breathless.

"Hungry."

"It's good." He ran his fingers over Trey, the touches random.

"It is. It's been so good, having our weekend."

"It has." No stress, no worry that this was it for months. It was easy and fun and good and sexy. He was going to fight tooth and nail to keep it. No sliding back to how it was before.

He jerked as Trey bit lightly on his nipple, surprised out of his thoughts.

"This is fun, love."

"It is. I love it when you get all toothy and tonguey on me."

"Tonguey?" Trey's voice was thick with laughter.

"Sure. It's a word. And if it isn't, it should be."

"I like it. I'll use it in a book. Later."

"Much later. Right now you're supposed to be tonguey with me."

Trey laughed and rolled them over, straddling his hips.

"Mmm." He ran his hands up along Trey's sides, admiring the slender body.

Trey arched into his touch, then grabbed his wrists, brought them over his head. "You be good. I'm touching."

"Does that mean I'm not allowed to touch, too?"

"Uh-huh."

"Bossy, bossy." Lucien kept his hands up above his head, though, watching Trey's face.

"That's me." Trey reached for him, fingers starting at the top of his head. They moved slowly, exploring every inch of him.

He stayed still, letting Trey look his fill, waiting for the sweet touches to shift, to become more sexual. It took forever, just to explore his face, his shoulders, his collarbones. He drew in one deep breath after another, enjoying each and every touch.

"You're beautiful." Trey's moan made him blush, head to toe.

"Not as beautiful as you." He had muscles, sure, but Trey stole his breath.

Trey shook his head. "No. No, you're stunning. I could touch you for lifetimes."

"You should touch yourself. Hey, have you? To look, I mean."

"Sure. I'm...me, but it's hard, because you're touching and feeling and that's super confusing."

"Ah. Yeah, I can understand that."

Trey grinned. "It's like if you touch your lip. Are you feeling your lip or is your lip feeling your finger?"

"Perv. Feeling up your finger."

"You know it." Trey sucked his own finger in, teasing.

He tried to laugh, but it came out more as a groan. "Damn, baby."

Trey's wet finger traced his nipple, so slowly. Arching, he groaned, his flesh drawing up.

"Mmm." Trey smiled as if Lucien had offered him a much-desired gift.

He wanted so badly to reach for his lover, to touch and make Trey feel good. But he was good and kept his hands where they were. For now. Trey wriggled his way down, spending a long moment rocking the heavy plug against his thighs.

He laughed softly and said the words he kept repeating. "I know what you're doing."

"Moving to suck your nipples?"

"No, the thing with your ass and the plug."

"I can't help it. It's so good."

"I wasn't complaining, only saying I knew what you were up to."

"You know... You can see. It's not that amazing."

Little shit! He slapped Trey's ass. "I can't see what the inside of your ass is doing!"

Trey leaned down, managed to bite his nipple through the giggles. He laughed and moaned together, his body jerking up toward Trey. His lover began sucking and biting, focusing on his left nipple until Lucien wanted to scream. He grabbed hold of the sheets, curling his fingers into them.

About the time he was going to demand that Trey stop, his lover switched nipples.

"Killing me."

"Loving you."

"Yeah, it's an amazing way to go," he teased, voice barely there.

"Never letting go." Trey set to sucking again, strong and steady.

"Oh..." He took a deep breath and unclenched his fingers from the sheets, moving them to slide through Trey's hair. His eyes filled with tears, the words rocking him to his core. "I love you, Trey."

"I know." Trey scooted down farther, lapping at his belly.

Groaning, he spread his legs restlessly, then cradled Trey's body. That fine ass was up in the air, hips rocking, body swaying.

"God, baby. So sexy. You'd make me want even if you weren't about to suck my cock."

But Trey was and he was going to watch every second. He moaned in anticipation. Trey braced himself on Lucien's thighs and started lapping at his erection.

"Baby!" Groaning, he laid his head back and panted.

"Yes. I have you."

"You do. Oh, fuck, you do."

Those tiny laps threatened to make him insane, the tiny laps and nuzzles near unbearable. He moved his hips restlessly, pushing his need toward Trey's mouth. Finally, blessedly, Trey took him in, pulling the head of Lucien's cock toward the back of his throat.

"Yes. Yes, Trey." He spread his legs wider, and rubbed Trey's sides against his inner thighs.

This time Trey didn't tease. He sucked, working every inch of Lucien's rod until he couldn't bear it.

"Baby, I'm going to come." He was going to shoot right down Trey's throat.

Trey made an amazing, happy sound that vibrated around his erection.

"Oh fuck!" He bucked up, cock going deep as he came, filling Trey's throat with his seed.

His lover didn't lose a drop, holding him in that amazing mouth. He reached for Trey's head, stroking his fingers through Trey's hair as he panted.

"Taste good, Sir."

"I'm glad you think so. It would suck otherwise, wouldn't it? Or not suck, I guess, if you hated the taste."

Trey chuckled softly, chest moving against his thigh.

"Come get a kiss, baby. I want to taste me, too."

Trey climbed his body, sweet heat dragging along his belly as he moved. Humming, he slid his hand behind Trey's head, guiding his lover down into a kiss. The flavor of his seed in Trey's mouth was delicious. Moaning, he rubbed Trey against him. His boy was still hard, eager, still working that plug. He could feel Trey's cock leaving wet spots on his belly as they rubbed. Now he needed to bind that pretty flesh, just like he'd promised.

"Not going to let you come." He stretched to the drawer, feeling around inside it.

"No fair."

"You've come already. Twice." Besides, there was no such thing as fair in love and sex.

"Uh-huh. You made me."

"Yeah, I did. And now I'm going to keep you from doing it again."

Trey craved the stretch, the control.

Lucien found a leather cock ring and wrapped his fingers around it. "Found it."

"Which one?"

"Black leather, about an inch and a half wide." It was good and solid and Trey would not be able to forget he had it on.

"Mmm." That was a look of pure happiness. His baby was pure hedonist.

He slid the ring down along Trey's back. Trey shuddered, lips open, parted. He traced Trey's lips with his tongue, rubbed the cock ring against Trey's ass. Trey started rocking, trying to get himself off.

He slapped Trey's ass. "Stop that."

"Huh?" Trey rocked faster, pushing him.

"No getting off!" He slapped Trey's ass a few more times.

"Okay! Okay! Damn!"

"Of course if you'd like some more swats…" They didn't spank that often. Pain wasn't really what got Trey off.

"No…" Trey shook his head, hid his ass with his hands.

"Okay, then. Let's get this ring on you before you shoot and actually earn a spanking."

Trey nodded, pushing his fist into his mouth.

Lucien stared for a moment. "What are you doing?"

"Huh?" There was a little mark on Trey's knuckle.

"Why are you stuffing your hand in your mouth?" He took Trey's hand and rubbed at the mark.

"It's how I make myself stop."

"Oh... Well, I don't want you hurting yourself."

Trey looked surprised, then pleased. "Yes, Sir."

He took a quick kiss then began to work the ring around Trey's needy erection. Trey's hot flesh dripped, leaked for him.

"Mmm. Gonna leave you needing for the rest of the day."

"No fair. No fair, Sir."

"Oh, it's very fair." He got the ring firmly set. Yeah, that was him. Totally unfair. "Now we can rub and pinch and play all night long and you'll still need me."

Trey laughed, the sound oddly strangled. "There hasn't been a moment in the last ten years I haven't needed you."

"Oh, baby." He kissed Trey hard because words couldn't make an appropriate response to that.

Trey's hand was on his cheek, holding him, and it was perfect.

"I love you," Lucien whispered fiercely.

"Love." Trey beamed at him, and they settled together, holding on tight.

Lucien wasn't even going to think about how tomorrow was Sunday and he'd have to go home in the evening. He would be seeing Trey again next weekend and that was new and wonderful.

Chapter Nine

Trey bashed at his word count, trying to hit his goal before the clock hit five. It was his weekend to deal with the date and that had been stressful, finding a place. He'd wasted hours researching it and now he was sweating getting his work done.

Brian knocked at his office door. "Is there anything else you need me to do before I go for the weekend, boss?"

"No." Go away. He had five hundred words left.

"Okay, so you're good with me leaving?"

"Go away, Brian. Shut the office door. Working."

"Ah. Got it."

He thought that maybe Brian was chuckling, but he ignored it and kept working.

He put his head down and typed hard, fingers banging on the keyboard. He wasn't even sure he was writing words that made sense. He just needed to get his word count in, though, before—

His thought was interrupted by his doorbell ringing, Dodger barking like mad.

Trey checked his word count. Fifty left. "Be right there!" *Come on. Come on.*

The doorbell rang again just as he finished up, Dodger running back and forth between him and the front door.

"Coming!" He hit save and headed down the hall. "I'm coming."

"Hey, baby. I was worried something was wrong." Lucien cupped his cheek.

"No. No, just trying to get my work done and now I have to get dressed really quick."

"I do believe I could help with that." Lucien chuckled. "Or I could not help, if you get my drift."

"I could use help. I'm running late. Reservations are coming up and I've already fucked my schedule."

"You have a schedule for our date?"

Trey heard the door close and Lucien put his hand on one arm, before walking him down the hallway.

"Yes. We have reservations. Tickets to that movie you said you wanted to see." He hated sitting through movies in the cinema — it was always so overwhelming — but Lucien loved them so.

"Oh, really?" Lucien sounded so pleased.

They turned into the bedroom, where his outfit was supposed to be out on the bed.

"Yep." He pulled off his T-shirt. "Tell me there are clothes on the bed."

"There are clothes on the bed. Nice ones. Where are we going?"

"Noir. We're at the early seating."

"Is it French?"

Trey shook his head. "It's a dining in the dark restaurant." He thought maybe that would make things more fair.

"Oh! Oh, Trey that is so cool!" Lucien actually sounded excited.

He pulled on his shirt, buttoned it and checked his watch. "The taxi will be here in five. How's my hair?"

"Let me just…" Lucien ran his fingers through it. "That's better."

"Thank you." He grabbed his wallet, put on his shoes. "Ta da." God, he was tired.

Lucien took his hand and put it on Lucien's arm again. "Do you remember the address? I'll put it in the GPS and are we taking Dodger?"

"I am taking Dodger and I called a cab. Did you want to drive?"

"Oh, a cab is fine. I like that you're taking total charge of the date."

"I said I would." The taxi honked just about the time he had Dodger harnessed.

"Are you okay?" Lucien asked. "You seem stressed."

"I am, but I'll calm down. I'm just a little grr."

"Let's get in the cab and then you can tell me all about it."

"Yeah. Yeah, that's good." They got to the cab and he gave the address.

Lucien put an arm around his shoulders. "So why are you stressed and grr?"

"The words didn't come easy today, even though I wanted them to so I could go."

"Yeah? Does that kind of thing happen a lot?"

"I don't know. I haven't dealt with it much."

"Even that last book that took nearly eight months to write?"

"I didn't leave the house, remember? There wasn't anywhere to go." He got into a story and that was everything, now there was so much more.

"Oh, so it didn't matter before if the words weren't flowing?"

"Not really. I just surfed. A lot."

Lucien chuckled for him. "You know if you get behind and need to put in some writing time Saturday or Sunday afternoons, I can just read a book or whatever."

Oh, that was sweet. Dear. "Right now I'm caught up, but thank you."

"Well, I'm trying to prove that you can have your writing and me, too."

He reached out, grabbed Lucien's leg. "How was your week?"

"It was good. We've got a new promo on and it kept things hopping."

"Neat." Trey knew Lucien liked his gym, cared about it.

"Yeah. I got a new client, too. She's working toward a triathlon. Really committed."

"Should I be jealous?"

"Of a chick?" Lucien chuckled. "Baby, she's got boobs."

"Ew." Trey cracked up, the old joke familiar and warm.

Lucien kissed his forehead. "So how did you hear about this place we're going to?"

"I asked one of the message boards I frequent. Lots of blind singles looking for places to take a date."

"That's cool. I'm looking forward to this."

"I am too." No one could see. No one. He'd be like everyone else.

The cab pulled up and Lucien told him the amount due to the driver. Trey paid and tipped, then asked Lucien if he knew which way to go. Hopefully they were right in front of the restaurant.

"Yeah, we're just to the right of the restaurant—up the curb and in we go." Lucien helped him and Dodger get out of the cab, then put Trey's free hand on his arm.

"Thank you." They got to the door and he heard it open. "Two for Germain, please."

"Certainly. Follow me, please."

They did, the hostess telling them about how the service worked and explaining that the meal would be starting in fifteen minutes and that's when the lights would go down. No one would be staring, no one would care if he made a mess.

Lucien made sure he was seated and Dodger was comfortable at his feet, then sat across from him. The table was small enough that their knees brushed together "It smells good, doesn't it?"

"It does." He inhaled deeply. He smelled meat and cinnamon, wine and citrus.

"The place is pretty crowded."

"Is it? I know they seat everyone at once."

"Yeah, she said fifteen minutes. We've got another ten minutes to wait. I'm looking forward to this. It's pretty cool."

"I wanted something…equal."

Lucien took his hand. "Yes, it will be that. Do you feel we're unequal a lot?"

"Not a lot, no. I mean, there are things we do that seem unequal, especially sexually, but we both know they're not. And money-wise, career-wise, we're fine. I guess, we're doing new things and I feel like I have to lean on you a lot for that."

"I can see where it seems like you're suddenly leaning on me a lot, because we're kind of changing tons of things. But as far as the sex goes… Well, first of all, you know as the sub you have the ultimate power and besides, even if you could see — well, it's called power play, isn't it?"

"It is. I just like the idea of eating without having to worry."

"Oh, for sure. It just made me curious if you felt…at a disadvantage with me."

"No. It's been a hard week, though, so I'm glad I can just sit and eat."

"Change usually isn't easy." Lucien spoke softly, stroking Trey's wrist with his thumb. "I think these changes are going to be worth it, though. I know I've really appreciated being able to spend more time with you."

"Yeah. Yeah, I get that." And he'd hit his goals.

A soft bell chimed.

"Oh, they're dimming the lights," Lucien told him.

"Don't be scared, love. I'm right here."

Lucien's fingers tightened around his. "I'm glad."

"I swear. You're the safest man in here."

That had Lucien chuckling. "Okay, it's all dark now. I'm assuming the wait staff is wearing night vision goggles."

"Amateurs." He reached down, murmuring to Dodger.

Lucien laughed for him.

"Good evening, welcome to the sensual experience of dining in the dark." The speaker was a woman, trying to be erotic and husky, but Trey just chuckled.

"Shh. This is supposed to be hot," Lucien whispered loudly.

That set Trey off, covering his mouth with his hand as he cackled. Lucien's deep laughter joined his and Dodger shifted slightly at his feet.

"Behave," Lucien stage-whispered.

"Try…trying!" he answered, but he was tickled now, and everything seemed funny. Hell, after this week, it was a welcome thing.

"Oh, don't try too hard, baby. You know I love the sound of your laughter. Only one sound I like better."

Trey felt his cheeks heat. Yeah. Yeah, Lucien loved to hear him beg.

A waiter came by and there was the soft thunk of plates hitting the table. "Directly in front of you and this dish is not hot," murmured the man.

"Your first course is now being served," came the voice of the woman over the intercom. "A trio of smoked pig. Plump, juicy figs wrapped in bacon, baked and cooled, served with a cold maple berry gastrique. Honeydew melon wrapped in prosciutto de Parma. And diced apple with crispy lardons in a red wine vinaigrette."

The smells were amazing—tart and smoky—and they made his mouth water. He searched the plate, finding a small bowl, then the figs and the melon. "Which one do you want to start with?"

"Let's do the fig—it's finger food."

"Sure." The skin was the slightest bit crinkly, and the bacon felt heavier, tougher.

"Oh my God." Lucien's words were somewhat muffled. "I can't believe how good this tastes."

He ate his, nibbling—sweet and salty together did amazing things in his mouth.

"It's amazing how much more I'm focused on the taste," Lucien told him. "And how that affects the taste, too."

He didn't know what to say to that. This was his life, all the time. Well, okay. Most of the time he was eating pizza.

"This was such a good idea, baby. Thanks for bringing me."

"You're welcome. Thanks for being willing to try."

"I will try anything with you."

He found Lucien's leg under the table, squeezed the man's knee.

Lucien's fingers slid over his hand. "You want to try the melon next? I'm kind of avoiding the one we have to use a fork to eat.

"You can use your fingers. No one can see, and you have a napkin." He found himself remarkably protective of Lucien like this.

"Yeah? It is cold…"

"However you're comfortable, huh?"

"Works for me. I'm going to have to brave the utensils eventually, though."

"True." He took his fork and tasted the apple. Oh. Oh, wow. It tasted like tart heaven. "Try it. It's so good."

After a moment, Lucien groaned. "Damn. Damn. That is the best of the three and I thought the other two were good. Wow."

"You ate your melon already? That's cheating." He was saving his.

"Oh. Oops?"

Trey started laughing again, enjoying the hell out of this.

A soup course came next and Lucien chuckled. "Okay, at least a spoon will be easier than a fork."

"The soup is a clear consommé with chives and mushrooms and topped with fried basil," their narrator-hostess told them.

"People fry basil?" Trey asked.

Lucien laughed softly. "You sound like that's the craziest thing you've ever heard of."

"Not the craziest. Just odd. How do you fry it?"

"I don't know. Probably put it in the deep fryer."

"Huh." He wasn't exactly sure how that worked, really, but at least he'd smelled basil. Mom used to keep it in the pantry. It smelled like grassy pepper.

"Okay. Let's give this a try."

He heard Lucien's spoon banging against his bowl. He found the edge of his own bowl and explored with his spoon, nudging the mushrooms out of the way.

Lucien laughed softly. "Man, I missed my mouth. It's right where it always is. How could I miss it?"

"I don't know. You can't see it when the lights are on, can you?"

Oh, man. That would mean he didn't understand this vision thing at all.

"No, but I can see where the spoon is going. I guess I figured I could hit my mouth no problem, even if I couldn't see it."

"Ah." Oh, good. Yay.

"It amazes me more than ever that you do this all time. Just finding the bowl with my spoon is awkward."

"I've never known any different." He always thought it would be harder to go blind.

"Yeah, that makes sense. It's like how I just know colors and stuff, how to eat with vision—you know how to eat without." Lucien laughed suddenly. "Man, I just spilled like a lot. This is making me more impressed with you, baby."

"Do you need another napkin?"

"If I don't, the table does."

"No worries, sir. We'll handle it for you." The waiter was close and Trey decided to eat his own soup.

"Thanks," murmured Lucien. "I'll try not to make any other messes."

"Just enjoy the experience," Trey said. How many times had Lucien said that to him?

Lucien's hand touched his knee, squeezed a moment. "I will. I promise."

"Good." He picked something up with his spoon. A leaf. A crispy leaf. "There's a leaf in my soup."

"I'm guessing that's the fried basil."

"What?" He didn't understand.

"That's what they said, right? Consommé with chives, mushrooms and topped with fried basil." Lucien felt around and touched his spoon. "Yeah, that's the fried basil leaf."

"That is not what basil is." Basil was little flakes. He knew this.

"What? Oh! I know what's going on. Basil is a plant and they take the leaves and dry them, then crumble them up to make what you know of as basil. This would be the leaf, deep fried."

"Oh." God. God, sometimes he was a moron. How embarrassing. He put the spoon down, leaving the rest of the soup. "How cool!"

"Did you like it?" Lucien asked him.

"The figs were the best so far."

"I liked the apple and lardon thing. The soup was the hardest to eat. I'm really glad we did this, you know? It makes me feel closer to you."

"I'm glad you're happy, Lucien. I wanted to give you something special."

"It is. It's very special. How often do I get to walk in your shoes?"

He chuckled softly. No one wanted to be blind, but this was supposed to be a neat experience, a new one.

Their next course was announced—seared duck breast with foie gras, roasted potatoes and vegetables.

He had to wonder if the meat came pre-cut. He'd bet so. Knife skills were hard to master and no one here had practice.

"I've never had foie gras before," Lucien told him. "But I've always kind of wondered what it was like."

"It's liver, right?" He wasn't eating that.

"Duck liver. It's not anything like actual liver. At least I hope not. That stuff is gross."

"I hope not, too."

Their waiter set the plates down in front of them.

Lucien whispered to him, "How do I work a fork and knife?"

He touched the plate, exploring. "The meat's cut for you, love. You can just eat."

"Oh, yay." Lucien chuckled and soon he heard the sound of Lucien's fork hitting the plate.

Yeah, that was tough. He used his fingers, knowing no one could see him.

"I think I like the foie gras better than the duck breast," Lucien noted. "If I'm guessing correctly which one is which."

"The duck breast is the chewy one. The other is just…smooth." He didn't love either one, but the potatoes were delicious.

"I still liked the apple lardon thing best."

"The potatoes are good."

"Yeah, and the vegetables, too. I just don't think the main is as yummy as the aps were."

Trey smiled, nodded. "You just like apples." Maybe there'd be an apple dessert.

Lucien's laughter was soft, happy. "Yeah, I do. But with those little squares of bacon fat? So damn good."

"I would never have thought it, either."

"Yeah. Pretty cool. Are you looking forward to going swimming tomorrow?"

"I am, believe it or not. The house felt very confining this week." He hadn't even put his finger on it, until just now.

"Well, if you ever need to go out during the week, you know you only need to call and I'll be there."

"I know. I know. I need to give it time." The temptation to go and feel and learn was huge.

"We'll figure it out, baby. We're motivated." Lucien sounded utterly sure. Completely. "I like the sauce they've put with it. And the wine is a great pairing."

He hadn't tried the wine—he hadn't even realized they'd put it on the table—and he felt around carefully, searching for a stem. There wasn't one, but his hand hit a rounded bottomed glass. It felt like a wine glass without the base. He held the glass to his nose, the scent of grapes and cherries and tobacco in his nose. It did go well with the food, complementing it.

"I just love how much more I notice the smells and tastes," Lucien told him.

"Do you?"

"I do. It's really neat. And it makes me think how it's like this for you all the time."

"It is." It was his life.

Lucien's hand squeezed his knee under the table. He squeezed back, rubbing Lucien's knuckles with his thumb.

"Love you." The words were soft, but he could hear how sincere Lucien's words were.

"Love." He had to smile. Had to.

Lucien just held his knee until their plates were cleared away.

"I smell cherries," he noted. Sweet and tart at the same time. It was a great combination.

"Oh, dessert." He heard Lucien sniffing loudly. "I don't smell it yet, though."

"I do. Cherries and pastry and cinnamon." He could practically taste it already.

"That sounds wonderful. I love dessert. Do you think they'll have ice cream with it?" Lucien loved pies à la mode, as he called it.

"I hope so. I love when you get ice cream." It made Lucien wicked.

"Oh you do, do you?" That note was already in Lucien's voice.

"I do. I like how it makes you feel."

"Me, too. You think if the cherry thing doesn't come with ice cream, we could ask for some anyway?"

"We can ask." Asking never hurt anything, right?

"Or we can make a stop on the way home if we have to." Lucien chuckled. "I've got it in my head now. I can almost taste it."

"You like having cold lips." He wiggled, loving the way teasing made his cock fill.

Lucien's chuckle was damn sexy. Trey reached down, adjusted himself. He knew no one could see him do it and that was really neat.

Their waiter set their dessert dishes in front of them.

"Ladies and gentlemen, your final course of cherry clafoutis and cinnamon ice cream."

"Score!" Lucien's voice was joyous. He heard Lucien rubbing his hands together, then the sound of his lover's spoon ringing against the ceramic bowl.

Trey lifted the bowl, holding it as he ate. Oh, man. Sweet, tart. Yummy.

"This is so good. I've never had cinnamon ice cream before. I wonder if the…uh, sensation later would be hot from the cinnamon and cold from the ice cream?"

"We'll have to get some at the store. Try it."

"Yeah." Lucien's voice lowered in pitch. "You'll have to tell me what it feels like."

"I want to." His cock pressed against his zipper.

"We should definitely find some place on the way home, then, because this is an experiment I can't wait to try." The need in Lucien's voice was not helping his erection deflate any.

"We'll have the cab take us somewhere."

"Sounds good to me. We can Google it when we're done here."

"After. Enjoy your dessert."

"Yes, boss." He could hear the teasing fondness in Lucien's voice.

"That's right." He cackled, ate another bite. He did love cherries.

Lucien's laughter joined his and they finished their meal on a high note.

"I did well, love?" Trey asked.

"You did fantastic. This was a fabulous date and I've had a fun time."

"Did you want to go to the movies, too?" He wanted to make sure Lucien still wanted to go.

"Oh, that's right, there's movies too. Terrific! What are we going to again?"

"That sci-fi one you wanted to see."

"I might have to put you in charge of every date night. You're doing a great job."

Oh, that didn't seem fair. In fact, that seemed like a little bit of hell.

"No?" He could hear the teasing note in Lucien's voice now.

"No. No, I'm glad to take my turn, but it's hard. A challenge. You're worth it," he continued, not wanting to offend.

"And you're used to me being in charge. I think it's good, though, for you to do it now and then. I know it's one of the things you worry about having me around more."

"I said I would do it. Just not every Friday."

"I know, baby. And I just said that's good." Lucien took his hand, thumb rubbing his knuckles.

Trey nodded. God, his mood was swinging wildly from up to down and it didn't seem to want to settle.

"We'd like to thank you for dining with us tonight. We'll be bringing the lights up a little bit at a time."

At least he didn't have to worry about that.

"Oh wow." Lucien laughed. "Man, I made a mess at my plate. You didn't."

"No?" He'd hope not. He was practiced at this whole thing, right?

"Nope. I really did love doing this, having a new insight into what everyday things are like for you."

"I'll have to buy you a blindfold."

"Oh, that gives me an idea." There was a note of excitement in Lucien's voice. "You get me a blindfold and we'll do some scenes with me wearing it."

"If you want to, sure." Silly man.

"I think it'll be great. I don't know why I didn't think of it sooner."

"Because blind men don't need blindfolds?"

"Well yeah, but if you weren't blind, I probably wouldn't blindfold myself for scenes, just you. This is going to be more fun."

He wasn't sure how, but Lucien was excited, so he went with it.

"The lights are up. Do we need to get going for the movie?"

He brushed his fingers across his watch. "Yes, let's grab a cab."

"Cool." Lucien pushed his chair back and once Trey had stood and grabbed Dodger's harness, Lucien took his hand and put it on Lucien's arm.

"Let's go finish your date," Lucien said.

"*Our* date," Trey corrected.

"Our date."

He nodded and wished, not for the first time, that he'd slipped earplugs in his pocket.

Chapter Ten

Lucien got Trey inside, slowing Dodger's happy bouncing so the dog didn't knock Trey over. It had been a great afternoon of swimming, but once they'd gotten out of the water, Lucien had seen how wiped out Trey was. It had been a busy couple of days and he knew Trey had been stressed out about his word count—at least on Friday, if not longer.

A relaxing, lazy afternoon was on order. Time for recharging.

Trey made a beeline for the back door, opening it so Dodger could use the doggie door at will. His lover was a good man. And so wasn't relying on him for everything. Lucien though that was one fear that Trey didn't really have to worry about.

"You want a Coke?" Trey asked.

"How about some hot chocolate?"

"That sounds good…"

"Come on. I'll make it. You can keep me company in the kitchen."

"Yeah? That would rock." Trey made it to the kitchen island and plopped down. "God, I'm tired."

"It's been a busy few days, hasn't it?" They had this afternoon and tomorrow to relax, for him to help his boy be lazy and rejuvenate.

"Yeah. Yeah, I'm a little worn out."

"Is it a good worn out, though?" He moved around Trey's kitchen easily.

"I think so, yes."

He had the sneaking suspicion it would be a while before Trey volunteered to see another movie at the theater, though. The noise had overwhelmed both Trey and Dodger last night.

"How would you like to spend the afternoon cuddled together? I could read to you from your latest book."

"You could just read to me. It can be anything. The touching part sounds good."

"The touching part sounds fantastic. And if it isn't a sneak peek into your latest book, it should be something you want to read."

"Did you bring anything? All I have are audio books and books in Braille…"

"I have my laptop." Lucien was sure he could find something.

"Oh, cool. E-books on demand, baby!"

Okay, that was adorable. He did love Trey with all his heart. Humming, he got the milk boiling and poured in the hot chocolate mix he'd made.

"I love that smell." Trey's eyes were closed and he was breathing hard.

"The hot chocolate or me?"

"Yes." The answer was immediate.

"Have I told you lately that I love you?"

"Yes, but you can tell me again."

He went over to Trey and cupped one cheek, turning Trey's face up. "I love you, very much."

"Love." Trey smiled at him as if he was magical.

He pressed his lips against Trey's, his lover's skin just a touch cooler than usual from the swimming. He would soon have them warmed right up.

"Cocoa is ready," Trey warned him.

"I'd better grab it then before it burns."

He dropped a last kiss onto Trey's mouth, then went and grabbed the pot from the stove, poured the cocoa into two mugs. His baby had an amazing sniffer.

"Sofa in the living room sound good?" They had never spent a lot of time there. Of course, they never used to spend weekends together.

"Perfect, yeah. You have the cocoa?"

"I do. Oh, just a second, marshmallows." He found them in the cupboard and added a bunch to both cups. "Okay. We're good to go."

"Marshmallows are proof that there is a god and he loves us."

"I love that something so simple makes you so happy."

"You know what? I do too."

Chuckling, he joined Trey on the couch, reached for his laptop. Trey handed him the remote, too, then drank deep, slurping up the marshmallows.

"You want a movie instead of a book, baby?"

"I'm totally easy. Either way I'm going to end up in your lap, napping."

"A movie would make that easier." Lucien turned the TV on. "I'll find something on Netflix. What are you in the mood to nap to?"

"*Avengers*?"

"Oh, good choice." And Trey knew it was one of his favorites. His baby was good to him.

Trey finished his hot chocolate, then pushed in close, begging attention. With the movie as background, he pressed his lips to Trey's. The kiss was slow, lazy and Trey ended up cuddled close.

"You know, I like watching movies at home with you way better than at the theater." He rubbed Trey's ass, squeezing his lover's cheeks and pondering getting a plug to give his boy some stretch.

"Me too. The theater is so loud."

"Yeah, I realized that yesterday, plus I can't do this." He squeezed Trey's ass again, fingers pushing into Trey's crack.

Trey gasped, hips rolling back instinctively.

"Yeah, you couldn't do that, either." Grinning, he took another kiss and continued to play with Trey's ass.

"No. No, someone would complain."

"And what we have together isn't for public consumption. It's ours." He was definitely getting a plug for Trey, though. Just because they were taking it easy, didn't mean they couldn't play at all.

"No. No, I'm yours, Sir."

"You are." It still gave him a thrill to hear Trey call him Sir, even after all these years.

Trey nodded, begged another sweet kiss. He was more than willing to give it, his tongue dancing along Trey's as they shared breath. He worked Trey's jeans open, tugging at his belt, his fly. He loved his boy's body, the slender limbs with their fine skin. He pushed the jeans away, fingers sliding down Trey's crack, the base of the plug there making him gasp.

Wicked boy!

"You weren't wearing this in the pool!" He was surprised, delighted, and more in love than ever.

"Magic." Trey had a look a pure innocence going on.

He couldn't do anything but laugh. "Such a naughty boy."

"Mmm-hmm." Trey wriggled for him.

"Let's see which one you used." He hadn't even seen Trey put the thing in his bag.

He encouraged Trey to move over his thighs, spread so he could see. Metal, firm — it was either the ball or the medium sized one. Knowing his beautiful size queen, it was the ball one. He tapped the end, then turned it. Trey rocked up, hips bucking toward his touch.

"Needy boy." He tugged the plug part way out, finding out that it was indeed the ball plug.

"Yes. Yes, Sir." His lover knew how to make it clear when he needed.

He pushed the plug back in, hard. "I have to find a bigger plug then."

Trey gave him a sharp, hungry little cry. Oh, that was a good idea.

He shifted Trey so his lover was on his hands and knees. Standing, he stroked Trey's butt. "Don't move, I'll be right back."

"Yes, Sir." Trey settled, eyes closed, trusting him totally.

He lingered a moment longer, stroking that super tempting ass.

Then he made himself go to the bedroom to look through their collection of plugs. He usually brought a new one every time he came over when he was only seeing Trey between books, so there were quite a few to choose from. His boy needed, though, so that dictated his choice. He grabbed the heavy, thick plug that they'd only used a few times. Trey needed to *feel* the plug inside him all the time.

Pleased with his choice, he grabbed the lube and headed back to the living room. Trey was right where Lucien had left him, a peaceful look on his face.

Lucien stood for just a moment, watching. God, he loved this man.

"I brought the big, heavy one," he said, when he finally broke the silence.

Trey's lips parted, cheeks flushing dark.

"I hope that blush is for excitement." He didn't let Trey feel the least bit of shame for loving being really filled.

"God, yes. What else would it be?" That was his boy.

Grinning, he went over to kneel on the couch behind Trey. So fucking gorgeous. Groaning, he leaned in and took a lick. Trey's toes curled, clenched tight.

"You make me need, baby. I'm going to take you first. Fill you up then put in the plug."

"I love your cock, Sir. Love how you push me."

Groaning, he tugged the plug out of Trey's ass. How had he gotten so lucky?

He tapped the needy little hole, sensitizing it. He blew on it then pressed his finger in. Trey, the slut that he was, bore right back in. He pushed a second finger in, spreading them wide. Trey was so hot inside, body gripping his fingers.

"Yes..." Trey's head bobbed, swaying between his arms.

He pushed in another finger, sending all three deep to bang up against Trey's pleasure spot.

"Lucien! Yes! Yes, there."

"Here?" He pegged it again, loving the way Trey's whole body pushed back into it.

"God, yes. Please."

"You're not allowed to come." He continued to manipulate that little bit of flesh, loving the way it had woken up Trey's entire body.

"Yes, Sir." Trey's words were sure, firm. For now.

He kept working Trey's gland. "So tight."

Trey was, body gripping his fingers so tight. Trey's body began to flush, to burn for him, each touch to those sensitive bundle of nerves making Trey need. He used his free hand to touch Trey's ass, the small of Trey's back, and he reached around and found the sweet balls, playing with them. Every time they tried to draw up, Lucien tugged them down.

"Gonna leave my seed inside you before I put in the new plug."

"Please."

He didn't stop working Trey's gland, though. He loved the push. He waited until his own cock began dripping in anticipation, then he slid his fingers away and opened his jeans.

"Sir..." Trey rocked back, searching for his fingers.

"Easy, baby, you know you get what I give. And you know I won't leave you hanging...all day." Hell, he couldn't remember the last time he'd left Trey hanging at all. He always wanted Trey too badly.

"I know. I know. I need you."

"I know you do." He needed Trey, too. He pulled his jeans apart, his erection pushing out as soon as he did. He rubbed against Trey's ass.

"God, yes. Yours. Please." Needy, hungry slut.

He watched as his thick heat spread that sweet little hole, Trey opening up around him. He loved that, the sight of his dark shaft disappearing into Trey's pale, perfect ass. Groaning as Trey's body gripped him tightly, he grabbed Trey's hips, fingers digging in.

"Please." Trey humped back, hips rolling.

"I've got you, baby." He did. Totally.

"I know. I know. It's so good, Sir."

"It is. You're so wonderfully tight." And Trey was bearing down on him, too. It made him moan and moved faster, really taking Trey's ass now. His eyes were fastened on the sight of his cock pounding that tiny hole. "Love you, baby. Love you."

"Love."

Lucien buried himself deep at the happy word. Sliding his hand around Trey's body, he found his boy's hard flesh. He wrapped around him and let his thrusts push Trey's need through his fist every time.

"Master!"

Oh, nice. He pushed in again, hitting Trey's gland. Trey pushed up onto the arm of the sofa, meeting each thrust.

"Yeah, that's it, baby. Take what you need. Take me in deep." His words had Trey bouncing on him, riding him like a champion. He squeezed tightly around Trey's cock, working to push his baby to orgasm.

"Soon. Soon, Sir."

"Come on then." The couch would clean.

Trey's ass bore down, gripping his cock hard. Oh damn, that was good enough to make him come. He fisted Trey's flesh vigorously, determined to make sure Trey came first. His boy, though, was fighting him, playing with him. He started banging in, hitting that sweet spot as much as he could. Trey groaned, pushed up higher.

"You can't resist me for long."

"You can't either…"

"You first," he demanded, jerking in several times.

"Oh, damn…" Trey's body convulsed, seed pouring over his fingers.

"Yes!" He filled Trey immediately, his own spunk shooting out of him.

He kept himself pushed deep, buried in to the root. Leaning over Trey's body, he panted, rubbing Trey's cum into his boy's belly.

"Love you. Love this."

He knew, but he loved hearing it from Trey's lips. "Love you too, baby."

He grabbed the plug and slicked it up. Thick and wide, Trey would be filled to the top. He got the plug set next to his cock and made the switch—he was getting good at this. All Trey had time to do was gasp, body fighting to adjust.

"This'll keep you stretched all night long."

"Uh-huh. Please." Trey's hips still rocked, nice and steady.

He pushed against the base of the plug, letting Trey's own movements jerk it inside him. He loved how that made Trey grunt and groan, dance for him. He played with it a little, enjoying the grace of his lover's body in pleasure. He flicked his fingers along the man's perineum—hard enough to sting—and Trey's hips rolled, trying to hide that sensitive strip of skin.

No, Trey wasn't allowed to hide anything from him. He kept tapping that sweet spot. He loved how the rhythmic taps seemed to soften Trey, make him twist. He finally settled the plug in properly and turned his taps into rubs, easing Trey.

"Make me ache, love."

He knew. He kissed the small of Trey's back, then sat back and tugged Trey back into his arms. "It should be a lovely feeling for the rest of the afternoon."

"Gonna feel it." Trey was damn near asleep, though, dozing for him.

"I'll remind you I'm inside you."

"All the way. Deep."

"Mmm. Yeah." He kissed Trey's nose. "Go on. Nap. I have plans for you later."

"Good plans?"

"Oh, baby, you know they are."

"I do. I just like the words."

"I have amazing plans for you this evening, after you've napped and rejuvenated."

Trey smiled for him, cuddling in. He stroked Trey's shoulder and arm, looking back up at the TV. It didn't even matter where they were in the movie, most of his focus was still on Trey anyway.

Chapter Eleven

Fuck Wednesdays. Fuck Wednesdays and emails and drama and editors and computers. Trey sat on his bed, head in his hands. God, he was tired and his head hurt and he was lonely. He reached for his phone for the half millionth time and this time he let his hand wrap around it.

He nearly jumped out of his skin when it rang right there in his hand.

"Hello?" *Please be Lucien. Please. Please.*

"Hey, baby." Oh, that voice filled him right up.

"Oh. Hey." He found himself near tears, just hysterical.

"How are you doing? Are you okay?" Lucien asked. "You don't sound like you're okay, but that could just be because I had this feeling."

"I... I need you. Can you come? Nothing bad happened. I just..." He was so tired.

"Of course I can come. I just need to lock my office and walk to the car. I can be there in a half hour, okay?"

"Yes. Yes, thank you."

"Okay, baby. Whatever it is, I'll be there soon, so just relax, okay?"

"Yeah. Yeah, okay. See you soon." He needed… Hell, he needed a hug. Just Lucien's solid presence.

"I'm ready to go home, boss." Brian knocked on his door. "Is there anything you need before I go?"

"No. No. Call before you come in tomorrow, huh?"

"Whatever you say, boss. Have a good night."

"You too." He heard the door shut then curled up on his bed, his head throbbing.

* * * *

He didn't realize he'd dozed off, but he must have because the next thing he knew, there was banging on his front door, the doorbell was ringing, and Dodger was going crazy.

"Coming! Coming!" He ran for the door, hip slamming into the couch as he took a wrong turn. "God damn it!" He hadn't done that in forever. Dodger nudged him, whined.

"Trey? Are you okay? Baby?" Lucien sounded worried.

"I… Why don't you have a fucking key?" He got to the door, ripped it open. "You need your own key."

"I totally agree, baby. Jesus, baby." Lucien wrapped him in those strong arms. "You look like death warmed over."

"It's been a terrible day and I'm just… Thank you for coming." He held on, tightly.

"You look like you're getting sick." Lucien lifted him right up. "Let's grab a shower."

He nodded. So long as someone else was helping, he was easy.

"I knew you needed me." Lucien set him down in the bathroom. He could hear the slight echo of Lucien's words.

"I did. I was reaching to call." He swallowed. Everything sounded funny.

"That's actually pretty cool. Speaking of cool…" Lucien put a hand on his forehead. "I'm pretty sure you've got a fever. Let's make it a cool shower and you need some Tylenol to help bring down the fever." Lucien began stripping him down.

"I'm not sick." Just tired and stressed and worried. Still, a cool shower sounded fine. "I want you to have a key, Lucien."

"Thank you, baby. I want to have one, too. I have for a long time, but I didn't want to push for it." Lucien kissed the top of his head. "And I think you're getting sick."

"We'll get you one."

Lucien had called. He'd known.

"Thank you." Lucien got him in the shower, following him in a moment later. "I've got two Tylenol I'm going to pop into your mouth."

"Okay." He opened up, then gulped a mouthful of liquid. The sound of the water echoed everywhere and it seemed almost cold, but it felt good, too. Lucien was hot against his back, the big muscles supporting him.

"It's been such a bad day. I was dialing your number when you called."

"I knew you needed me. I could feel it. If I lived here I would have come home early." Lucien began soaping him up, hands sliding on his skin.

"Uh-huh." He felt like crying. So stupid. The touches felt so good and that made him want to cry even more.

"Oh, baby." Lucien kissed his eyelids, his wet lashes. "I've got you."

"I'm sorry."

"No, you don't need to apologize. I've got you."

He leaned in and sobbed, trusting Lucien to get it, to understand that he didn't know what was wrong. Lucien simply held him, rocked him as he cried. The storm passed, leaving him totally wiped out.

He let Lucien support him and when the water was turned off, he let Lucien dry him and carry him to his bedroom. Then Lucien eased him into the bed, wrapping him in a light sheet.

Lucien cuddled up with him. "I've got you."

"Thank you." And even though it was only early evening, he let Lucien hold him and he fell asleep.

* * * *

Lucien woke up at six and called the gym to let them know he wasn't coming in today. He'd had a hunch Trey was getting sick and today it was conclusive—Trey had a miserable cold. After his call, he slipped out of bed and went to make some hot tea and porridge.

Trey's home phone rang and he answered, "'lo?"

"Uh… Lucien? It's Brian. He told me to call and make sure he wanted me."

"Hey, Brian. He's sick, actually. You can probably have the day off."

"Okay. If you guys need anything before Monday, call. I'm studying all weekend."

"Good luck on your exams, Bri. We'll call if we need you." He hung up and poured a glass of orange juice—lots of vitamin C in that.

Getting back to the bedroom, he found Trey sniffling and coughing, twisting and throwing the blankets off.

Lucien put his tray down and sat, cupping Trey's cheek. Yeah, time for some meds.

He grabbed some cough syrup and Dayquil from the medicine cabinet. He needed to go shopping. God knew how old this stuff was. He found the expiration dates and put the cough syrup in the garbage. The Dayquil was okay, though, and he brought it back to set on the tray next to the orange juice.

"You awake, baby?" he asked quietly.

"Lucien?" Trey flailed, reaching for him. "Everything sounds funny."

"You've got a bad cold and I bet your ears are blocked." He took Trey's hands and held onto them. "I have some Dayquil for you to take and juice, oatmeal and hot tea"

"'Kay. You should go, if I'm sick. Don' want you to get it."

"I'm not going anywhere, baby. I'm going to stay right here and play doctor." There was no way in hell he was leaving Trey while his lover was sick.

He fed Trey the pills first with the juice, then started the process of tempting food into him. He even resorted to making airplane noises at one point, both of them laughing. The tea went down easily, though, and Trey even asked for more.

Then he sat with Trey curled up in his arms. "When you go back to sleep, I'm going to zip to the drug store and get you more meds. Is there anything you can't take?"

"Uh-uh." Trey was drooping. "Sorry. My head hurts."

"Go to sleep, baby. I'll be here when you wake back up."

"Promise?"

"I promise. Unless of course you wake up five minutes after you fall asleep."

Trey laughed, but the laughter ended up as harsh coughs, racking his lean body.

"Oh, baby." He rubbed Trey's back. "Okay, laughing is bad."

"Laughing is good. Coughing is bad."

"Yeah, but at the moment one leads to the other." He kissed the top of Trey's head and held his lover close.

Trey was burning up, but rested hard against him, snuggled in. He hoped the medicine would help bring that down. He was also going to get a thermometer while he was out and if Trey's fever got too bad, he'd have to take his lover to Emergency. Chicken soup and Sprite, more tea, maybe some rice...

Trey grew heavier and heavier in his arms and he finally shifted his lover out of his lap and slipped from the bed. He gave it a few minutes to make sure Trey really was asleep, then grabbed his wallet and Trey's keys, and headed out to buy supplies.

* * * *

Trey hated this. He couldn't hear. He couldn't balance. He was dizzy and grumpy and tired. Thank God Lucien was here. He was given pills and juice, carried into the shower where Lucien held him in the lukewarm flow of water.

Now there was soup, which felt amazing going down his throat—hot and soothing.

"Just a little more—it's good for you." Lucien coaxed him to eat some more.

"It's good. Really good."

"Cool. I picked it up from the deli near the drug store. I bought stuff to make you potato soup tomorrow. It's really easy to make from scratch."

"I like soup." Every time he swallowed, his ears popped.

Lucien fed him spoonful after spoonful.

"My ears hurt." He squeezed his hands over his ears and suddenly the world disappeared.

Lucien's hands slid over his, pulled them away. "I asked if you thought you needed to see the doctor."

"I don't know. This is weird. So weird." And freaky.

"I wish I could wave my magic wand and make it go away."

"Me too. It's just a cold, though, right?" Not the plague. Not some dread disease.

"Yeah, seems like it. If you aren't a little bit better by tomorrow, though, I'm going to take you to the clinic."

"Okay." He couldn't lose his hearing.

Lucien wrapped him in a tight hug. "It's going to be all right, baby."

"Am I keeping you from something more fun?"

"There's nothing more fun than spending time with you."

That was sweet to say, even if it wasn't true.

"I've got *The Stand* cued up to read to you when we're done eating," Lucien told him.

"Yeah? I love that book. Love it."

"Me too. And as you've already read it, if you doze off, you won't get lost."

"It'll take you a hundred and eighty days to read it to me."

"Then it takes a hundred and eighty days. Unless there's a different book you'd prefer?"

"No. No, I like the idea of you reading to me for months." In fact, he *loved* that idea.

"And that's the first really bright smile you've had since you came down with this, so I believe you."

What was there to believe? He'd always loved Lucien's voice. "I just hope my ears unstuff soon. It's crazy-making."

"I bet. Nothing I found specifically mentioned helping ears. Only sinuses. Like I said, if you're not showing improvement tomorrow, we'll go to the doctor. I'm not taking chances with your health."

The words made him blush, made his heart beat a bit faster.

"What's this for?" Lucien asked, fingers sliding along his hot cheek.

"I…" He shook his head. How could he admit that he loved having someone to care for him?

"I think it's kind of charming that you can still be shy with me sometimes after all these years together."

"I just… I love it, how much you love me."

"I do, Trey. You're…" Lucien paused, as if he was searching for the right word. "You're amazing to me — and beautiful. And sexy and fun, and I just do. I love you so much.

Oh. Oh wow. Trey cuddled in, fingers trailing over Lucien's face. Lucien stayed still and quiet, like he always did when Trey did this. Somehow Lucien always knew the difference, too — when he was actually looking and when he was just touching. He loved the way the textures differed between hint of stubble and smooth lips, the way Lucien's nostrils flared when he traced the bridge of the man's nose.

Lucien's eyes were closed as his fingers passed over them, eyelashes fluttering slightly, giving him little butterfly kisses. Trey relaxed, the act of 'seeing' Lucien easing his soul.

"Mmm." Lucien kissed his fingertips as they ghosted by again.

"Yeah. Better." He hated the distance that his stuffed ears gave him.

Lucien tugged him close, kissing the top of his head. "I hate that you're sick."

"Me too." It sucked, but then that wasn't surprising.

"You'll get better fast." Lucien sounded sure.

"Mmm-hmm." He'd have to, with Lucien taking care of him.

"You need anything before I start reading?"

"No, love. I have everything I need."

"Okay, then, here we go. *The Stand* by Steven King."

He cuddled in, warm and comfy, Lucien's voice cutting through the weirdness in his ears. It took only a few paragraphs before he was caught, lost in his lover's words.

* * * *

Lucien had told Brian not to bother coming in for the rest of the week and they'd canceled going out on Friday. Still, by Friday morning Trey was clearly feeling better and Lucien felt a rush of relief go through him.

"How's your hearing today?" he asked, as he set two bowls of oatmeal down on the table.

"Better. Much better. I feel less like running around screaming." Trey was all smiles this morning.

"I'd only let you do that if you were naked—more entertaining that way."

The soft laughter suited him to the ground. "I think I'll take it easy for another day."

"Cool. I'm glad we canceled tonight's date—means we can just be lazy and enjoy each other's company." Lucien gave Trey a spoon and showed him where the bowl was. "Bit of milk and brown sugar in that."

"Thank you." Trey picked the bowl up and began eating. "Oh, that feels good on my throat."

"I love porridge when I'm sick." Which might explain why this was the third time he'd served it to Trey since his lover had gotten sick.

He ate his own, the food filling and warm.

"Yeah. I've only had instant. This is amazing."

"Only the best for my baby. You know I like cooking, right? You'd eat much better if I was here to cook for you every day. You eat too much junk food."

"You're prejudiced."

"Hey, I've eaten plenty of pizza with you. I just know my cooking is so much better tasting and better for you."

"It is and you have."

"If we lived together, I could make you delicious food every night.

"You could."

Wait. That wasn't an immediate no. Lucien sat there with his spoon halfway to his mouth for a moment, staring at Trey.

Trey kept eating, spoonful after spoonful. Lucien went back to his own food, wondering if it was a good time to broach the subject of them living together again. He had his own key now, after all, made on one of his runs out for supplies.

Trey beat him to opening the subject. "Do you think you'd be comfortable here?"

"I do." He'd thought it for a while. He knew them moving in together would be easier if Trey didn't have to learn a whole new house. That would be an enormous change for his lover. "I like your place a lot."

"I do too and I know the neighborhood."

"We could maybe redo some of the painting. I don't think the walls have been touched since you moved in." And more than that, Lucien thought maybe it showed he was serious, if he wanted to redecorate a little—make the place theirs instead of just Trey's.

"Oh, I don't know… I sorta like the color…" Little ass.

He swatted Trey's butt. "We can *keep* the color. Butt head."

"Do they actually have color?"

"They're cream. It's probably got some fancy name. I wouldn't make any changes without discussing it with you."

"Lucien, I don't know if you know this, but I'm blind."

Lucien gasped. "Really?" He could be an ass, too.

"I know. And that means I don't know what colors are."

"I know. You're the one who started with the whole color thing, though."

"I just meant that you're welcome to decorate, love. I mean, if you move the furniture, that'll be a problem."

"I know. That would be something we'd have to discuss. I think I'd just want to trade your chair in for my big huge comfy one."

It occurred to him suddenly that Trey had never seen his place. He supposed it made sense, up until the last few weeks—they'd only had four or five days together at a time.

"Do you have a big one?" Trey asked.

"You know I do, baby." He put a leer into his voice.

Trey's laughter filled the air.

"I also happen to have a big chair. It's huge and comfy."

"Cool." Trey smiled, the look a little dazed. "Are we really talking about this?"

"We really are. You haven't officially asked me to move in, though. So for now we're just talking." He wasn't going to steamroller Trey. No way.

"Yeah. It's exciting."

"I just love the idea of being *home* with you."

"Yeah. I love the idea of sleeping together every night."

"Every single night. Coming home from work to you…" There were so many pluses to living together.

Trey nodded. "I want you to like it, being here."

"I would. I do." Was this Trey asking him? Or were they still just talking about it?

"I do, too."

"I hope so. It's your place. That would really suck if you'd been here as long as you have been and you didn't like it."

"Shut up. You know what I mean."

Chuckling, he leaned across the table to kiss Trey.

When their lips parted, Trey touched his face. "So, will you?" There, that was a clear offer.

"I'd love to."

"I've never asked anyone to move in before."

"And I've never been asked to move in with anyone either."

"We'll have to figure it out together." Trey was vibrating.

"We've already done the hard part." They'd survived ten years together.

"Have we? It didn't feel hard."

"I meant the getting to know each other part."

"I know what you mean. That was amazing."

"*We* are amazing." Lucien grinned at them. God, they were being sappy dorks.

"You're moving in with me," Trey said.

"I am. I'm going to have full time access to the awesomeness that is you." This was what he'd wanted, what he'd hoped for when he'd suggested they see each other more often.

"Wow." Trey reached for him.

Getting up from the table, he then went to Trey, taking his boy's hands in his and pulling Trey up against him.

"It's pretty damn momentous," he suggested.

"Yeah. It's the biggest question I've ever asked."

"We should celebrate. Are you up to celebrating?" His plan did not include leaving the house.

"Do we get to stay home?"

"God, yes." His plans were very much of the staying home variety.

"Our home."

That felt so good, to hear Trey say that.

"Our home," he repeated.

Trey's smile blossomed over his face.

"God, I love you." He pressed their mouths together, taking a long, slow kiss.

"Love you, Sir. Lucien."

"Good."

In the end, that was what mattered.

He picked Trey up and carried his boy to the bedroom. Time to play.

Chapter Twelve

There were boxes — everywhere. Trey locked himself in his office and refused to leave until Lucien and his friends were done. Lucien wasn't even bringing most of his furniture, but somehow he had so much stuff — so much stuff and so many people in his house. And cardboard smelled. So did sweaty people. So he was staying out of the way until things got back to something more normal.

A soft knock sounded on his door. "Baby?"

"Yeah?"

"It's done. The guys went to get pizza."

"Oh. That didn't take long."

"There wasn't a whole lot. I haven't put everything away, but I did put all the boxes as out of the way as possible."

"I'm sorry. I don't mean to be that guy." But everything was changing, everything.

"What guy is that?" Lucien asked.

"The hidey in the office type of guy."

"You're not. You're the stay away from the landmines type of guy."

"Yeah. Yeah. Is the third bedroom going to work for you as an office?" He never went in there, so it wouldn't matter what happened to it, which made it easy to focus on.

"It is. I really just need my laptop. Most of my paperwork and stuff gets done at the office at the gym." Lucien slid a hand on his shoulder, rubbing.

Trey let Lucien's touch relax him. "Did you hire a service to clean your place out?"

"I did. I waffled for a bit first. It's a lot of money for something I could do myself. Then I decided that I'd rather spent my time with you and settling in, and it's not like I can't afford it."

"I think that's good. We have lots to learn about this."

"Yeah, I've never lived with anyone before."

"Me either, not since school." He couldn't decide whether to be freaked or excited.

"Honestly, it should be like my sleeping over except I just never go."

"I bet I have a hard-on for the first few days, just because I hear your voice."

"Oh, baby, you say the nicest things." Lucien's hand moved down his chest right into his lap.

"Just true." He reached up, fingers sliding on Lucien's arm. "Show me your chair?"

"Oh, yeah. It's awesome and we'll both fit wonderfully." Lucien took his hand and tugged him up.

"Are there lots of boxes?"

"No, maybe a dozen. Books, plates and stuff. And they're all up against the walls and stuff, so they're out of the way. I've done my best to make sure they won't trip you up." Lucien led him to the living room. "It's where your chair used to be, next to the couch."

He reached out, searching, needing to explore. "Tell me."

"It's dark brown leather—it still smells like leather, too, even though I've had it for four years. It reclines. It rocks when it's upright. It hugs my body. I love it."

"I remember how excited you were when you bought it." It was soft, puffy, cold to the touch.

"Yeah. Silly to be so excited about a piece of furniture, but it really is the most comfy spot. Why don't you sit in it on your own first?"

He slid into it, the thing lower than he'd anticipated.

Lucien took his hand and brought it down along the side of the chair. "This is the lever that controls the footrest."

"It's a big chair." He popped the footrest up, chuckling. It smelled like Lucien.

"It's huge. It goes up one more and the back goes almost as far as lying you down horizontally." Lucien showed him.

"Oh. Oh, wow. That's...cushy."

"Yeah. I'm going to bring you back up so we can sit in it together."

"Cool." Trey understood why Lucien loved this chair.

Lucien sat and tugged Trey down onto his ample lap. "Rocking first." Lucien's leg muscles worked beneath his ass, the chair beginning to rock.

Every motion pushed him into Lucien's body, nudged them together.

"Oh, it hadn't occurred to me how perfect this would be for making love." Lucien sounded like now that it had, he wouldn't be forgetting it.

"No?" It hadn't taken long for the thought to occur to him. Not long at all.

"We should test it out, have you ride me."

"You're not worried about your chair?"

"Baby, the chair is replaceable."

"Still. It's your favorite. I should get a towel for under us."

"No, we're being spontaneous." Lucien's hands slid over his ass, squeezed.

"Am I ever spontaneous?" He liked his routine. He wiggled, rocked back and forth in Lucien's hands.

"I make you be. Usually in the bedroom." Lucien chuckled, one hand pushing up his shirt.

He loved the sensation of Lucien's fingers on his skin. "Usually." God, Lucien made him shivery.

"Not today. Today we're bringing the bedroom in here."

Lucien's mouth covered his, the kiss making him forget any other objections he might have had, or even if he had any. Really, he didn't have any. If Lucien didn't care if his chair stained, it wasn't like Trey would.

Lucien went back to tugging his shirt off and they had to break off their kiss to pull it over his head.

"You locked the door? Your buddies aren't coming back?"

"Door is locked, nobody's coming back and I have a tube of lube in my pocket."

"Boy scout!" He laughed, pushed back into the kiss. He'd raised plenty of concerns.

Lucien laughed against his lips, shaking his head, which made their lips slide together sideways. He nibbled on the full bottom lip, tugging it idly. Groaning, Lucien pushed up against him, thick cock hot against his ass, even through their clothing.

Oh, it was more than he could bear, not to reach down, touch.

Lucien moaned for him. "We need more naked."

"I like naked. I'm a fan."

"Me, too." Chuckling, Lucien began undoing his pants.

He tugged Lucien's shirt from his waistband, hunting for skin. He found it, Lucien's muscles shifting beneath his fingertips. The tiny hairs on Lucien's belly felt like steel wool, rough, scrubby.

"Love your touch, baby." Lucien pulled down his zipper, fingertips teasing his cock.

"Love..." Oh. His head fell back, and he swallowed.

"Right here, baby." Lucien's mouth landed on his throat, tongue licking along his Adam's apple.

"God, you make me want to just laugh, the happiness is so large."

"I love your laugh."

"Is... This is real. You're here—with me."

"It's real, Trey. And it'll be real every night that we go to bed together and every day that we wake up together."

"I'll probably ask a lot."

"Okay, baby. I'll keep telling you—and showing you—that it's real." Lucien fished his cock out. "Does this feel real enough?"

"I don't know," he teased. "Try again."

Laughing for him, Lucien squeezed a little harder, rubbed a thumb across his tip. Shivers rocketed through him, made his nipples hard.

"I can smell you." Lucien squeezed him tighter.

"I can too. Do you like it?"

"I love it when I can smell how much you need me." Lucien kept touching him, kept dragging along his cock.

"Gonna have to make you get up to get your pants off."

"Uh-huh." Right. Moving.

Lucien was laughing again, mouth covering his own as the laughter faded and Lucien kissed him. The soft sounds kept coming, though, as they explored each other. It was different now. They weren't Sir and boy. They weren't fuck buddies. They were a couple.

They kissed for a long time, Lucien playing with his cock, distracting him. Enough that he hardly even noticed that suddenly he was standing, Lucien tugging off his jeans. He felt as if he was wrapped in cotton wool, as if nothing on earth could harm him.

Then Lucien stood, still kissing Trey as he took off his own pants. And just like that they were back on chair, their naked bodies pressed together. It was a unique sensation, to be holding one another, the leather against his knees, his thighs.

"I want you to ride me, baby. I want to feel you hot and tight around my cock."

Hell, yes. He wanted that too. He lifted up to tall kneeling, giving Lucien access to slick him up.

"Oh, God, you look incredible, torso stretched for me, cock reaching up for your belly." Lucien touched his nipples, dragging those big fingers down his chest and over his abdomen, then patted his cock, rolled his balls.

Trey arched into the touch, ass cheeks clenching.

"God. My lover is the sexiest man in the world." Lucien's fingers teased along his crease.

"Lots of men you haven't seen." And Trey had Lucien. So he knew there were men sexier than him.

"I don't care. I don't believe any of them could be sexier than you are."

One finger pressed against Trey's hole, pushing in. He groaned and bore down, rocking down onto the touch.

"You feel like silk inside." The rest of Lucien's fingers slid along his ass as the one went deep inside him.

"Oh..." He moaned low, riding nice and slow, luxuriating in the easy pressure.

Every time he lifted up, Lucien's finger slid away, pushing inside him as he came back down again. There was a lovely extra zing every time Lucien breached his hole.

"Don't stop, Trey. I want to see everything." Lucien's words were like another caress, to hear them in that amazing, arousing voice felt so good. "I'm going to spend hours opening you up."

"Oh, God." Lucien knew how he needed, knew how he craved ass play.

The finger inside him went in deep, bumping up against his gland.

"There. Sir. Lucien. Love. Right there."

"Are you sure?" He could hear the teasing laughter in Lucien's voice. "Maybe it's here." Lucien's next push of his finger totally missed his gland this time.

He groaned, head thrown back. Lucien's body pressed against his as Lucien wrapped hot lips around Trey's throat. This time when Lucien's finger pushed in, it hit Trey's gland bang on. A wild sound tore from him, desperate, needy.

Lucien's moan vibrated across his throat, and Lucien hit that spot again, staying on it now. His entire body clenched, so tight that he could barely suck in a breath.

"Easy, baby. I'm just going to do it again."

"Uh... Uh-huh." God. He felt like he was going to shake apart.

Lucien did do it again—and again and again. Trey's entire body was lit up, burning. Lucien was still using just one finger, playing him like a Master. He tried to pull away, but Lucien held him, kept him right there.

"You're staying right here, baby, dancing for me."

"I'm gonna go crazy." His erection was dripping, his need growing bigger and bigger.

"Yeah, that's the point." There was a wealth of satisfaction in Lucien's voice — and also need.

The tapping felt endless, so strong he couldn't bear it. Finally it stopped, but only long enough for Lucien to push two digits in, stretching him a little more, but still ending up against his gland.

He was going to scream. He couldn't think, couldn't breathe. He needed it to stop and he wanted it to go on and on.

Lucien spread his fingers wide, then twisted them together and hit his gland. There was a rhythm to it, one he could follow. His legs began to shake, his muscles overwhelmed. Lucien wrapped his free arm around Trey's waist and guided him down so his strong thighs were supporting him.

"Easy, easy." Lucien twisted and turned inside him, but gave his prostate a break.

"Sir. Sir..." He pressed close as he fought to catch his breath.

"I have you, Trey." Lucien rubbed his back.

"Sorry. Sorry, that was getting intense." Wild. Crazy.

"We can ramp it back up again."

He shook his head, nodded. Shook again.

"We will, but I'll give you a minute to catch your breath." Lucien rubbed their cheeks together.

"You have to be getting tired."

"It's a good workout. I'll have to do it every day to keep them in shape."

"Every day? That?" No way.

"You aren't enjoying it?" Lucien wriggled inside Trey.

"Hush." He was soaring.

Lucien laughed softly and kissed him, tongue finding the same rhythm as his hand. He moaned, the excitement gearing up even faster this time. A third finger worked into him, stretching him out wider. He pulled up, keeping Lucien off his gland.

"Oh, baby." Lucien pushed deeper, finding his sweet spot.

"Sir..." He was going out of his mind.

"Right here."

Like he didn't know that. He was fully aware of where his Sir was.

Three fingers always felt so much bigger than two and today was no different. Lucien made him feel everything. Everything. He was soon wild again, crying out as he rode, body begging for more. The touches to his prostate made him gasp, made him twist.

"Love watching you while I open you up." Lucien's voice had a rough, needy edge to it.

"Driving me insane."

"I know."

That wasn't helping.

Chuckling, Lucien pulled out, away. Leaving him empty. He cried out, shaking hard, desperate.

"Easy, baby, it's me now."

He loved how the head of Lucien's erection pushed at his hole. He pressed down, demanding more, harder, faster.

"Pushy, needy, sexy boy." Lucien's fingers wrapped around his hips.

"Yes." He was going to scream.

He moved up and down, Lucien guiding him. He stretched around the base of Lucien's cock, feeling his lover deep. Groaning, Lucien nuzzled against his neck, lips and tongue sliding on his skin.

"More. More, please. God, you make me want to scream."

"Then scream, baby."

Trey threw his head back, a cry ringing out.

"Yes!" Lucien thrust deep inside him.

He bounced off Lucien's thighs.

"Love you," Lucien told him, bringing him down hard.

"Sir!" He knew they weren't doing a scene, he knew it. But still he needed to use that word. It was what Lucien was.

Lucien kept them moving, making him not care what they were doing as long as they kept doing it. Time stopped still.

When Lucien wrapped his hand around Trey's cock and whispered, "Come," Trey had no choice but to obey. He shot so hard his bones rattled and Lucien cried out his name and filled him with heat.

He ended up snuggled against Lucien's chest, cradled close as they rocked together.

Lucien gave him a squeeze. "This is ours. Every day now."

"Ours. Damn." He couldn't quite believe it. Every day.

"I know." Lucien kissed him. "Thank you."

"You're the one that did all the work."

"But you invited me to come, opened your home to me full-time," Lucien said.

"I did." It had been a long time coming, but he'd done it.

Lucien kissed the top of his head. "This is going to be a good thing, baby. I promise."

"It's going to be an adventure, that's for sure."

"Yeah. A wonderful adventure we take together."

"Together." Trey was more and more fond of that word.

"Yep. We're a real couple now."

"We were pretty real before." Trey had never thought they weren't.

"I know," Lucien said. "But now it's full-time. It's we live together. I'm just really happy to be able to do all the things that couples who live together get to do."

Trey nodded, not sure what all those things were, but he was willing to see.

Lucien rested his head against Trey's and they breathed together, bodies still connected. He knew that Lucien would be hungry, would need a shower and some down time, but right now, he'd just take this. He wasn't even going to stress about where he was on his word count. It felt too good to stress.

"Love you," Lucien murmured again.

"Good." He took a deep breath and relaxed, melted.

He was pretty sure he was going to like this living together thing.

Chapter Thirteen

Lucien spent two days unpacking his stuff and finding a home for everything. It helped him stay out of Trey's way while his lover worked as he knew that the extra stuff was making Trey a little crazy. His lover had to relearn his own home and Lucien knew that wasn't easy — that it messed with Trey's head — so he was determined to be done as quickly as possible.

He was glad he'd arranged to be away from work for the whole week. Moving, even a fairly easy one like this where it wasn't an entire house move, was stressful and he was pleased to not have to go in.

The back bedroom worked perfectly as his office. He had a desk for it, along with some workout equipment. He actually wanted to get Trey working out a little now that he had the stuff in the house. Not that he thought Trey was out of shape or anything, but working out was good for the body and he wanted Trey to have that freedom of knowing he could work out if he wanted to.

He'd gone grocery shopping, too, and now he was making supper. He didn't know yet if Trey usually broke at a specific time or just ate supper when he was finished writing for the day, but Lucien knew Trey hadn't had more than an apple and a handful of carrots since breakfast, so now that it was six, he was making supper and he was going to insist Trey stop to eat it, too. He had more pull than Brian did, who'd gone home at five.

Trey came wandering in, headphone on, dictating into a digital recorder. "...scares me. Sometimes you get something in your mind — like the idea of a cut out tongue — and you fixate on it. You can't let it go for anything."

Trey went to the fridge, found a Coke on his shelf — and thank God Brian had warned him about not interfering with the man's shelf — and wandered back off, still talking.

It left him smiling. This was the kind of thing he'd been missing with their setup, the little things like what had just happened. And look — Lucien hadn't interfered with Trey's routine or tried to do things for Trey while he worked. Trey was strong and independent and Lucien didn't believe that was going to change because he moved in — especially as aware of it as Trey was.

Whistling, he continued working on supper.

About twenty minutes later, Trey was back, Coke in hand. "Something smells good."

"That would be our supper — shrimp stir fry. I've just started frying it off, so it should be ready in about five minutes. Hopefully you can take a break and eat."

"Uh-huh. I got my blog posts done." Trey wandered, a little aimlessly.

"Yeah? You still doing one a week on the Guy Wilks' blog?"

He followed that blog religiously. He loved everything Trey wrote, be it a novel, a short story, or his blog posts.

"I am, yeah. Brian will transcribe it for me tomorrow. They've got voice software now, but I can't tell if it's read me right and this way Brian has something to do."

"That's cool. Why don't you sit?"

Trey made his way to the other side of the bar, perched on a stool. "Have you had a good day?"

"I have. I got the last of my boxes unpacked, so you won't accidentally run into any of them. I'll take you on a tour of my office later."

"I'd like that. I think I'd like to go through the whole house together, find the new things."

"Sounds good. We can do it after supper if you're done for the day."

"I am. It was a good day."

He could see that on Trey's face, his boy was relaxed, easy in his skin. "That's great. It's a plan, then."

"Now if you could just remember not to whistle so loudly…"

"Uh-oh, did I disturb your writing?" He hadn't even realized that the sound might carry.

"It's easier to keep going if I try to forget that you're here, and that's hard to do if you're making a lot of noise."

"I'll do my best not to do it again. You can also call out and tell me to shush," Lucien noted.

"Yeah, I guess I could. I'll remember that."

"Good."

Lucien put plates out at the little table for both of them, along with a pair of forks and glasses filled with water. Then he tossed the shrimp into the stir fry pan.

Trey explored the counter in front of him, fingers finding the odds and ends he'd unpacked. A salt and pepper shaker, a closed pocketknife, a little funny toothpick holder that had been his grandfather's.

"That was my Papi's," he told Trey, when those clever fingers reached it.

"Oh, yeah?" Trey picked it up. The little wooden cup was hand-carved, a face of an old man smoking a pipe on it.

"I think his father might have carved it for him when he was young."

"Oh, wow. That's cool. It's old, huh?"

"It is. One of the few things I have that's from the family."

"We should put it away. I could break it, accidentally."

"Then I'll glue it back together. There's nothing here more precious than you, baby."

"Still. I'm not used to things that are decorations. I'd hate to destroy your memories."

"I'll have my memories whether the toothpick holder is in one piece or not, but I'll put it in the windowsill so you don't worry about it."

"Okay. I just worry about your things."

He shrugged. "Things break. I try not to worry too hard on stuff like that."

The shrimp were done, so he plated it for the two of them.

"Do you want to eat here or at the table?" Trey asked.

"I've set the table with glasses and forks."

"Oh. Cool. I'm starving!"

"It's a stir fry, tasty, quick, good for you and, I figured, easy to eat." Everything was chopped and he'd even split the noodles so they weren't long.

"Yum. I'm going to get spoiled."

"You deserve to be spoiled." He put Trey's hand on the back of his chair. "This is you, I'm sitting right across from you."

"Okay. Thank you." Trey pulled the chair out, sat down then explored the bowl, fingers so curious.

"I cut everything fairly small so it would be easy to pick up, and the shrimp are the biggest thing on the plate. Hey, have you ever tried eating with chopsticks?" He'd bet those clever fingers would get it in no time.

"Uh-huh. I'm pretty good at it, really."

"Oh, fantastic! I'll buy some so we have them handy."

"You'll have to explore drawers. I know there's probably tons from take out. Brian loves Chinese food."

"Cool, I'll do that next time I serve something Asian."

Trey dug in, obviously both hungry and enjoying it. He ate too, pleased with how it had turned out." He was going to have to buy lamps, things for the living room and office walls. The emptiness was disconcerting as fuck.

"Do you think your publisher would send you posters of your book covers?" The hall would look amazing with a row of those.

"I have them in the hall closet in tubes."

"Awesome. Any objections to me getting them framed and putting them up in the hall?"

"None at all. Are they neat?"

"Has no one ever told you what they look like? They're awesome."

"I'm sure people have but... They don't make an impact."

"Yeah, I suppose not." He thought about it, about how they might mean something to Trey. "Well, the best one is the cover for *Darkness Rising*. It looks like fear."

Trey's head tilted. "Yeah? Tell me about it."

"It's the feeling more than the images. There's this little bit of light in one corner and it fades away on the rest of the cover."

"When you look at dark things, do you feel heavy?"

"Depending on the dark, yeah, that's probably a good description."

"Are you dark?"

"I am. I'm a dark brown."

"What am I?"

"You're pale. Not white, but pretty pale."

"I wish I knew what that meant."

"Me, too." And he wished he was better with words so he could explain things better to Trey.

"I'm not being a whiner. I just... I want to know."

"No one said you were being a whiner."

"Yeah, but I feel like it. I mean, I have this great life, but...I burn to get it. It's like something everyone but me understands."

He reached out and took Trey's hand, held tight. "You keep asking and I'll keep trying to explain, okay? Because you're not a whiner. I just wish I was better with words."

"That's my job, huh? Describing things I can't see?"

"I know. It's pretty amazing that you can do it."

Of course he thought Trey was pretty damn amazing all around.

Trey had lived so long on his own, supporting himself, being successful. "You know I'm so proud of you, right?"

"Yeah. Yeah, I do." Trey grinned, the expression so pleased. "You've always let me know that."

"Good. I should tell you that—and I love you— every single day."

"You do." Trey finished his noodles with gusto. "Oh, man. Those were delicious."

"Excellent. I'll put it in the rotation."

"What do you like best?"

"I'm a big fan of seafood and steak, actually."

"I like beef tips and rice."

"I can do that." He would make anything Trey wanted. "What else?"

"Hrm. I eat mostly burgers and pizza, but I love bacon sandwiches. I like turkey and dressing. I like pasta salad."

"Noted. I think tomorrow I'm going to make pizza. It tastes way better when you do it yourself."

"No shit? Can I help?"

"You can! I wanted to ask actually, do you usually have supper at a set time? Do you want to have supper at a set time?"

"I haven't. I try to be done around six or six thirty. If I push myself longer, it just makes me bitchy."

"Then I will plan to have supper around six thirty most nights, because I do not want a bitchy lover."

"You know that I'll buy supper when you want. I didn't ask you to move in to cook for me all the time."

"I like a treat now and then, but I don't mind cooking, and homemade is better for you. You've got a health nut living with you now, baby."

Trey chuckled. "Do I? My gym owner."

"Yep. And personal training includes guiding people's diet, too. Now that I'm here full time, I'm going to make sure you eat more than just pizza for dinner." They could work out together. Trey wasn't in bad shape, but he sat all day. It would give his lover more stamina for swimming, too.

"I was thinking about coming home for lunch. Maybe we can do a twenty minute workout and have a small meal together?"

Trey tilted his head. "Don't you work out all day?"

"No, baby. I have paperwork first thing in the morning, then I have clients. I do often work out with my clients, but my job is to make sure they work out. When I have lulls between clients, I definitely work out."

"Oh. We can try. I don't know how it'll work. Brian takes care of my schedule during the day."

"I'll talk to him then about what the best time for lunch would be. I have a bunch of equipment in my office."

"Yeah, I want to see. I mean, I promise not to go in there, but... I'm curious."

"Oh, baby, it's not sacrosanct. I'll take you in and show you where everything is, but I'll leave the door open—unless I'd rather not be disturbed—and you can go in any time you want."

This was Trey's home after all.

"Still, I'm not a snooper."

"If I've already showed you everything, that means you aren't snooping."

Trey was such a sweet love.

"Good. I need to know where things are."

"I know. I was really careful not to move anything. I added some stuff to shelves and bookcases, but I didn't move furniture."

"Yeah? Excellent. I love how the house smells now that the cardboard is gone."

"Did the cardboard smell bad?" It had only been a couple days and he hadn't noticed it at all himself. It wasn't that he forgot that Trey's nose was so much more sensitive than his own, but he just didn't think about how certain things might affect that.

"It does. It smells like…glue."

"Huh. Well, I'm glad it's gone then. You should say something, next time there's a smell you don't like."

Trey shrugged. "It's not like you could do anything about it, love. You had to use them."

"Well, I could have been quicker getting them out of the house." Smiling, he took Trey's hand. "I want this to be a totally positive experience for you."

"Oh, I know we'll have weirdness. It's inevitable. I'm ready for it."

"We're probably going to have fight or two, too."

"Yeah. And I'll warn you, they'll be my fault. If the writing gets intense, I'm awful.

Lucien shook his head, before reminding himself that Trey couldn't see that and wasn't close enough to feel it happen.

"I'm sure it'll be a learning curve. It takes two to fight, though, and I know that things get intense with your writing. It's not like you're springing it on me." Grinning suddenly, he relaxed back in his chair. "Besides, you've got Brian to abuse when that happens. I'll hide out at the gym or in my office if I need to stay out of the line of fire."

"I do. And trust me, Brian can scream right back. We have huge wars."

"The gym then. And I'll try to remember that and not interfere if I hear yelling." That wouldn't be the easiest, as it would always be in him to run to Trey's aid.

"Brian might like that."

"What, me interfering? Baby, I'd be on your side."

"Until you hear me having a melt down over something ridiculous."

He chuckled. "Does it make me weird that I'm looking forward to it?" He just wanted to know all of Trey, not just the good bits.

"A little, yeah."

"It's a part of who you are, you know?" And if that made him weird, then so be it.

"Yeah. Not my favorite part. I hate when I get in that head space."

"Well, maybe some of the time I could try to bring you out of it." Lucien was all for being helpful.

"Maybe. If anyone could…"

He hummed, sliding his hand along Trey's arm. "I will certainly give it my best effort." God, he could just eat Trey up.

Trey chuckled for him, then suddenly he had a lap full of warm man.

"Mmm." He took a kiss, Trey tasting like dinner, and that beautiful flavor that was simply Trey himself.

He could hardly believe he was having supper with Trey in the middle of the week, and now he was making out with his boy. He had to wonder what Trey did in the evenings, what the routine was. "So if I wasn't here—what would you do now?"

"Chat on the computer. Surf. Read."

"We could do another chapter of *The Stand*." Lucien had discovered he loved reading out loud, Trey curled up in his lap.

"Yeah? You don't mind?" The eager response proved Trey enjoyed it too.

"Do I mind having my lover curled up in my lap as I read one of my favorite books to him? I think I can suffer through it."

"I think that sounds like a perfect way to spend an evening.

"That's tonight taken care of, then. Let me just get the dishes done and I'll meet you in the living room? My big chair should be perfect for this."

"I'll help. I load the dishwasher a lot."

"Cool." He loved watching Trey move around and do things like that, just normal every day stuff. His baby was awesome.

There was a rhythm to everything Trey did. He checked the thing on the dishwasher that said clean or dirty. Then he emptied the handful of glasses and the two plates, along with the blender from his morning smoothie. "Where does this go now?"

"On the counter at the far left end. So it's easy access but out of the way."

Trey followed the edge of the counter, found the base of the blender. Lucien wondered if he'd ever not be impressed by the way Trey managed, if it would become old hat to him. He hoped not. Trey did everything in the sink, not going for the cutting board and knife, the wok.

"I'll get the hand washing done," he told Trey, once everything else had been cleaned up. "Won't take any time at all."

"You sure? I'll turn some music on."

"You don't need to. There's, like, just three things to wash up." Did Trey find it weird not to have music on?

"Oh. Okay." Trey wandered out of the kitchen, touching random things, exploring almost idly.

Lucien made short work of the hand washing, and decided not to put on the dishwasher—there was more than enough room for their breakfast dishes to go in there and he could get it going before heading off to work. He detoured into the bedroom to grab the book from the bedside table, then headed back to the living room, whistling happily.

Trey was grooming Dodger, the pup's tongue lolling.

"Oh, now there's a happy dog."

Dodger's tail thumped on the floor, but he didn't move to come see Lucien.

"He's a good boy." Trey leaned down, cuddled Dodger.

Oh, God. That was adorable. Lucien just watched for a while. He found he could do that a lot—watch Trey at his everyday life. Did it make him weird that he enjoyed watching when Trey couldn't? Was that creepy?

Trey scratched Dodger's belly, playing and laughing. "It's so neat, having you here."

"It's awesome being here. I like just watching you be." There, it wasn't creepy if Trey knew, right?

"Yeah?" Trey grinned toward him. "Show me your office, love?"

"Oh yeah. Let's do that before we read." He put the book down on the arm of his chair, then took Trey's hand in his.

"How exciting. I don't know that I've been in that room in years."

"Really?" He couldn't imagine having a room he never went into.

"It was just a room. Storage. I had Brian clean it out."

"My place wasn't big enough for storage."

"No? I don't... I mean, I sort of know what was in there... Is that weird? To not know?"

"Nah. That's what storage areas are for, right?"

"Yeah. Yeah. I guess. That's why I write horror, you know? So much of it happens in the dark?"

"Yeah, the dark can be a spooky place. At least... Is it scary for you?"

"No. No, the idea of light is harder. The whole thing. It burns and it blisters."

Okay. Okay, that was totally unexpected. "Light hurts you?"

"No. No, isn't that what people say? The light burns you?"

"Well, it can, if it's too hot, like the center of the sun."

"Yeah? I know light bulbs are hot."

"Yeah, they burn." He chuckled. "This is like a big time philosophical question, I think."

"Yeah. It's weird, huh? Having a blind... I'm not a boyfriend..."

"Lover." It sounded good, calling Trey that out loud. "And it's different but not weird."

"It's amazing. It's fucking amazing." Trey laughed, pushed up and hugged him, the move sudden and surprising and oddly young.

He wrapped his arms around Trey automatically, then bent to take a kiss. "You are amazing."

"We are." Trey chuckled. "I want to do everything — fuck and explore and read and listen to a movie and everything."

"The really cool this is we don't have to do them all tonight. We have all the nights."

"Yeah." Trey leaned against him, hard. "Yeah. All the nights."

"So tonight we check out my office, then we go read. Tomorrow night, we can do something else." He loved being able to support Trey.

"Make love, maybe?"

"Mmm. We could do that tonight, too, after our reading. Unless of course the sound of my voice puts you to sleep."

"Man, a guy falls asleep once…"

Lucien chuckled. "Yep, it will live on in infamy."

He grabbed Trey's hand. Time to explore, show his lover his office.

Chapter Fourteen

"Get the fuck out of here!" Trey slammed his office door and locked it, put his headphones on and started talking. No more interruptions from Brian. No more bullshit. No talking. He had a novel to finish and the serial killer was in his head.

He paced and talked, paced and talked, his body aching and his head pounding. He thought he heard knocking, but that could have just been this headache.

The next thing he knew, a hand landed on his arm.

He screamed, the sound shocking him. "Don't! Don't." Fuck. Fuck. It had finally happened. His stories had come to life. He shouted at the top of his lungs. "Lucien!"

The earphones were pulled out from his ears. "Baby. Trey. I'm right here. It's me."

"Oh. Oh, God. Oh, God. I thought... I thought... Oh, God."

Lucien wrapped around him, tugging him in close. "Shh. Easy, baby. I'm right here. Just me."

He shook so hard his teeth chattered and he fought to breathe.

"Okay, Trey. One breath after another. In and out. I've got you."

"Sorry. God, sorry. I… The story… It was big."

"I'll say. You got up at, like…two in the morning to come work. I sent Brian home, by the way." Lucien's big hands were rubbing him, sliding on his arms, up and down his back.

"I need to… God. I'm trying to get it down. All of it." He sounded like a crow.

"You're not doing the book any favors by making yourself crazy. You haven't slept in a day and you only had a few hours then."

"I don't know what time it is. My throat hurts."

"It's almost eight. Come on." Lucien helped him untangle from his earphones. "Do you need to save anything before we go get you something for your throat, maybe get some food into you too?"

"Save. Save all." The computer would do the work for him.

"Send Serial dot doc to Agnes."

"Okay?" Lucien asked. When he nodded, his lover led him from his office.

"I'm sorry."

"Hey, you didn't yell at me." Lucien sat him at the kitchen table and a moment later a glass was placed in his hand. "Juice."

He sniffed. *Oh. Orange. Yay.*

"I've got leftover mashed potatoes and roast beef with Brussels sprouts. Sound good?"

"Uh-huh." He was cooling off, the sweat drying on his skin.

"Good." He heard a plate go into the microwave and it got turned on.

"I bet you're starving."

"I guess?" The juice was good.

"Oh, you've hit that point."

"What does that mean?"

"There's a point where you're so hungry you don't even realize it anymore.

The microwave dinged and the smell of food hit his nose as Lucien put his plate in front of him. He almost burst into tears and his belly cramped.

"Oh, love." Lucien dragged a chair close to him and that big, warm hand landed on his back. "Easy, baby. You just need to start slow."

"I'm not doing so well, Lucien."

"Twenty hours working after only three hours of sleep with almost no food will do that, baby."

"Uh-huh."

"Open up, baby."

He opened his lips, trusting Lucien with his soul. A forkful of mashed potatoes slipped into his mouth. *Oh. Oh, yum.* He swallowed and opened for another bite. This mouthful had potatoes and beef. He swallowed again, his throat so sore.

Lucien kept feeding him, offering him drinks in between each bite. He felt weirdly disconnected, as if his body wasn't his own. Lucien kept feeding him, talking softly to him, just murmurs and soft words of encouragement.

He kept apologizing, kept tearing up.

"Stop it, baby. You just need to relax."

"Uh-uh."

"No? What do you mean no?"

"Did I say no? I meant to…" Hell, he didn't know what he meant.

Lucien kissed him, ending his need to figure out what he'd meant to say. "Shh. It's okay, baby. You don't need to do anything right now — not even think."

"No?" *Oh, God. Promise?*

"No. I've got you covered."

"Okay." *Please.*

Another mouthful of food slid between his lips. "If that was enough, we're having a shower now."

"Shower." That sounded perfect.

"Yeah. You, me and as much hot water as the heater holds." Lucien helped him up and put his hand on one big arm.

He followed along, just stumbling a bit. Lucien didn't let him fall, though—his lover right there to catch him, guide him.

"I'm sorry, huh? It's a big story."

"Does this happen a lot?" Lucien undressed him, and he heard the clothes dropping into the bags.

He nodded. It happened all too often.

"Ah, baby. There's got to be a better way." Lucien kissed the top of his head and drew him into the shower, the water hot and wet as it hit him.

He started crying, head down, entire body shaking hard.

Lucien held him, hands sliding up and down his back. "It's okay, baby. It's okay. I have you."

"I'm sorry. I'm so stupid." And tired.

"Not stupid, just exhausted. You've overworked yourself. Hush now. I mean it. You don't have to think anymore. I've got you. I'll take care of you."

He nodded, cuddled in close.

Lucien washed him, hands moving slickly on him, cleaning him and soothing him at once. Soon he was done sobbing, just clinging to Lucien's shoulders. Lucien hummed for him, the sounds calming and sweet. Finally the water stopped and he was being dried, drawn down the hall.

Their bed felt like heaven, soft and warm all around him.

Lucien kissed the top of his head. "Sleep, baby. I have you."

"Promise? Promise you'll stay?"

"I promise. I'm not going anywhere, Trey."

"Okay. I need you to stay."

"Trey. I live here with you. I've committed to staying right here with you. Always."

He squeezed Lucien's fingers and let himself relax, believe.

"I tell you what, baby. I'm going to make love to you and then plug my seed inside you. Maybe that'll help convince you."

"Please. Please, I've wanted to... Always."

Lucien's lips covered his, tongue sliding on his, demanding his focus. He opened up, crying out into his lover's mouth. Lucien found his ass, squeezing and kneading. He nodded, almost hysterical, needing Lucien to make things better.

Lucien's kiss stole his breath, tongue fucking his lips as the strong fingers slid into his crack. God, yes. Make it go away. Make it better. One finger breached him, opening him up.

"More," Trey demanded.

"Lube first." Lucien leaned away from him, but before he could protest, was back, fingers slick now.

"Yes. Yes, please." He needed this.

"I've got you, boy." Lucien pushed two fingers into him, opening him wider.

His toes curled, and he turned over, exposing his ass, his hole.

"My needy boy." He could hear Lucien's pleasure, Lucien's need in the words.

"Yours. I need this. You. Now."

"I know." Lucien pulled his fingers away, then he felt the thick heat of Lucien's cock pressing against into him.

He bore back, taking that fat rod in to the root, their bodies slapping together.

"Trey!" Lucien called out to him, then slammed into him again.

"Yes." He forced himself back, over and over.

Lucien met him each time, cock driving into him. Then those big hands wrapped around his hips, Lucien pulling him back with even more force. That was what he needed. Lucien's control.

"No coming until I say." Lucien growled the words out, the speed of those thrusts increasing.

"I…"

Lucien slammed into him hard. "You heard me, boy."

"Yes!" His worry shattered, the universe suddenly perfect.

The pounding continued, and Lucien had total control, choosing the speed, the strength, the angle, beginning to bang away at his gland. His head fell between his arms, lightly swaying back and forth.

"That's it, baby. You're mine and I've got you."

He loved that idea, that truth. He was Lucien's.

Lucien didn't touch his cock, fingers digging into his hips and leaving bruises. He loved it, pushing back, over and over, low cries on the air.

"Love you, baby. My boy."

The words made everything even better.

"Yes. Yes. Love."

"When I say," Lucien reminded him, moving even faster, beginning to lose that rhythm, movements become jerky. It would be soon.

"Soon. Soon, please."

"Uh-huh." Lucien thrust a few more times, then called out to him. "Now, Trey! Now!"

Spunk poured from him, his balls emptying themselves so quickly they hurt. Lucien cried out, punching into him throughout his orgasm, making it stronger, better. He sobbed softly, soaring with the sheer pleasure. A few more thrusts and Lucien cried out, froze inside him, and filled him with heat.

He gripped Lucien tightly, squeezing hard. Lucien rested his head on Trey's back, panting hard. He could feel each breath on his skin. He slowly lowered himself onto the mattress, his whole world spinning. Lucien went with him, staying buried deep. In a minute there would be a plug.

"Stay with me, love. Stay close." He needed Lucien with him

"I'm not going anywhere." Lucien stayed right there, heavy on him without crushing him.

"I love you. I'm so sorry about the freak out." He was exhausted.

"It's okay, baby. We worked it out." Lucien slid a plug along his arm.

"Uh-huh." His ass clenched. "We did."

Lucien's lips slid along the back of his neck as he felt the thick plug press against his perineum, Lucien's cock beginning to slide out. He groaned, body fighting Lucien.

"Shh. Love. I need to come out. I need to put the plug in. That will keep me inside you."

Trey nodded. He knew. He knew that.

"Easy then, love." Lucien kissed the back of his neck again.

It was more than he could do, to deny his Master.

Lucien eased out, the heavy plug pushing in to keep his spunk inside. He pressed up, bore down, taking it in.

"That's my baby. It's a nice one, good and heavy. You'll feel it all night, even while you're asleep."

His body snapped around the base of the plug, and it felt so fucking good.

Lucien dropped another kiss on his neck and lay next to him, pulling him into that warm embrace. His world eased, and he sank into a deep sleep without a hint of dreams.

* * * *

Lucien woke up with Trey still curled up against him, dead to the world. He wasn't surprised, Trey had been going for about twenty hours straight and on only about three hours sleep at that. He hadn't seen it coming, but from what he was gathering, it was — while not something that happened *all* the time — something that happened at least once with every new book, usually near the end.

He hated to think what Trey used to do before he was here full time. All his boy would have had to do was give him a call and he would have come, helped Trey through the craziness. Of course, that would have meant that Trey realized he was being nutso.

The fear in Trey's eyes had been horrifying, as if Lucien had been a monster. He would have to be on the lookout for that kind of intensity and focus and overwork. Because he was pretty sure it would happen again and if he could catch it sooner...then maybe Trey wouldn't get to that point.

Trey's eyes popped open, went wide, then eased closed for a second.

"Hey, baby. Morning." He touched Trey's arm, sliding his hand along it.

"Morning." Trey's voice sounded like a crow's.

"My poor love." He took a kiss.

Trey moaned softly, tongue sliding on his. Now that was better, calm and sexy. He let one hand slide down, move on to stroke Trey's cleft. To play with the plug that still held his boy open wide.

"I should get up." Trey moaned into his lips.

"Why?"

"Uh…" Trey moaned and licked his way back into Lucien's mouth.

Laughing softly, Lucien pulled in Trey's tongue, sucking on it. Maybe he could convince his boy to have a day off, a scene. That was just the thing.

Letting go of Trey's tongue, he filled his boy's mouth with his. Lucien didn't give Trey a chance to argue, either. He wanted his lover's total attention. Rolling Trey onto his back, he followed, letting Trey feel his weight.

"Master."

Lucien nodded, loving the way that word sounded in Trey's mouth. "Gonna give you a good day, baby."

"A good day…"

"Uh-huh." He licked from Trey's throat, up to his lips.

"I should work…"

"You should do as your Master says."

Lucien felt the reaction underneath him, Trey's jerk, Trey's shudder. Oh yeah, he had Trey's attention now.

He tugged at Trey's lower lip. "Keeping you here all day. Keeping you busy." He rubbed them together, biting down harder on that sweet lip.

"Working." Trey wasn't even really arguing.

"Working on a scene. Working to make your Master happy."

"Thank you for last night."

"I'm glad I was here to help." So glad.

"I was just totally in Ranger's headspace."

Yeah, and while that served Trey well in writing, it had to be painful to Trey's psyche.

"And you had been for hours and hours. Today you're going to be in Trey's head space."

"Am I?" There was an obvious hunger in his boy's face.

"You are. I'm going to turn you inside out and right side in again." He licked at Trey's earlobe, then bit it.

Trey grabbed his shoulders, tugged at him, whether to keep him closer or pull him away, Lucien couldn't tell. It didn't matter, he was giving Trey himself back and that was that. He brought their mouths together, taking a long, hard kiss.

As soon as their lips parted, Trey said, "He's a bad man, Ranger. He hates, so much."

"It amazing me how someone as loving and wonderful as you can tap into that kind of character."

"It's something inside me. Something scary."

"There's probably something like that in all of us. You just tap into it for your books."

"I think so. I think that's why people read them."

"Could be. Better to read them than to become a serial killer, eh?" He traced Trey's lips with his tongue.

"Uh-huh…" Trey followed him, head turning.

He kept licking, tracing, enjoying the way Trey moved. How did his boy escape the monsters alone? So brave. So fucking strong.

"You don't ever have to fight alone anymore." He was here now, with Trey,

"Never?"

"I'm your forever man, baby."

"Oh… That's a great title."

"It's my truth."

Trey stilled then those sightless eyes filled with tears.

"Baby? What's wrong?" That was supposed to be a good thing. It *was* a good thing.

"I love you. You… You don't know how much that means. Your words, I mean."

"Oh." He kissed Trey gently, licked away the tears. "So these are good."

"They are. They're thankful."

"You made me worried." He kept kissing and licking, making the tears his own.

"I'm stupid with emotions today."

"I'm here to help you hold on."

Trey nodded, leaned back and opened his arms. "Sir."

"My beautiful boy." He pounced, devouring Trey's mouth, making plans to fill that sweet ass over and over. He found the ties that lived around Trey's headboard, drew them up to bind his lover. "You're going to be at my mercy all day long. I'm going to make you fly."

"I have to work…" Trey didn't pull his arms down.

"No, you're going to fly." He pressed a kiss to Trey's forehead, then his nose.

"I want you to make it huge."

"I will, baby. I promise." He so would.

He fastened Trey's wrists, making sure that there was enough slack to spin his boy. Then he began touching, sliding his fingers over Trey's body, mapping every line. He scratched and tugged Trey's nips, pinching firmly.

"I want to get rings in these, baby. I want to be able to play."

Trey moaned, but he got a nod. Just a single nod.

"When you've completely finished this novel... When you're done with Ranger... We'll mark the end of the book with a piercing." He'd just discovered a new way to mark each one. Instead of him coming over, they'd get something pierced.

"Oh, God..." Trey pulled at the bonds, cock slapping against Trey's belly.

"Master," he corrected. Then he bit at Trey's right nipple. "Will do this one first."

Trey was caught. He knew that fascinated look.

He lapped at the nipple, giving sweet before the sharp. "One at a time so there's always one I can still play with."

"What will you do after?"

"After this one is pierced..." He bit down hard and quick on the nipple he'd been teasing. Then he lapped his way over to the other one. "Then I pierce this one."

"Yes..." Trey nodded, chest arching to push up into his lips.

He pulled back, teasing, then moved back in to bite and tug at the hard little nip. He used his teeth to rock and squeeze, to drive his boy higher.

Then he eased the pain with flicks of his tongue. "You want to know what I'll do when both the nipples are done and healed?"

"Yes. God, yes."

He did love having a lover with imagination.

"We're going to head down this way." He started kissing his way along Trey's chest toward his navel.

"Belly button ring?"

He laughed against Trey's skin. "Oh, no. I'm not stopping at your navel on this journey."

"No?"

Lucien felt the tight abs ripple under his lips. He nibbled at them, dampening the warm skin. He was going to start working out with Trey, give his boy another outlet for all that energy. He licked his way down to the hair around Trey's cock. Tugging on it, he then moved on to that lovely hard cock. He lapped at the top. "Right here."

"No..." Trey arched for him, liquid salt touching his tongue.

"Oh yes." He licked again, then wrapped his lips around the tip and sucked until more drops flavored his mouth. He was going to make Trey absolutely wild just thinking about all the places he was going to pierce.

Trey tugged at the bonds, pulled at them. "No. Oh, fuck..."

"Yes, baby." He loved the fight, that Trey knew he could let go with Lucien.

Trey gasped. "I'll never be able to stop touching it."

"Then I'll tie your hands behind your back until you learn not to." He slid his tongue around the tip of Trey's cock. "Can you imagine that, baby? Writing with your hands behind your back, your cock throbbing with every beat of your heart?"

"Shh..." He knew that wasn't what Trey needed. His boy needed him to tell Trey all about it. All about everything.

He wrapped his lips around the side of Trey's erection and let him feel his teeth without biting. Then he moved and did the same thing an inch down, then another inch. "This is where your ladder will be."

Trey's expression was a study in need, eyes wide, lips parted.

"One rung each time you finish a book. It's going to take us years to get everything done." He kissed the base of the silky flesh, licked it. "The last rung will be down here."

"Then I'll be done?" Trey shifted his hips restlessly.

"Oh, no, baby. I think you have more books than that left in you and that means you have more piercings to come." He nosed at Trey's balls, giving his boy a hint.

Trey arched, heels digging into the mattress.

"Your balls need decoration." Several rings climbing up along them. "At least three rings. Maybe four."

"No... No way." Trey's belly was flushed dark, ball sac drawn up tight.

"Yes way. We haven't even gotten to your guiche yet." He flicked his tongue back and forth across the smooth, hot skin between Trey's balls and his hole. "I think we could get three in here, no problem."

"Lucien!" Someone was thinking hard, visualizing.

"I'll be able to play with them all, eventually. Imagine me tugging. Imagine me pushing the ladder through your skin, back and forth, rubbing you from the inside."

"I-I can't... Oh, please, Sir."

"One day you won't have to imagine." Lucien made it a promise, a vow. "When this book is finished, when you've put Ranger to bed, we'll start." He bit at the sensitive flesh behind Trey's balls.

Trey barked out a sharp scream, his feet pounding at the mattress.

"You're allowed to come, boy." He slapped at Trey's balls with his tongue.

The scent of spunk was sharp, strong—his boy shooting for him.

Moaning happily, he licked his way up, cleaning Trey's belly for him. Trey's face was lax, his boy dizzy with pleasure. He rubbed his thickness against Trey's thigh as he kissed his way up Trey's slender body. Trey wrapped his legs around him, held him close, lips searching for his.

He pressed their mouths together, tongue slipping in. He loved the way Trey tasted, the heat inside his lover.

"Did you mean it?" Trey whispered.

"I did. I do. And when we've run out of piercings, I'll come up with some other way to mark the passing of your books."

Trey shuddered, rolled against him. "You... You can't say things like that."

"I just did." He rubbed them together, letting their cocks slide and bump.

"I know. I know. I'm... I can imagine it. Every second."

"Good. That means you'll remember it when you need to. It's a promise. All those things we're going to do are a promise."

"A promise. I promise. Make love to me, Sir."

"Yes." After slicking up his cock, Lucien tugged at the plug with his free hand, turning it slowly as he pulled it out.

Trey's eyes rolled, body arching impossibly. His boy was so stunning, so beautiful. Trey made his heart ache. Moaning, Lucien lined up and slid in, needing to be inside Trey, needing to join with his baby.

"Mine." Trey sucked in a deep breath, fingers wrapped around his cuffs.

"I am. Every inch of me, baby. All yours." Lucien thrust as he spoke, pushing every word into Trey's body.

Trey's moan echoed, his baby not holding back. He loved that best about Trey, he never doubted that Trey wanted this, loved it—needed it.

Lucien rocked in again, over and over, watching the emotions chase themselves across Trey's face. He really could do this all day long. Okay, maybe not physically, but emotionally he was right there.

Trey grabbed the bonds and used them to drive himself down, add his strength to Lucien's.

"You were made for this, baby. Made for me."

Trey's chin dipped, but his writer didn't have any words left, just low moans. He moved in harder, just pounding Trey's needy ass. He buried himself in to the root, then started pushing in with short, fast thrusts. Their bodies were both shining with sweat, the scent of them strong. It was intoxicating.

He touched Trey's lips and his boy reached up, wrapped his lips around his finger and sucked.

"Fuck," muttered Trey, body bucking.

Trey was amazing. He proved that every damn day. Trey's head bobbed, fellating his finger in time with the way their bodies met. He hung his head, concentrating on not coming yet. Control. Control. Fuck, his Trey was hot.

He started counting his thrusts, like they were reps. He was well into the eighth set when Trey threw his head back and screamed. Cum bubbled up out of his baby and he cried out, coming hard and filling Trey up with pulse after pulse of spunk. Trey's face was a study in pleasure, in need.

He collapsed, careful not to put any pressure on Trey. He pressed kisses on his baby's face, though, one after the other, breathing heavily.

"Love." Trey nuzzled him, cheek sliding on his. "You didn't have to go to work?"

"I texted last night to let my assistant know I wasn't coming in."

"Oh. Did I fire Brian again or just send him home?"

Lucien chuckled. "You fired him, but he told me he'd give you a couple days to cool off and be back on Thursday."

Trey blushed, skin going dark red. "I... Yeah."

Lucien pressed a kiss against Trey's cheek. "It's okay, baby. He knows it's a part of your 'process'."

"Yeah, the asshole part."

"Good thing you're so loveable ninety-nine percent of the time."

"Yeah. Good thing I pay well."

"He loves working for you."

"He's a good kid. I'm going to be devastated when he graduates. I hate training a new assistant, but you know that. We're on number, what? Five together?

"Yeah, something like that. I'll be able to help you with this time, though."

"Yeah. If I remember, you made sure Brian wasn't an ax murderer."

"I did." He'd found out that Trey didn't run a check on his potential assistants and had fixed that. No one was going to take advantage of Trey. Ever.

He pressed kisses on Trey, fingers sliding up the slender arms to the cuffs.

"Leave them on, Sir. Just a little longer."

"Anything you want, baby." He slid his hand back down along Trey's arms, fingers working the slender muscles.

"I want to be with you."

"I'm not going anywhere." He kissed Trey's cheek and settled next to him.

Trey was quiet, still, and he could tell that his boy's thoughts were rushing.

"Talk to me, baby."

"Huh?" Trey shook his head. "I'm just thinking."

"I know. I can smell the smoke."

Trey's eyes rolled, but that did get him a laugh. "I guess I'm just worrying about the book."

"I haven't done my job right if you're still worrying about the book," Trey noted.

"You know that it gets into me, won't let go."

"I know, but today you're supposed to be relaxing, coming out of it." Lucien wanted Trey to have a real break.

"I don't know if I understand how to do that."

"That's what I'm here for, eh? To keep you in the here and now." It was his job.

"To save me from the serial killers, right?" Trey asked.

"Yeah. No evil is taking my boy away from me." Lucien wouldn't let that happen.

"Do you think I'm crazy? For getting in so deep?"

"I think it's what makes you an amazing writer."

Trey's smile made Lucien feel ten feet tall.

He kissed each of Trey's eyelids. "Love you, baby."

"Love you. I do. Thank you for everything."

"Always my pleasure, baby."

And it was. Everything about Trey was.

Chapter Fifteen

Trey woke up in the middle of the night with an idea of how to finish the book and he stumbled from the bed and started working, curled into an old quilt. At some point, Brian brought him coffee and took his tapes to start transcribing and he nodded, voice cracking as he continued to speak.

A soft knock sounded after his second cup of coffee, Lucien speaking quietly. "You okay, baby?"

"Uh-huh. Working. Not now, love. Not now." He needed this, more than breathing. The story was tearing out of him, screaming through his synapses.

"Okay, but I'm making you a sandwich and you have to eat it."

He shooed Lucien with his hand, Lucien's voice echoing in his ears.

At one point a sandwich was put in his hand. "Eat it, Trey. I mean it. You don't have to stop, just eat it."

He sniffed, smelling peanut butter and jelly, and he took a bite, then another. "Milk?"

Lucien pressed a plastic cup into his hand. "It has a lid and a straw."

"Thank you. Thank you." He drank deeply, the cold washing his mouth clean, and he was off again. The Reaper had his final victim, or did she have him? It was bad to kidnap and rape a pyrokenetic. Bad.

He was given water as he was rounding the last bend. He gulped it, tears streaking his cheeks. He rejoiced for Amy, mourned his dead killer and the end of other one. By the time he said "The End" he was sobbing, wrecked and lost, in that horrible place in between writing.

"Lucien!" he called. He needed his Sir.

Lucien wrapped strong, warm arms around him, Lucien right there and holding on. "I'm here, baby. I'm here."

"I need you. I need you, now." This one had been hard and he wasn't sure he'd kept his soul intact.

Lucien's lips closed over his and he felt his chair disappear as Lucien picked him up, cradling him against the broad chest.

He heard Brian slide into the office. "I'll have these done in a few days, Trey."

He nodded. Whatever. Go away.

"Thanks, Brian. Work on them at home and take a couple days off when you're done." Lucien's voice rumbled in the big chest against his ear.

"You got it, man. You want me to arrange pizza for later?"

"No, we've got it covered. Thanks, man."

If Brian said anything else, Trey didn't hear it. Lucien took him into the bathroom and closed the door.

"I did it." He was so proud, so lost, so sad and mad and tickled all at once.

"You did!" Lucien laughed. "Your first book that you finished while I was here. And now you don't have to call me and wait for me to show up."

"Uh-huh. I didn't scare you away." It was more a happy surprise than a question.

"Nope. It gave me insight into what goes on while you write. Why you need so badly by the time I get to you."

"It's a hard place to be sometimes, my brain."

"I think your brain is special." Lucien was stripping him, tugging his clothes off.

He nodded. So did he. Honestly. "Need you, Sir."

"I know."

Lucien bundled him into the shower and followed, curling around him. No waiting. No worrying. Lucien was right there for him. It was rather stunning.

Lucien tilted his head back, took a long, lingering kiss. He opened, begging to be taken, to be touched and dominated. Pushed—maybe punished. Lucien's hands traveled over him, coming back to his ass again and again, lingering on his crack and pushing at his hole.

Yes. Yes, more. He didn't talk, his voice was spent. He just trusted in Lucien to give him what he needed. His hands were placed against the tile, Lucien spreading his ass cheeks apart and dropping down behind him. He could feel it, but before he could say anything, Lucien's tongue slid along his crack.

He made a high squeaking sound, his belly going tight at the caress. Lucien's chuckle blew air over his wet skin.

"T-tease." *Fill me. Stretch me. Please, love.*

"Just getting you ready." Lucien began to lick at him again.

Oh. Oh, please. He went up on tiptoes, rocking back and forth. Lucien pushed that tongue in quickly, fucking him with strong strokes. It wasn't enough, but it was a start. He reached down, tugged his balls, rolled them a bit.

Lucien's growl was immediate. "No touching, boy."

"Sir!" *God, yes.*

"You heard me. I'll give you what you need. All you have to do is trust me." Then Lucien's tongue pushed into him again.

He did. He'd proven that trust again and again, from their first meeting.

After Lucien had tongue-fucked him long enough that he thought he was going to go crazy, the warm, solid body slid up along his back and Lucien slid into him. Right into him, just like that. He bore down, riding the pressure inside him with a furor. Lucien's hands wrapped around his hips, pulling him back into every thrust.

They ground together, then Lucien slammed him up against the tile. The thrusts were hard and solid, undeniable. Right there for him. Lucien filled him up over and over, reminding him who he was. Whose he was.

His ass felt like it was stuffed full and he wanted more. Lucien gave it to him, moving harder and faster, changing the angle and finding his gland, banging against it. He went up on tiptoe, swallowing again and again as he fought to remember how to breathe.

"Gonna make you come, and I'm going to plug my cum inside you." Lucien's sounded like he was speaking through gravel. "Going to use a big one, going to stuff you full." Two more thrusts filled him. "Going to keep you open all night long."

Trey spread his legs, taking more, taking it all.

"You're going to come for me without a touch to your cock. You're going to do it because I tell you to."

"Make me." *Please. Make me.*

"That's what I'm doing, baby." Lucien leaned in harder, pressing him against the tile, body hot against his back. "I know your balls are hot, aching. You need so much."

"Yes. Yes. I'm so empty."

"No, I'm inside you. I'm filling you up."

Trey squeezed hard, feeling every inch.

"You ready, baby? Ready to shoot and feel me inside you all night?"

He nodded, trusting in Lucien to know, to have him.

"Then come, boy. Come for me now." The words were accompanied by a twist to his nipple, a reminder of Lucien's promise. He was going to have a nipple pierced.

"Now," demanded Lucien, slamming into him again.

His balls tightened and he jerked, seed spurting from him.

"Yes. Yes!" Lucien shouted, jerking into him and filling him with more heat.

Yes. He groaned, head hanging down between his forearms. There was a plug, Lucien pushing it into him as that thick, hot cock slid out of him.

"There. Now I'm inside you."

He groaned, lips open, just out of his mind.

Turning him, Lucien took his mouth, tongue-fucking it just like that amazing cock had fucked his ass. His ass worked the big plug, squeezing it, making it shift inside him.

"I know what you're doing," Lucien told him, hand sliding on his ass and squeezing his right butt cheek.

"Nothing." He couldn't stop.

"You're working that plug." Lucien kissed the corner of his mouth. "I'm not suggesting you stop — that's why it's there."

"Feels so big," Trey confessed.

"It is. As big as I am. I have a new one, too, that's even bigger."

His body jerked, his cock threatening to come to life again at the thought.

He felt Lucien's smile against his lips. "We'll put that one in later — once you've worked this one to death."

"What time is it? Is it night-time? Lunchtime?"

"It's late afternoon. You got up at, like, two a.m. and just monstered through it."

"He needed to talk."

"Is it always like that at the end?" Lucien's hands slid soap over him, cleaning him top to bottom.

"Most of the times, yeah. Beginnings and endings are huge, middles are harder."

"You did it, though." Lucien sounded so proud of him.

"I did. And you stayed and didn't hate me at the end."

"I don't hate you at all. It was fascinating, watching your process."

"You don't hate me. Thank you. Thank you so much."

"You're amazing to me, baby. Absolutely amazing."

"And I think you're the reason I don't get lost."

"That's a role I take seriously." Lucien turned off the water and lifted him out of the shower before wrapping a towel around him.

He reached out, sliding his hands over Lucien's shoulders, arms. God, he loved how Lucien felt. He could feel each muscle contracting, flexing as his fingers slid by them.

"Beautiful man," he whispered.

"For you, baby." Now Lucien was showing off, muscles dancing beneath his fingertips.

"Yes." He moaned, even though he wasn't horny anymore.

"Come on. My chair and some movie await."

Oh, he did love that chair.

Picking him up, towel and all, Lucien carried him to the living room, sitting in the big chair with him.

"Music? Movie?"

"It's all the same to me, Sir."

"I'm going to put some music on. My focus is on you and I'd probably miss most of the movie."

He nodded, head on Lucien's shoulder. He could hear their heartbeats, pounding together.

"Do we still get a week or so before you dive into the next book?"

"Maybe two this time. I'll have to do edits before it goes to my editor."

"I'm going to make an appointment for tomorrow at the Happy Piercer."

"The Happy Piercer?" Was that seriously a place?

"I know, right? He's got this tiny little shop, just him and his lover, a tattoo artist."

"That's adorable and totally going into a book."

"Everything goes into a book," Lucien pointed out. "It's neat. Like the whole world exists just for your books."

"It's my gift. My stories."

"It's a great gift. Mine is making people sweat."

"Yeah. I missed my last pool day."

"I noticed." Lucien wrapped a hand around his right bicep. "These are looking good, though, since we started doing it."

"Are they? Good. I have to use your gift, too."

"Yeah. You're getting some definition."

"Is that hot? Definition?"

"It is." Lucien took his hand and slid it over the muscles of Lucien's chest. "This is definition."

"Mmm." Yes. Hot.

"See? Definition is hot."

"Uh-huh." He liked that idea, the thought of being hot.

"Smart on the other hand, is sexy. You, baby, are smart."

"I am. Creative too." He'd read his own press.

"And the most beautiful size queen I've ever known."

He started laughing, so happy he couldn't bear to hold it inside.

"God, I love that sound. I know I've told you before, but I do."

He did too. He loved being able to laugh.

"You looking forward to getting your nipple pierced, baby?" Lucien played with his right nipple.

"I don't know if I'm looking forward to it, but it's a turn on.

"I should play with this one a lot tonight. Really make you feel it. Because I won't be able to after it's done."

"It'll heal, though, right?"

"God, yes. I should be able to play with it in a few months. Sooner if you're a fast healer." Lucien pinched his right tit.

"I don't know if I am." He arched into the touch.

"We're going to find out." Flicking at his nipple, Lucien made it ache.

"Uh. Uh-huh." His toes curled, body arching.

Humming, Lucien wrapped thick, warm lips around his skin, sucking hard on it. Trey could feel the blood rushing to it, feel his flesh swell. Lucien's teeth threatened and Trey could feel himself going tense, waiting for the bite. His breath caught in his throat, but Lucien waited and waited. Another flick of Lucien's tongue had him crying out and bucking. It was only then that Lucien bit him, sharp and quick.

"Ow!" Oh, fuck. So good.

Lucien's chuckles vibrated against his skin.

"L-laughing at me." He was laughing too, though, so it was okay.

"Uh-huh. Because you make me so happy."

He grabbed Lucien's face and took a hard, happy kiss. Lucien wrapped a hand around the back of his head, holding him there to keep the things going. They connected, the kiss continuing on and on.

First taking his hands, Lucien tugged them behind his back and held them there. He sucked in a breath, loving the pressure, the pull. With his other hand, Lucien grabbed his nipple, twisting and pinching. Trey made wild sounds, moaning into Lucien's lips.

Shifting him, Lucien moved him until he straddled his lover's thighs. The plug moved, shifted inside him. Lucien made it shift even more, pressing against the base.

"Sir." His sir.

"Right here. And right here." Lucien pushed the base of the plug again.

He nodded, ass squeezing so tight. Lucien tugged the plug partway out, then pushed it back in.

"Oh." His eyes closed, his body squeezing.

"I know what you like." Lucien did it again. There was no question of that. None. "I know how to make you crazy." Lucien was proving that, again, too.

"Crazy. Fucking out of my mind."

That got him a laugh. He nipped Lucien's bottom lip.

"That's my job," complained Lucien.

"Nibbling?" Trey teased.

"Changing it up, giving you every sensation you can imagine and then all the ones you can't."

"Oh." He could imagine an enormous amount.

Lucien stroked his right nipple some more, then pinched again, not leaving it alone. The pressure began to build, the ache setting his teeth on edge. Just as he thought he couldn't stand it another second, Lucien used his nails against Trey's skin, the sharp bite almost shocking. He pulled away, nearly overbalancing, but Lucien held him, strong arms supporting him.

"Good surprise?" Lucien asked before tonguing his skin and soothing the hurt.

"Uh. Uh-huh. Intense."

"Yeah. You need intense. You need soft and hard and sharp and easy and sensuous—and everything."

He liked that idea.

Lucien's lips slid on his own, the kiss gentle and easy, like the hands stroking him were now.

"I did it." he whispered. "I finished another one."

"You did. You continue to amaze me, Trey. Every damn day and twice on the days you finish your novels."

"Maybe three times that day."

"Maybe even four. Hell, let's go for five."

"Now that's just self-indulgent."

"Nothing wrong with a little self-indulgence, baby — especially when you've just finished a book."

"Another book." And he thought this one was good, special.

"This one really had you by the balls."

"Lots of them do, but this one… Yeah."

"I'm glad. Your first piercing should mark a big one."

"If I don't like it, we'll take it out, right?"

"We'll talk about it, anyway."

"Okay. It's a weird thought, something foreign inside me."

Lucien tapped the base of the plug. "Isn't that what this is?"

"No. No, I mean, yes, but that's different." And he hadn't thought about it.

"Is it?" Lucien pulled the plug almost, but not quite all the way out. Then he pushed it back in again, angling it and hitting his gland.

Trey's head fell back. *Oh. Oh, God. Oh, God yes.*

"Someone's ready for another go." Lucien got a good hold of the base of the plug and began fucking him with it in earnest.

He hadn't been. He shouldn't be. But he was. He totally was.

Groaning, Lucien sucked on his neck as he continued to push the plug in over and over.

"Master. Sir. Fuck…" He needed this more than he needed to breathe.

"Love that. Those words in your mouth."

He loved saying them, loved knowing they were the truth.

Lucien picked him up and laid him out on what had to be the couch. Then Lucien's lips wrapped around the head of his cock, sucking as Lucien continued to hit his gland with the plug.

"Sir!" He arched up, his scream echoing in the house. The pressure inside and outside was absolutely perfect.

Lucien didn't miss a beat, sucking him all the way in until he could feel the swallow around the head of his erection. He barked out another, desperate sound before he shot, his balls aching. Lucien swallowed over and over before pulling slowly off, lips tight around his cock.

All Trey could do was moan.

It seemed to take forever before Lucien came all the way off, then he cleaned Trey with his tongue, making him writhe. His world spun and he had to trust Lucien to hold him there. When his cock was clean to Lucien's satisfaction, his Master started in on his balls.

"Gonna kill me," he muttered.

"Gonna try." He could hear Lucien's grin.

"E-evil Master."

"No, evil would be telling you that you can't come anymore today."

"I've already come a thousand times."

"Twice. You've come twice."

"It has to be more than that."

"I don't think so. Anyway. We already called for four or five today. You've got plenty more coming your way — if I let you."

"Oh, God." He was going to die. Die happy, but die nonetheless.

"Name's Lucien, but you can call me God if you want."

He groaned. "Not punny."

"I thought it was hilarious." Lucien's smile felt good against his lips.

"My amazing, sort of hilarious, Master."

"Sort of?" Lucien raspberried his belly.

God, he was a happy man. "Uh. Uh-huh."

"I'll have you know I'm freaking hysterical." Lucien began tickling his ribs.

"Are you sure?" He couldn't stop giggling.

"You're laughing, aren't you?" He could hear laughter in Lucien's voice, his Master clearly happy, too.

"You know it."

"Then we're all good." Lucien's big body covered his, full of promise.

Yeah, they were good. Really, really good.

Chapter Sixteen

Lucien put the egg-white omelets on two plates, along with some toast, and set them on the table.

"You've toast at the top right, the omelet taking up the entire left side." He wasn't sure how much he was going to be able to eat himself. Excitement coursed through him.

"Smells good. What's in them?"

"Spinach and mushrooms. I didn't want to do anything too heavy. Our appointment is at eleven."

"So early?"

"Yeah. It won't be very busy, so you'll be able to enjoy the experience better."

"Enjoy it." Trey shook his head. "Maybe we should wait."

"No, you finished the book. That means you get the piercing. You're going to love it, baby." He was sure of it. He could see how this might be a bit scary, though.

"I'm worried."

"Tell me about your worries and I'll see if I can alleviate them."

"It's going to hurt!" Trey looked so affronted.

He had to bite his lip to keep from chuckling at Trey's expression. "Not for long, though."

"What if it makes me crazy?"

"You mean what if it turns you on?"

"Uh-huh. I mean, all the time."

"Then we'll find a way to deal with that."

Trey picked at his food, moving the omelet in circles. Getting up, Lucien then went to Trey and picked him up, carrying him to the living room.

"You didn't eat."

"Neither did you, baby. We'll have some juice or something before we go. Right now, you need a little distraction."

Trey shook his head, frowning mightily.

"What this all about?" Lucien asked, rubbing at the wrinkles between Trey's eyes.

"I don't know. I don't know what to expect."

"The shop will be quiet. We have an appointment with Brundy. He's going to clean your nipple with disinfectant. Then he's going to take a pen and mark where he's putting the ring in."

"And you'll check it?"

"You know I will. I'll make sure it's straight and where we want it." He slid his hand beneath Trey's T-shirt to lightly stroke over the nipple in question.

Trey hummed for him, the sound soft, wanton.

"Baby it's going to be amazing. You'll always know it's there, but eventually it'll fade into the background. Then when you come to bed, I'll grab it and bam, you'll be awake again."

Trey's nipple hardened under his touch.

"I love how sensitive your nipples are."

"I-I bet they're worse this afternoon."

He chuckled. "I imagine they will be."

"Or at least the right one will be. I'll have to give extra attention the left once the right is off limits."

"You'll be with me the entire time?"

"For every single second. I promise." He wasn't letting Trey experience a moment of this without him.

"Okay. Okay. I just… Big nerves."

"I know, baby." He wrapped his lips around Trey's right nipple and started sucking,

"Oh!" Trey grabbed his head, arching, bending for him.

Humming, he slapped at the tip with his tongue, loving driving his boy nuts. He wanted Trey too revved up to be worried, scared.

Biting at the tip of Trey's nipple, he pushed two fingers into his boy's mouth, trusting Trey would start sucking. Sure enough, Trey began to pull at him like a starving man. That made his cock stand up and pay full attention.

He knew that Trey was missing the plug he'd removed this morning, craved it. He would put another one in, something Trey could wear when they went out. He knew just the one, too.

He bit down, rolling that taut nipple between his teeth and each of Trey's responses made him love his boy more.

"Need you. Please. I… Need."

"I know, baby." He put his wet fingers at Trey's hole, pressed in.

"Master…" Sweet size queen.

"Right here, baby." He pushed them deeper, then began to fuck Trey with them.

Trey groaned, one leg pulling up to spread himself more.

"Get the lube, baby. There should be some under the cushions above your head."

"Uh-huh." Trey reached up, and Lucien moaned at the sight. Look at his baby. All stretched out for him, needy and wanton. Trey made his mouth dry.

He took the tube of lube from his boy, and tugged his fingers out of Trey's body. He was going to use four fingers on Trey, possibly even his whole hand if that's what Trey needed this morning.

"Don't go," Trey moaned.

"Where am I going?"

"I don't know!"

"I'm not going anywhere, baby." He took a kiss to ease his boy. His lover was on edge, ramped up and near hysteria.

He got his fingers slicked up as he kissed Trey. Then he pushed four of them in.

"Uhn." Trey rolled up, knees on his chest.

"Better, hmm?" He wriggled his fingers inside Trey's body.

Trey nodded, shook his head, nodded again. He knew, though. He knew this was what his boy needed. He moved his hand in and out, slowly fucking Trey. Trey moaned, the sounds getting louder, more desperate.

"You need my hand, baby."

"Oh, God. God. Master. Please."

Lucien pulled his fingers out then added more lube. He was going to make his boy fly. "I'm giving you my whole hand now, baby. Every finger, my thumb. My knuckles, my palm."

Trey stilled, holding himself open, holding himself wide.

"Don't forget to breathe, boy."

"Trying. Trying to."

Setting his fingers back at Trey's hole, he reached up with his other hand and pinched the about-to-be-pierced nipple. Trey sucked in a deep, sharp breath. Better.

He pressed the tips in and twisted Trey's nipple again. Trey's ass gripped him, squeezed him tightly.

"Easy, baby. Let me in." He wriggled the tips of his fingers, then pushed them in deeper.

"Oh..." Trey's face was flushed, entire body shuddering.

"Just keep breathing." Leaning up, he licked at Trey's pretty little abused nipple.

"Breathing. Please."

He bit at the nub of flesh as he pushed his hand past the second knuckles. Trey cried out, barking out a wild sound. There was only a little farther to go to get his whole hand into his boy. Crooning softly, he went for it. Trey's body shuddered, shook all around him, but let him in.

"That's it, baby. You're opening right up for me."

That tiny ring gave and gave, just spreading wide under his ministrations.

"Such a beautiful size queen. You rock my world, baby."

"Love. I love you enough to let you in."

"I know. You make me feel so good." He kissed the tip of Trey's needy cock. Salt bloomed on his lips, sharp and perfect. Groaning, he lapped a bit more of the pre-cum, then he went back to concentrating on fucking Trey with his entire hand.

He could feel Trey everywhere around him. So fucking amazing. Trey blew his goddamn mind. Trey called out, cried for him, entire body shuddering.

"I've got you, baby. I have you so hard. Holding you in my hand."

"In your hand."

"That's right." He closed his hand into a fist, then opened it again, fingers pushing over Trey's gland.

He felt Trey's body clench around his wrist, grip tight. Leaning in, he flicked his tongue across Trey's cock again, drawing in more of the clear, salty liquid. Trey rocked, holding his knees, riding his hand in the tiniest motions.

"That's it, baby. Take it. Take what you want—what you need."

"Take…" Trey kept moving, sliding on Lucien. There was nothing but pleasure left.

Lucien watched Trey's face, taking it all in. The trust there, the need—it humbled him.

"Trey… I love you, baby. You're my soul."

"Yours. Please." His boy whimpered softly.

"You are. Every inch. Outside and in."

Trey nodded, eyes rolling madly.

"I want you to come, baby." He dove onto Trey's erection, sucking hard.

"Me too. Me too."

He had to fight the urge to chuckle.

He tapped the tip with his tongue every time he came up Trey's cock. Trey's body stiffened, then the needy flesh swelled in his lips. He touched Trey's gland with his fingers, swallowing hard. Spunk filled his lips, hot and bitter. He took it all in, filling his belly with Trey's seed.

Lapping and licking, he kept it up until Trey begged him to stop. Letting Trey's penis slide from his lips, he wriggled his fingers.

"Lucien!" His boy was out of his mind.

"I've got you," he said again, because he so did, Trey's body gripping his hand—his whole hand—so hard.

Trey wasn't worrying about the nipple piercing right now. Trey wasn't thinking about anything except this. Hell, he wasn't sure Trey *could* think right now.

Lucien applied more lube to his wrist and pushed in a little more, getting Trey's stretched hole a little slicker. Then he started the careful process of pulling out, crooning at Trey all the while. Trey muttered softly, head shaking back and forth.

"Breathe, baby. Relax and let me come out." He covered Trey's mouth and pushed air in.

His hand popped out, Trey's eyes moving frantically, rolling, and he turned the breathing into a kiss, tongue pushing in, his body pressing against Trey's. He burned with passion, hips rolling, erection rubbing against Trey's thigh. Shifting, he settled between Trey's legs and drove into his lover's body. Trey was ready for him and so hot inside, like a fire.

"Master," Trey moaned, stretched muscles rippling around him.

"Right here, boy. Loving on you." He moved his hips slowly, pushing in, tugging out again only to thrust back in. It was the perfect fucking circle.

"Love. Yes, God. Love."

He brought their mouths together again, intent on giving Trey a good, long fucking. If his boy was melted, there wouldn't be any worry. No stress. No fear. Just peace.

He moved a little faster, hips pumping. This was magical, being connected like this.

Lucien closed his eyes and focused on the pressure, the need, the way Trey's muscles gripped him tight. He breathed into Trey as they kissed, sharing air as well as bodies. Lucien felt his control slipping, felt the kisses growing desperate, and Trey grabbed his head, kissing him back, giving that back to him. His hips lost their rhythm as he punched into Trey, chasing his orgasm.

His balls clenched, drew up painfully tight, and he thought, for a second, that he wouldn't be able to shoot. Then Trey squeezed tight around his cock and he cried out, jerking as he came hard.

"Love you." Trey moaned the words against his lips. "God, I love you."

"Me, too, Trey. So much." Trey was his world. They rested together, their heartbeats slowing. "God, Trey, you just do it for me."

"That's good, huh? Given that we're together."

He had to chuckle—had to. "I *knew* you were going to tell me that."

He felt Trey's laugh all around his cock. "Either you know me or I'm super predictable."

"I think I know you pretty damn well." Shifting slightly, he opened the drawer in the little side table by the couch. He grabbed the smaller of the two plugs hiding in there, and the tube of lube. "I'm going to keep you inside me." He wanted that for while Trey got his nipple pierced.

His size queen moaned, chin dipping in a nod.

He slicked up the little plug and pressed it where his flesh and Trey's body were joined. Taking his time, he pulled out and replaced his cock with the plug.

"Gonna feel you for days."

"That's the plan."

Between that and the new nipple ring, Lucien figured Trey was going to be horny for days, too. He liked it. He liked it a lot.

Chapter Seventeen

Trey sat in the car, the sun beating through the window. He was going to do this. His poor nipple.

Lucien's hand landed on his thigh, squeezed gently. "Stop fretting, baby."

"I'm not fretting." He was stressing.

"What would you call it, then?" The car slowed and angled, then stopped.

"Stressing. Worried, maybe." Not a ton.

"Then stop stressing, baby. You don't need to worry."

"No? It's going to be hot, huh?"

"It is. It'll be hot, just having it there, but when it heals and I can play with it. Damn, Trey, it's going to incinerate us both."

Trey was totally going to write a pyrokenetic carnival freak show character. Totally.

"We're here. I'll come around and help you out." Lucien got out of the car and a moment later opened his door, helping him out.

He held on, the world feeling a little off without Dodger there. Lucien put his hand on one arm.

"I found a spot right outside the shop, so we don't have far to go and there's no stairs."

"I trust you."

"I know." Lucien patted his hand. "It's one of the things I love about you."

They headed into a door and the smell was weird — oil and deodorant, sweat and... Something he didn't get.

"Hi there, how can I help you?" The voice was female, cheerful.

"Lucien and Trey. We have an appointment for a nipple piercing."

"Ah, yes. Brundy is waiting for you. Come back." She hesitated. "Should I... Is there some way I can help?"

"No, we've got it covered. Thank you for asking." They moved deeper into the place.

"Lucien? That you, man?" The man's voice was soft, low, gentle. Not nervous in the least.

"Hey, Brundy. How's it going, man?

"Good. Good. Trey, I assume. Nice to meet you."

"Pleased."

"Trey, this is Brundy. He's the one who's going to put the little ring of metal in your nipple."

"Brundy. Hey. Lucien can stay, yeah?" Trey wasn't doing this if Lucien wasn't allowed.

"Of course. We often have partners in here. Especially for a more intimate piercing."

Lucien led him to a chair and helped him to sit. "Those are coming later. This one first." Lucien sounded so sure.

Brundy chuckled. "So is this your first piercing, Trey?"

"Yeah. Yeah, I'm a little wigged."

"That's understandable. I can tell you that I run a licensed, clean shop, that I've been doing this for seventeen years and that if you follow the aftercare instructions, you shouldn't have any problems."

"Lucien will help." He knew that. He suspected that Lucien was eager to help.

"I will. I'll make sure it doesn't get infected."

"Good deal. Have you chosen jewelry?"

"Just a simple gold ring for now. Once Trey's used to it, we may go for something more fancy." Lucien's hand was solid and warm on his shoulder.

"Absolutely. Would you like to feel it, Trey? I can sterilize it after." A little piece of metal was placed in his hand. It felt tiny, smooth, with a bump on one edge.

"If you'd like to lift your shirt up, we can get started." Brundy took the ring back.

"I can help." Lucien helped him to get his T-shirt up to his underarms. It was Lucien's shirt, really. Lucien had said it would be easier after to have a loose, soft T-shirt. The best part was how it smelled like his lover, how it smelled familiar, superseding the scents here.

"So Trey, I'm going to use an alcohol swab to clean it. Then I'm going to mark where I'll pierce you and Lucien will make sure it's where you want it. The piercing itself will only take seconds."

"Okay." His hands moved restlessly for a moment, searching for a place to land.

Lucien grabbed them and placed them, palms down, on his thighs. "Your arms are out of the way like this."

"'K." He squeezed his eyes shut, thinking about this morning, how his ass ached now. How when he clenched, the plug shifted.

Lucien put his hand back on Trey's shoulder, giving him that connection.

A cold touch hit his nipple and he reached up, grabbed the man's wrist.

"Okay, honey. Okay. You can't do that when I'm piercing you. One of us could get hurt, okay?"

"Sorry! Sorry. I didn't expect it right then."

"Ah, okay, I can be more vocal about what I'm doing."

"Hands on the rests, Trey. Hold tight," Lucien suggested.

"Okay. I'm sorry." He'd just been surprised.

"It's okay, man. At least this happened when it was just the marker." Brundy patted his hand.

Lucien squeezed his shoulders. "I'm right here, baby."

"Thank you." He leaned his head over, his jaw against Lucien's hand.

Lucien kissed the top of his head.

"Okay, I'm going to mark it now. There will be a touch of the pen on both sides."

Trey nodded, the touch barely noticeable this time.

"Okay, Lucien, come look."

Lucien squeezed his shoulder and moved away. "Oh, that's perfect, Brundy."

"Cool."

Then Lucien's hand was back on his shoulder, the warmth good.

"There's going to be a pinch now. It won't hurt, just ache a little."

Lucien's fingers dug into his shoulder. "I'm right here."

"Okay. Okay. I'm ready." Trey wasn't even lying. He'd had Lucien's hand inside him. He could do this.

"Okay. I need you to stay absolutely still. I'm doing it now."

There was a terrible pain, but it only lasted a moment, then something slid through his flesh.

He didn't even have time to gasp. "Is it done?"

"Yep. I just need to spray and you're good to go. That's coming now."

Something cold sprayed against his nipple.

Trey jerked, ass leaving the chair. "Oh."

"That was the good part," Brundy said, chuckling.

Lucien squeezed his shoulder. "Was it?"

"You know it. Looks good, doesn't it?" He didn't want it to be crooked or look funky or anything.

"It looks fantastic. It'll be okay if he feels it, right? Just gives it a look?" Lucien asked.

"Sure. You can clean it again after."

Trey shook his head. "I don't want to touch."

"Are you sure, baby?"

He nodded, then he did it anyway. He touched the metal inside his body. It felt weird, hurting a bit but not as much as he'd expected. "It's... Can we go home?"

"Of course we can." Lucien kissed the top of his head.

"You're good to go," Brundy added.

Lucien helped him get the T-shirt back down, then took his hands and tugged him upward.

"Did I need to pay or something?"

"I've got it covered, baby." Lucien kissed him softly. "You okay?"

He tilted his head, thinking about it. "Yeah. Yeah, a little buzzed, that's all."

"Okay. Let's go home and enjoy the buzz." Lucien kissed him again, hands sliding down to cup his ass. "You look amazingly sexy."

"Do I look different?"

"You're flushed a little, and I know it's there. I saw it."

"I did okay?" He felt flushed, like he was feverish.

"You did amazing, baby. You didn't even say ow." Lucien put his hand on Lucien's arm to lead him out.

"It went fast." Now the nipple just throbbed more than anything.

"I told you it would be fine."

"Yeah. Yeah, you did." Not that he hadn't loved Lucien's distraction techniques.

Lucien stopped at the desk on the way out to pay, then they were on their way to the car. The touch of the T-shirt was a little maddening as he walked, teasing his skin.

"We can take the T-shirt off when we get home." He could hear the smile in Lucien's voice.

"Laughing at me," he teased.

"Oh, no. I'm anticipating having you shirtless for days."

Trey felt… He felt like he was drunk.

Lucien got him into the car and buckled his seatbelt, then wrapped his hand around the shoulder part. "Hold this so it doesn't press against the ring."

"Okay. Yeah. Is it hot? Looking at it?"

"Uh-huh. And I can't wait to get you home so I can look at it a lot. So I can help you deal with all that stuff buzzing around inside you."

"Yeah. Yeah, that sounds perfect."

"You working that plug?" Lucien asked as he started the car.

He nodded, swallowing hard. "I have to."

"I can tell. And it makes me so hard, knowing what you're doing."

He reached out, searching for Lucien's fly. When he found it, Lucien groaned, legs shifting a little.

"Oh, God." He traced the length of his lover's cock.

"We'll be home in two minutes, baby." He could hear the need in Lucien's voice.

"Uh-huh. Home." He forced himself to stop touching.

The tires actually squealed as Lucien came to a stop. "Home." Lucien was unbuckled and out of the car before he could reply, the driver's door slamming shut.

He worked the seatbelt open right before Lucien flung the door wide.

"Come on, baby. I don't mean to drag you around, but God, I want you."

"Want. Now. Now is good."

Lucien laughed, the sound full-bodied and husky. "Now is very good, though I think we're going to have to fend Dodger off first."

They went up the steps and Lucien opened the door and sure enough, they were met by a very eager Dodger. His best friend fussed at him, vocalizing loudly, expressing how Trey was not supposed to go outside without him.

"It's okay, Dodger. I took good care of him." Lucien loved on Dodger for a moment. "I'm going to go unlock the doggie door. I'll meet you in bed."

"Okay." He scratched Dodger's ears for another second, then he headed for the bedroom.

It wasn't long before he heard Lucien's footsteps coming back. "Mmm. Let's get you naked, baby."

"That won't take long." He stepped out of his shoes.

"No, but what comes after probably will." Lucien's fingers slid on his belly, the T-shirt he wore carefully tugged up.

"Is it pretty?"

"It's stunning. Small and gold and shiny against your pale skin."

Lucien ran his finger in a circle around the piercing. His nipple throbbed and he swore he could feel the piercing move.

"I won't be able to do more than this and this – " On the second 'this', Lucien blew across his pierced nipple. "Until it's healed."

Trey whimpered softly, chest lifting.

"You can feel it with your whole body, can't you?"

"Uh-huh. Uh-huh." He found himself shivering, shaking.

"Good. It's going to be amazing when we can play with it, but it'll be fun until then, too. So new."

"I need to sit down." The adrenaline buzz was making his knees weak.

"You need to lie down." Lucien picked him up and set him down on the bed, the comforter soft against his back.

"I'm okay. Just buzzy." Like his head was filled with bees.

"Uh-huh." Lucien opened his pants, undid the zipper and tugged them down over his hips. The movements of his lower body seemed to vibrate the ring.

"You're leaking." Lucien tapped the tip of his erection, playing.

Then Lucien's lips wrapped around his head, tongue lapping at the liquid there, before beginning to suck.

"Sir."

The suction was easy, gentle, almost maddening. Lucien flicked across the tip again, tongue slick and easy. Trey explored the comforter, the stitches, the puffy parts, his hips moving constantly as he did.

Lucien brought a hand up, playing with his balls. His legs spread, and he nodded. *Yes. God, yes.*

The touches stayed at his balls at first, then Lucien reached farther back and pushed at the base of the little plug he wore.

"Please. Please, yes." That's what he needed.

Lucien tugged the plug right out but before he could complain, Lucien's cock slammed in instead. He grabbed for Lucien's shoulders, scrabbling for connection. Lucien kept thrusting, filling him up over and over. And yeah, yeah, the ring was definitely moving as Lucien pushed into him.

"Harder. Harder, love."

"Pushy boy." Lucien gave him what he needed, though, pounding into him.

"Yours." And Lucien loved him.

"One hundred percent mine."

Air blew across his new piercing. His entire body clenched tight, and Lucien gasped, slammed in. "Fuck. Baby." Lucien twisted his unpierced nipple, making the pierced one ache all the harder.

"Yes. Yes. Yes." He was like a broken record, a word processor with a stuck 'Paste' function.

Lucien wasn't complaining, his lover just thrusting into him, groaning and moaning, panting. Trey reached up, barely nudging the bottom of his new ring.

"No touching," growled Lucien, one hand grabbing his wrist and holding tight.

That shocked him, surprised him. More than that, it turned him on.

Holding his hand over his head, Lucien kept pushing into him, sliding home again and again, so damn deep. His feet were braced on the mattress, helping out, meeting thrust after thrust. Lucien made no move to touch his cock, instead squeezed his wrist even tighter as his free hand dragged along Trey's side. He tried to tilt, get pressure, friction on his cock, but he couldn't.

"My rhythm, baby."

"Trying. Trying, damn it."

"I'm not touching your cock. You're going to have to come anyway."

"I…" He twisted, his body straining. "Damn it."

"I'll do this all day long, baby."

"No way." Also, no fair.

"You can come any time you want."

He felt Lucien's breath first, then his Master's teeth on his bare nipple, the bite sharp. *Oh, Jesus*. What was that going to feel like on his pierced nipple?

Lucien kept punching into him, finding his gland and pegging it over and over. The world shattered, splintered into a million different pieces. Lucien kept pushing into him, making his orgasm go on and on like it was never going to end.

When he floated back into his body, tears streaked his cheeks. Lucien was still buried deep, and was licking his cheeks clean.

"Master." He moaned the word out.

"Right here, baby. God, I love you."

"Love." He didn't have any more words. Not right now.

"I know." Lucien kissed him and rested against him.

Trey rested, the silence in his brain like heaven.

Epilogue

"He's fired me again." Brian walked out of the office, winked at Lucien. "This one's been a bitch. I hate when he writes about things he's really scared of."

Lucien heard that. Trey hadn't been to bed in a week and the last time they'd spoken, Trey had thrown a cup at him, sobbing the entire time. The man was close, though. Lucien knew the end was near — like in the next hour.

"Do you want me to hang around for the last tapes so I can give you guys a week of privacy?" Looked like Brian knew the end was coming, too.

"Sounds good, Bri. You're a star." He thought maybe Brian deserved a raise this time.

"No worries, man. He works hard."

"I know he was worried about losing you when you graduated. He was pleased you were doing your master's. I think he's hoping you go for a PhD next, so you stay on." Lucien had half an ear cocked for the signs that Trey was almost done.

"Oh, I don't know. But, I'm not ready to be done. His process is amazing."

"Well, we both hope you'll stay on. It would be hell to have to train someone new. And he adores you."

"Yeah. Yeah, me too."

There was a crash, the sounds of soft sobs.

"That's your cue, Lucien."

"I'll get him and you can go rescue the tapes. Have a good week, Bri." He was halfway there before he was finished talking.

Knocking—he always knocked so that Trey knew he was coming—he went in. "All done, baby?"

"I hate this book." Trey was on the floor, sweating, crying. "I hate this book!"

Leaning down, he picked his boy up into his arms. "It's finished, eh?"

"Uh-huh." Trey was lean, muscled, fine. They worked out almost every day, except in the last weeks of a novel.

Today there would be working out of another kind. And tomorrow they would visit Brundy at the Happy Piercer and get Trey his Prince Albert.

Three novels down, two and a half years living together, and they were flying. Things just got better and better the longer they were together.

He kissed the tears from Trey's cheeks as he carried his lover to the bedroom.

"I'm tired, Sir. So tired."

"I know, baby. Tired and empty."

Laying Trey down on the bed, he began stripping off the clothes that separated their skin. Tired and empty and ready to be filled by him, by love and hope and pleasure.

It was time to do his part in vanquishing the monsters.

It was time to be Trey's hero.

About the Author

Often referred to as 'Space Cowboy' and 'Gangsta of Love' while still striving for the moniker of 'Maurice', Sean Michael spends his days surfing, smutting, organising his immense gourd collection and fantasizing about one day retiring on a small secluded island peopled entirely by horseshoe crabs. While collecting vast amounts of vintage gay pulp novels and mood rings, Sean whiles away the hours between dropping the f-bomb and pursuing the Kama Sutra by channelling the long lost spirit of John Wayne and singing along with the soundtrack to 'Chicago'.

A long-time writer of complicated haiku, currently Sean is attempting to learn the advanced arts of plate spinning and soap carving sex toys.

Barring any of that? He'll stick with writing his stories, thanks, and rubbing pretty bodies together to see if they spark.

Sean Michael loves to hear from readers. You can find her contact information, website details and author profile page at http://www.totallybound.com.

Totally Bound Publishing